ABOUT THE AUTHOR

Rian is a bestselling non-fiction author and YouTube content creator with a life as varied as it is extraordinary. Born in the rugged landscape of Alberta, he has worked as a rancher and logger in British Columbia's interior, served 13 years in the Royal Canadian Navy on Vancouver Island, and held executive corporate positions in Montreal, Quebec, and Toronto, Ontario. He holds two degrees—one in Graphic Design with a major in Art History, and another in Business and Information Security—and has earned certifications in Harmonized Threat and Risk Assessment from CSIS, Canada's intelligence service. He is also recognized as one of the Canadian Forces' top 30 technical experts in information security and cyber warfare.

A Tae Kwon Do regional champion in college, Rian has taught at Fleet School in Esquimalt, deployed to the Horn of Africa to combat piracy with the U.S. Seventh Fleet, and circumnavigated the globe. He holds several prestigious honors, including the Order of Magellan, the Order of the Ditch, the Order of the Suez, and the Order of the Rock.

From military service to international travel, Rian's life is a testament to adventure, expertise, and ambition. Now, you're reading his fifth book—and his first work of fiction.

The
Dog Walker
R A Stone

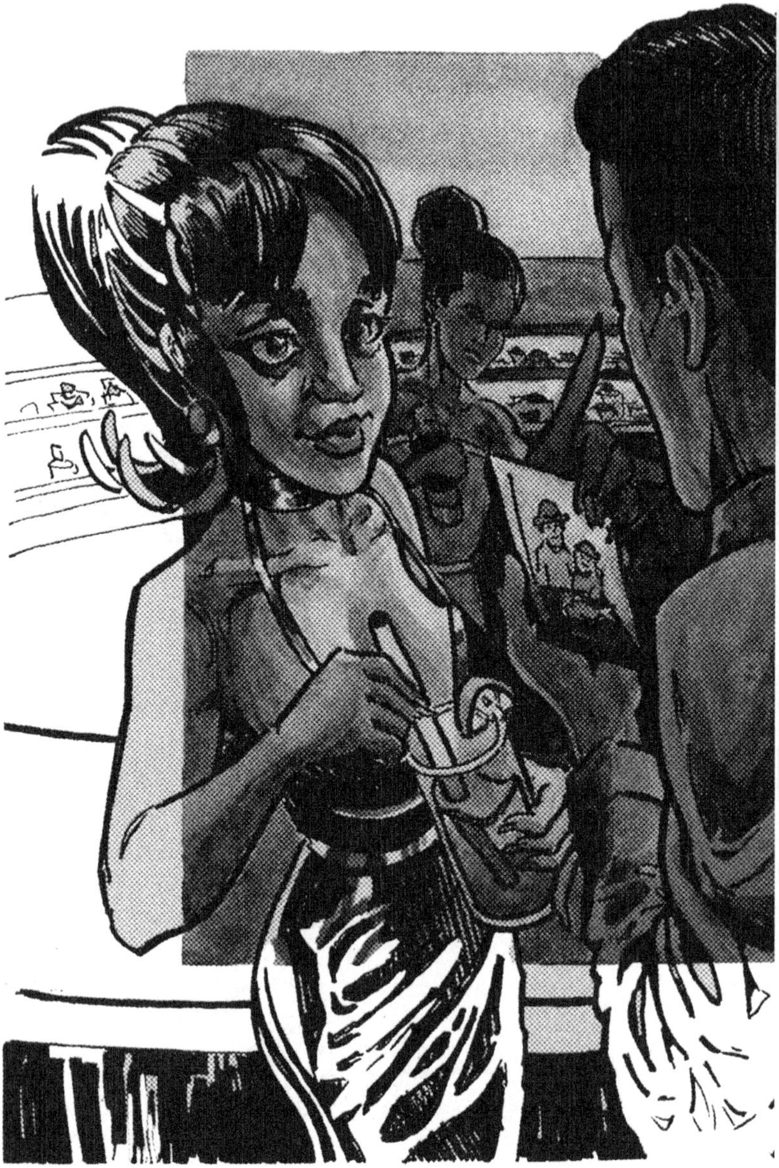

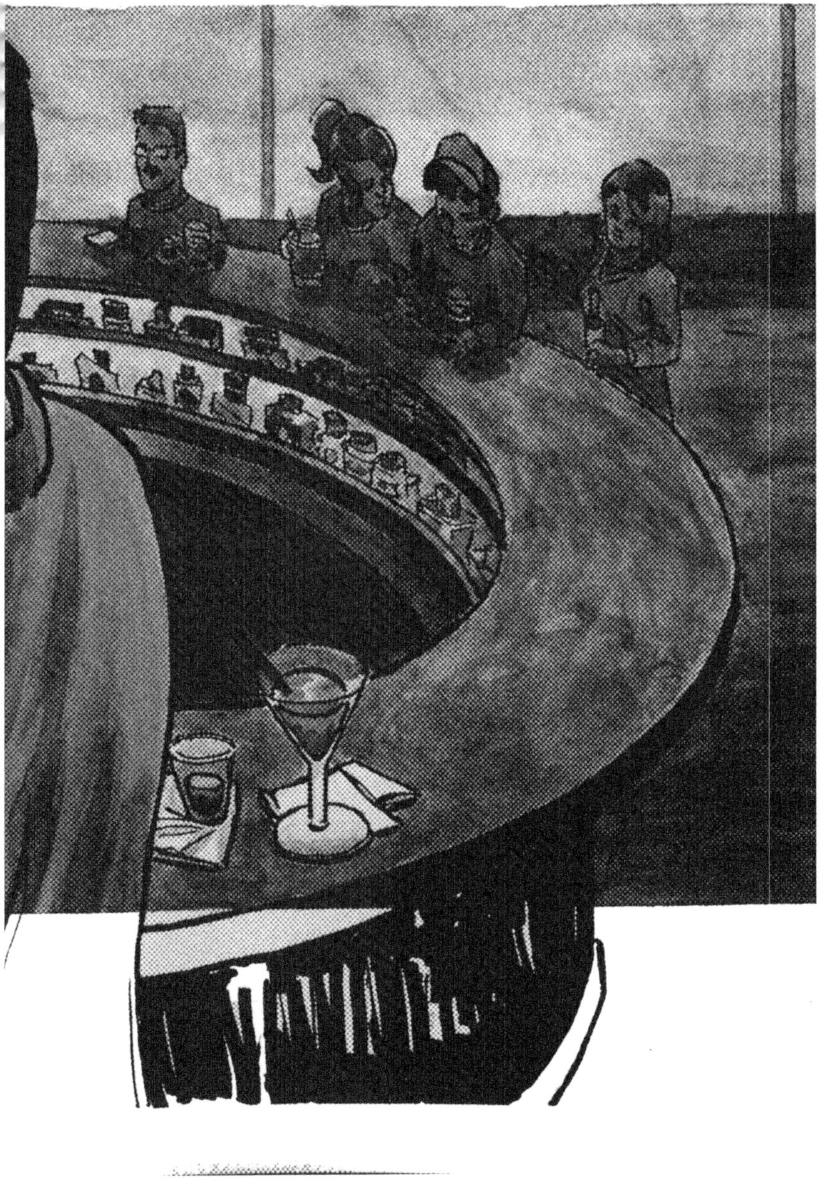

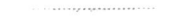

4R Books
Canada

4R Books
Find all my work at https://www.rianstone.com

Copyright © 2025 R A Stone

All rights reserved.

No part of this book may be reproduced, distributed, or transmitted in any form or by any means, including photocopying, recording, or other electronic or mechanical methods, without the prior written permission of the author, except in the case of brief quotations embodied in critical reviews and certain other noncommercial uses permitted by copyright law.

For permission requests, email the author at StonePimpleTilists@rianstone.com

ISBN: 9798305009835

Printed in Canada

Cover design by rayrayisHappy (rayrayisHappy.com)

Book design by R A Stone

First Edition

This book is a work of fiction. Any resemblance to actual events, locales, or persons, living or dead, is purely coincidental.

Table of Contents

Dedication i
1. The Dog Walker 1
2. Shirley..9
3. Rose 27
4. Sara 41
5. Melissa..63
6. Kelly...83
7. Kate 109
8. Alyssa...133
9. Charli...145
10. Rex 177
11. Megan 191
12. Marie..205
13. Kim..219
14. Jason 231
15. A Choice 247
16. Keep the hat on. 269

Dedication

Who do I dedicate this to, and why?

The easy answer is Nick August. From him, I learned to write better prose, craft more compelling characters, and tighten a plot. He's a man who's studied literature and read more in his lifetime than everyone else I know combined. But that's the easy answer—and I pay him on time, which is all the thanks he's ever wanted.

I could thank my friends, family, or even my wife. But they don't read my books. I've written five, and not one of them cares. Not that they should care, or that I need them to. It is what it is.

So, perhaps I should dedicate this book to the broads. Their nonsense inspired the entire story. To Melissa, Sara, Kate, whose names I remember, and the others whose names I can no longer recall. I remember the situations—the collection of war trophies they destroyed in my house. I remember the one girl etched into my memory only by a number. She turned me into the unreliable narrator I am today. I call her 27. She was 23, 24, or 25. She definitely wasn't 26 or 27. I couldn't pick her out of a lineup, but I remember our conversations clearly. For that, I'm grateful, because I still don't write dialog as well as I'd like to.

But no, I don't want to dedicate this to those broads. None of them would appreciate being immortalized as the inspiration for the characters in this book. I'm almost certain that Melissa or Sara's husbands, assuming they're still married, would try to punch me or post a passive-aggressive rant online if they read their vivid depictions.

I could dedicate this to you, my readers. Without you, none of this would work. I couldn't have spent the inordinate amount of time I've spent writing without your financial support. But I've always provided something in return—information, entertainment, or both. To dedicate this to you would cheapen the work. If you didn't like it, you wouldn't have bought it. Dedicating it to you would feel like telling you I think you have no taste—as if I were just a panhandler with a smartphone.

Perhaps I should dedicate this to Rollo Tomassi. Developing a character like Rex was easier because of the archetypes he's fleshed out so thoroughly. Making Rex into a Promise Keeper already came with a rich backstory. Rollo's essays on modern men ensured every character here is not just believable but uncomfortably relatable. Yet, I've already dedicated my four non-fiction books to him. This is my own thing, not just building on established canon. So he's out.

So, who's left? Just the dogs—Chomsky, Sagan, and Hitchens. They love me for no reason other than my ability to open their Tupperware containers and buy the raw food that fills them. If this book does well, they'll continue eating raw beef for the rest of their days.

The Dog Walker

Alissa was playing with me like a science experiment.

"What are you doing?"

"I've never seen one from a dark guy before. It's usually pink." She continued examining me as if David Attenborough were narrating.

"Well, take a look now. It's getting late."

"Are you kicking me out?" She looked as surprised as the last time or anytime I've kicked her out.

"No, no. Not right away. But, you know, soon. Actually, wait …"

If Alissa put on a shirt she would be the girl next door. Hair long enough to tickle her collarbone with a face straight out of a wheat field. She wasn't supermodel thin but attainable thin. Gym membership thin, willpower thin. Not cocaine thin or purge thin.

"Where's my clothes?" She snapped up her white panties. She never wears the comfortable panties when she comes over.

"In the dryer."

"Thanks." She tiptoed out of the room.

"Yeah, least I could do, it was kind of my fault."

She pulled out a slim-legged pair of denim jeans and a white cotton shirt. Just how you'd expect a woman to dress for a movie, or the malt shoppe. A small Christian girl from a small

Christian town. I've been to that town. I've met women from that town. Most were cockteases. She threw her shirt on and just like that, her wholesome disguise was complete. I sat up in bed and reached for my bathrobe, a big white fuzzy towel of a robe.

"Wait. I want to ask you something."

"Oh, so I don't have to leave yet?" She picked up her purse and gave a sharp glance my way. Not angry, more…offended. That's fair.

It had been a half a year of the same surprise. She would come over after one or both of us went to the bar and struck out. We fooled around. I'd learn about a new kink that I either loved or hated. Then I'd kick her out.

I got out of bed and went to the living room and played XBOX. Queen and Country and sex and silence; ideology for the modern man.

She walked into the living room fully dressed.

"You don't owe me an answer," I said, "but I want to know something."

That stain on her shirt was completely gone. I love that damned washing machine machine. It was worth every penny. My deployment exempted me from income tax, so I finally had the money for designer furniture and appliances.

I think she was Irish. In Canada, that's code for looking like an English girl but with straight teeth and a proper set, big enough. Not cartoonish or absurd. A healthy handful. More than that is a waste. Besides, I'm not greedy and there are starving children in Africa. Stop drifting, Rex. Don't lose this thought. Don't you fucking dare.

"Yes, the stain is gone," she said.

"No, not that."

"I'm not fucking Mike anymore."

"Not that either. I know that. It's that, the worse I treat you, the better you act."

"OK?" she laughs nervously. She's uncomfortable with this conversation that hasn't even started yet.

1 The Dog Walker

"I kicked you out of my condo and the next weekend you gave me a blowjob in the hallway. You gave me that whip to play with then you told me I was a better lay than Mike. I don't even call you by your real name. I don't get it."

I'm stalling. Just say it.

"Why do you let me treat you like this?"

"Like what?"

"Like this."

"I dunno. I'm having fun aren't you?" She would rather me cum in her mouth than have this conversation. I should have never put her shirt in the wash. I should have been back on her like a dirty shirt. I should have never opened my stupid mouth. If I could be two people, I would slap the other guy. I saw the look. She saw right through me. She knew I wasn't her me. I was mine.

"I'm getting a glass of water," I said. "Want one?"

"Thanks."

I didn't even want water. I wasn't great at this. I was good enough to know when the only play left was to exit and change the subject.

I needed a second to think. If she's enjoying it, is it really that bad? Yes. She's stupid and doesn't know what's good for her. Maybe the problem was me? It couldn't be. I wasn't really an asshole, not like Jon was, not like she wanted me to be. But she doesn't know all that. She couldn't appreciate the real me. I could see it in her eyes. The minute she heard real me ask a question, to attempt a real moment, to be myself, she checked out. I cleaned her shirt like a nice guy and soiled her fantasy.

Fuck, other me seemed to be saying. I knew you couldn't shut up.

Real me had been trying to get laid for so long that maybe that was the real me. Her image of me was better than the real me. That me never got laid and never got so much as a smile. I needed to recover, put the real me in a box.

"Hey, I brought you a water," I said. "But it's not free."

"What do you mean?"

"Shut up, flip over."

"No, it's late. I called the cab already. It should be here any second." She walked out the door, and I walked over and turned the lock behind her. Then I poured the water in the sink and sat on the sofa. The ring on my XBOX was glowing, the screen flashing:

Waiting for players ...

I woke up tired and in a shitty mood until my feet touched the cold floor, cussing at no one in particular. I checked my Seamaster, a gift to myself for circumnavigating the world on my deployment. 0545. I had to shower, shave, and drive to work, and change into my uniform. Plenty of time. No terrorists to kill at present, so the only adventures were in the foreign ports. I wished there were more, but my income tax exemptions paid for the furniture and custom sheet sets and all my toys.

I sat on the chaise lounge of my white, Italian leather sectional sofa and drank my coffee. It's dark and drizzling outside. It's that time of year where you leave in the dark and come home in the dark. Everyone says it's depressing, but I found the cold darkness to be crisp, invigorating.

The side of my face itched. I had a scratch from a down feather sticking out of my duvet. I needed to buy a new duvet cover, and I was down to my last two sets of sheets. There used to be a few ivory and navy blue, three hundred thread count, Egyptian cotton. I was down to my last set and they are beat to hell. They were clean, but stained with regret. I washed them after every session with a woman. The good sheets don't pill. The pillowcases were discolored from all the makeup and vomit and sweat and sex stains from many late night adventures. The duvet cover had blood stains in the middle so it had to go. It wasn't a lot, but any amount of blood is too much.

My head was killing me. I was finishing my coffee and looking at my reflection in the patio door. This guy, real me, was really fucking it up for everyone. It was time to kick that loser out. Blue Jeans, grey henley, scruffy face, work boots. I look fit but tired. I look like someone who just met me and right off doesn't like me and wants to give me shit.

You're just like Jon, you know, the other guy said.

"No, I'm not. I will never be like him."

Sure you are. You didn't even like Alyssa. You hated her.

"Well, yeah. She called my cousin a whore."

Yet you slept with her anyway. You were on her like a dirty shirt!

"That's different."

Is it?

"Yes. She's not just some chick married to a skidder operator doing coke on the weekend. I'm not hurting anyone."

It probably hurt Mike since she was his girlfriend.

"Mike hurt himself. I didn't do anything except for once I won."

Right. I forgot about your rules.

"Fuck you."

Oh yeah. Your moral rules that make you better than all this. You know her name, you slot her into your notch count. Let me guess, she's number twenty?

"Twenty-three. Alyssa's twenty-three."

This is probably the first time you've said her real name and not flippantly calling her the Dog Walker.

"You're annoying me."

When Manjeet was sleeping around and having fun you didn't bat an eye. Why is it any different here?

"Manjeet. I hadn't thought about her since I was seventeen. How long have I been a hipocrite? I don't think I am. It doesn't matter. It's different when I do it, I do it the right way."

Yeah, sure. Whatever you say, friendo. I get it. Everyone else is wrong and you're right. Everyone else is stupid and immoral and they hurt the people they love, the people you love. But you're different

"I try to be."

Do you though?

"I want to."

Fine. When you're out getting the duvet cover, get it in that ivory color. Just like your truck used to be. The right duvet cover is such an important detail, makes a huge difference.

I needed a new duvet cover and some sheets. I needed this asshole to shut up. I'm not like Jon. I will never be like Jon.

You're going to be late. Get dressed and get to work.

♦

She was probably sitting in a meeting right now. I was back on board in the communications consoles beside Jason. He was six foot, five inches with a military crop. He wasn't fat fat. He was Fred Flinstone fat with a scar across his face from rugby as a teenager.

"Why do you call her the dog walker?" he asked me.

"Man. I'm busy. Laz is going to yell at us if we don't get all the morning traffic finished before stand easy."

"Oh whatever man. It'll get done when it gets done. We always figure it out. Is it because she only does doggy style or something?"

"It's because I don't like her. If I call her Alissa it makes her a human being."

"Dude, thats rough." Jason always found the humor in my most asshole behavior. He bit his tongue and laughed from the belly. He held himself together long enough for more questions,

"So you just call her a dog."

"A dog walker. I like dogs."

"Right. A dog walker, then just fool around and she's OK with it?"

"I guess so. I messed up last night though. I asked her why she liked it when I treated her that way and she hasn't talked to me since. I left a bright red hand print on her ass that would be there for work. She's a marketing director for Zellers."

"Sounds like a strong, independent woman type job."

"I guess so. But she walks foster dogs for the SPCA on the weekends, so I call her Dog Walker."

"Is that what Mike calls her?"

"Doesn't matter. We aren't building a life together. I don't even like her. Besides, nine times out of ten when we go out Mike is fucking whoever. He doesn't give a shit."

"I wouldn't be so sure about that, man. Have you ever seen him when a girl dumps him first? Beneath that whole *I'm an asshole who owns a truck* thing he does, he's actually a sensitive soul."

I didn't say anything, but it felt good to finally beat Mike without having to invent some Calvinball rules. He freaked out all the time, but this time I win. I fucked the girl and she told me I did it better. And that's the best part: not the sex, but the win.

"Are you like this with all the girls?" Jay asked.

"No. This is the first one. I have rules. I always try to make them breakfast, give them a coffee, offer a ride home. I make sure to remember everyone's name. I think it's important."

"Those are some weird rules, dude."

"Maybe. But I'm not an asshole."

"Except for when you are."

"That's different."

The tones of the bosun's call came over the intercom. Those notes, low, high, low: a general call.

Standeasy.

"Rex, you coming?" Jay asked.

"In a bit. I have to check something first."

I slid down the ladder and opened the hatch to number two mess to grab my cellphone from my locker. The comms office was wrapped in copper mesh forming a faraday cage. No signals in or out. Phones remained in our personal space as a security requirement. I checked the phone. The LED light wasn't blinking, but you never know.

"Hope you made it home all right." I sent it after she left. Still on read.

I don't blame her. There were two Rexes in my condo. One was having an existential crisis over turning into his asshole of a stepfather with a shitty moral compass; he's the nice guy. The other one fucked a chick he didn't like just because he could.

She loved asshole Rex and loathed the nice one. Asshole Rex marked his territory like he was pissing on a tree stump just because he could. She looked good and let him treat her like shit. He didn't care. He got laid. The reason both Rexes were going at it like Spinks and Ali was because she liked it. Nice guy Rex couldn't dismiss this as a broken woman who didn't know any better. She was pleasant. She did community service. She had a good job, good friends, a nice apartment. She didn't have a drinking problem. There were no pills in her medicine cabinet. She didn't do drugs. Her only vice was dick and degradation. There was nothing wrong with her.

The other Rex, the asshole, was pissed off at how the nice guy keeps ruining all of his fun with stupid, made-up rules and daddy issues. There was literally nothing seriously wrong with the dog walker, yet here we were. It was a situation with benefits. It was better than good.

It was good enough.

2

Shirley

It was the summer of 2001. There was a shirt on the floor of my truck covered in blood and reeking of gas and oil. Must have been for a chainsaw. It reminded me of her. I was sure she hated me. Well, she didn't hate my me, but her me. I'm not that guy. I'm a good guy. I'm not like him. This didn't count. I picked up the shirt. It was crusty and stiff. My trucks extended box was covered in cigarette butts and beer caps. On the floorboard was a flat bottle of Brisk Iced Tea. It reeked of cheap rum. I cleaned, placing everything in an old silage bag on top of the burn pile in our yard, then I went inside and started up the Nintendo in my room. The 8-bit sounds distracted me from this headache. I was feeling like I took a chainsaw bar to the head.

The game was a classic. I loved Mega Man II. It was hard to finish. I played it for years. Nothing that happened on the screen made any sense, not at first. It was like they put things in my way just to mess with me. I bought an issue of Nintendo Power just to learn how to win. According to the Howard and Nester comic,

the trick to beating that game was in the patterns.

I had to practice, to learn the pattern of every enemy. Everything was chaos but everything was predictable. Just have to watch the individuals then understand how it all comes together. They come out predictably and they act predictably. You have to see what they are doing and not what you think they would be doing.

At first, it was impossible and most of the time my muscle memory got me into trouble. They should have gone one way instead of the way they went, and I would get knocked into lava or something. It was frustrating and I used to cuss out the screen until I figured out the pattern and accepted that I can't make them do what I thought they should; then everything clicked. Then it was fun. The fun was in finding the patterns. Once I got there, I felt good. I still screwed up on occasion, but I always knew why which made it easier to stay calm.

My mom walked in. Was she checking on me after last night, or did she want to complain again?

"You need to put this stupid game down and go outside. All I hear is you losing. What's the point?" She was waiting for me to ask about last night. I knew she didn't want to talk about video games. I'm supposed to ask her what is wrong so she can get into it about Jon. That way it's not her fault for using me as a sound board. My head is throbbing. I can't be bothered to play today.

"It's because I have to practice. Once I know how not to die, I'll never die again. Plus, it makes me forget about this headache." Good enough lead-in. Time to hear about the asshole again. I fucking hate that guy.

"OK. Well, I'm just tired of all Jon's shit," she said. "I'm fucking tired."

He was working in the bush until eight. Maybe Jon did a line then fucked some married bitch before he got home. Maybe he didn't. After that, he would come home and yell at everyone, then get mad because the pepper wasn't on the table, so he ate alone. The rest of us scavenged food and ate in our rooms or at the bottom of the stairs like a city mouse in the country. Then he would get up at five the next morning and it would start again.

It's all about the patterns.

I hated him. I loved Dad, but Dad never stuck around. Jon

was the dad who stepped up. He may have been an abusive and overbearing bushman. He may have hated me and my brother. Mom may have hated him more than she hated dad. But he was here and I didn't know any better. He bought me video games every birthday and Christmas, and I got to spend the next eleven months out of his sight playing it. It was a fair trade.

He had forearms like tree trunks, a belly like Santa Claus. Burly and scruffy and wearing that same grey wool henley and stained jeans every day. He smelled like diesel and ass. He had recently come home after his annual Harley Davidson small town personal Sturgis event. He was high and drunk. We put railroad ties around the outside of the house so he would hit them instead of the house with his Harley. He passed out in the bathroom using my duvet as a blanket. When he finally got up to work, I got to inspect. It smelled like booze and vomit. I threw it out and slept on a cheap piece of shit acrylic blanket from Zeller's. Every time someone had a party, something I enjoyed got destroyed.

Jon fucked half the woman in town. Half his employees' wives were fucking him and the other half hated him. But NAFTA killed the mills in town, so if their husbands wanted work, he was the guy. Their only alternative was to help out the The Hells Angels. Him being *their guy* worked out for me. I got every toy a boy could want. Dirt Bikes, a quad, a one ton Chevy. Brand new Nintendo when it came out. They were all hot, but I didn't know any better. Jon could afford brand new. He just liked the idea of owning the neighbor's quad more.

I wasn't a criminal. I keep telling myself that I wasn't like that. I didn't know about any of this at the time, so for me it was just stuff around the house to do while I waited to graduate. He was the criminal. I was just a kid riding bikes and playing Nintendo, which didn't count.

"I'm getting food for dinner. Want to come?" I must have blanked out. How long had she been complaining for?

"Yeah, I'll get my shoes."

I was hungover on a Sunday, listening to my mom, the only

woman I've known who loved me unconditionally. The only one who has loved me since I was little. The most important woman in my life, and she's complaining about that asshole. I promised myself never to do this to another human being. I'm not that guy. I'll never be that guy.

Mom drove her brand new Bronco. Bright blue with black bumper and spare tire storage bar with rust speckled overtop. Next to the grocery store was a video rental spot. She could get food and I could rent a game. She hated him. She complained about him while driving her new truck, but she was weirdly loyal to him, too. She was old school. Being raised by a preacher will do that. You don't leave a man for hitting you or sleeping around or doing drugs and drinking or fucking or yelling or throwing shit around the room or getting high and riding his Harley into the side of the house while Cheech and Chong records are playing at full blast. It's what the lord would want. So long as he doesn't drag the kids into trouble and keeps food on the table, you just…endure, I guess. We were a traditional family with a Nintendo. Jon never asked her why she liked to be treated this way. Jon didn't care. Jon had three daughters and two bastard kids of hers plus a piece of tail on the weekends. Why ruin the good life with stupid questions?

I ended up staring at a kid in the mirror in the rental store. A kid with a hangover was staring back at me. He wants to give me a lecture or something.

"I will never do what he does to a woman. I never want to be the reason a woman complains like that."

Except you kind of did, the kid in the mirror pointed out.

"Yesterday didn't count."

If you say so.

"It wasn't my fault. That other chick walked in on us."

The cashier butted-in. "Hey. $5.34. Anything else?"

"Huh? Oh, no, thanks." I handed him a ten.

♦

Shirley

Graduation on Saturday. I didn't have a date for the grad party, or the ceremony or the dance. I never had a partner. I had one girlfriend in my life. It was in the seventh grade for maybe a week. Every time I tried to make it work with a girl, it was as if life knew and put obstacles in my way to mess with me. As long as I didn't do what Jon did, I felt like I knew it was only a matter of time before things worked out for me. Things can't happen the same way every time. I just had to be patient.

A lot of wealthy East Indian families moved to our town. All the doctors and lawyers in Pakistan decided they didn't want to live in their shithole and came to our shithole. The Canadian adults hated it. They would come by for a beer and some work in the bush, or be contracted out by the government to make fire breaks in the woods.

"Another Paki family moved in, you see that?" Blayne was pissed. Blayne was inbred. He was always pissed. After graduation I heard he went to jail for murder. He and Jon went on about it for a good half hour. I'm pretty sure Jon fucked Blayne's wife. I'm pretty sure that both of them were high on crack. The air smelled sour and everything was hilarious. Times were tough. He made do.

I visited my friend, Joey Chuti. His grandma gave me Samosas. He had a sister: Manjeet. She was an ugly duckling. Acne and dark skin. She mostly kept to herself. Joey and Manjeet lived up the hill, not far by bike. Now that I had the truck going up was easier. Manjeet didn't know any boys, and she had thirty cousins who would have beat up any guy she met, so she didn't date. She got to know me when I came over to hang with Joey. I'd bring the Nintendo. He'd provide the Samosas. She would hang around and banter. I never knew what she got out of it.

It was a few days before grad. I didn't have a partner. I was in art class with Joey and Shirley. Shirley was a year younger. She got bullied by the other girls, so it was easier for her to just sit beside the two nerds and quietly draw horses. I didn't care anymore. I just had to run out the clock then I never would have

13

to come back to that shithole. After graduation, I would be able to go to university, start a real life. No more puke-covered sheets and rants about Pakis ruining the neighborhood. I never have to smell crack again.

When I heard the bell, I was the first person out of the room. I grumbled as I walked down the hall to my locker. When I opened it, Manjeet was standing there.

Joey wasn't around.

What was she doing there?

She was waiting for me.

She had those big inset eyes. Big prescription glasses. Long hair with a slight wave in it. She looked like my mom only younger and a touch taller.

"If you don't have a partner for grad yet, do you want to go with me? I don't have anyone yet," she said.

I had never thought about it. She was very convenient.

"Yeah, Sure. Wait a minute. Your cousins won't mind? I don't want to get my ass beat."

"They know you, they know you're good. Grandma speaks highly of you. Says you can handle things spicier than the other white guys."

It's nice to know even the people who just arrived in Canada can see it. Now, I have to figure out what the fuck to do.

"So how does this work? Is this like a date or are we friends or…?"

"Not sure. I was hoping you would know."

"I have an idea. I'll pick you up tonight."

I don't have an idea. I had no idea how this was supposed to work. I was supposed to get a corsage and a limo, but who has a limo in buttfuck nowhere? I had a ranch, maybe horses? Jon had a ranch. He had a cement plant also, but no one wants to get picked up in a cement truck, so I got a horse and a carriage. The wood was weathered and the finish was bleached. The leather was cracked but it looked like a carriage. I bought a flower. It was fake, but it looked like a flower. Ivory, same color as my truck.

Jon wouldn't have done any of this. He probably would have brought his work truck and made a move, then drove her to the party and got drunk. He didn't care. I always cared.

I took Manjeet to meet my mom. Jon was there. She said "hi" to my sisters and brother, then we headed outside. Our ranch hand gave her a brief lesson on horses. She'd never seen one before. I guess India was more about the cows. Jon looked me in the eye. This was the first time he saw me as a person and not mom's little bastard kid. He even smiled. It was funny. For eighteen years, I never knew he had teeth. It was the first time I didn't see him scowl. He started talking normal, then his voice became constricted and excited as he delivered his fatherly advice.

"She's a looker," he said. "You better be on her like a dirty shirt! Jesus Christ!"

Mom slapped him on the arm. Sex at a time like that? What the hell? This was graduation!

I said nothing because, why bother? Fuck that guy and his bullshit. I'm better than this. He may have fucked whatsherface last week, but I'm better than him where it counts. I put thought into this. I made sure her family liked me first. I'm a gentleman.

If everything went perfectly, perhaps we could be something more, but that's why I was a good person and he was an asshole. I didn't care about getting laid as much as he did. It was the only thing he thought about. A dirty shirt and a warm hole. That wasn't me, not what I was about.

I wouldn't be showing up alone. That's what was important.

I wasn't looking forward to the trip. I wasn't looking forward to wearing a blazer. I wasn't looking forward to the diploma. I wasn't looking forward to hearing Aerosmith blasting "I don't want to miss a thing" on the dance floor while holding Manjeet at shoulder length. I cared that I was going to walk through those doors and no one would be able to say, Look at that loser, all by himself. I cared that I never would be like Jon. If it meant I wasn't getting laid that night, so be it.

I wasn't a loser. I was good. Halfway to the ceremony, the horses stopped and shit in the middle of the street. There's always something getting in my way. It was rancid, not very romantic. Manjeet laughed. It's like they put this in front of me just to kill the mood, which sucked. I had made so much progress.

We had the dance though, and that felt good enough. Her arms were thin, her back a little bony. All that work getting a carriage, preparing the horses, picking her up, buying the outfit, planning the night. It would have been a lot easier if I didn't have that asshole's voice in my head. On her like a dirty shirt. Fuck you, Jon. It's like every time I have an idea how to play this, life just throws things in my way to mess with me.

♦

The class gathered in the parking lot afterward sorting out their party plans. Every graduate piled into the box of one truck or another, looking for someone to boot for liquor. Manjeet and I stood by the horses.

"Thanks for coming with me, Manjeet. This was fun and I'm glad we came."

"I know. You're the only man my dad even lets me talk to who isn't family. So what are you doing after the ceremony?"

"After party at the farm. You're coming, right? Joey is coming, and we are going to drink at the fire. I hear we hired a DJ to play and everything."

"You know I don't drink. You should come over instead. We can play Nintendo while Joey gets drunk up there."

"Thanks, but rain check. It's the last party before I leave for college, and I don't want to miss it."

"Well, that's okay, I guess," she said. "I'll be there by myself. My parents are out looking for an apartment for me. I'm going to college, too."

"Then you should come out! It'll be fun, and they won't know."

2 Shirley

I got on the carriage, took Manjeet's hand, and put her in the seat next to mine. I took her home, then turned to go to mine. On the way, I started talking to one of the horses,

"It sucks. I hope it's not always going to be like this."

The fucking horses don't care. The one's bobbing his head and walking home.

"One of these days it has to work out. There's always stupid shit getting in my way."

The carriage stopped. I snapped the reigns to get moving, but the horses didn't respond.

The bastard is taking another shit on the street.

♦

This is what it must feel like to smuggle Mexicans across the border, I thought. I had twenty teenagers packed into the box of my truck driving up an abandoned mountain logging road. Joey wanted to ride in the box and drink with the others.

"Thanks for driving us man," he said.

"No problem. The cops know we're having a party tonight, so they have a checkstop on the road, guaranteed."

"What, they aren't going to stop us?"

"None of the cops have clearance to get over the drainage ditches, and I'm taking the back roads. They won't even see us."

Joey was bouncing around like a rag doll.

"Well fuck, man," he said. "slow the fuck down!"

I could have taken a quad on the trails. It would have been quicker, but it was nice to have a group of friends for a bit. I got to show up to the party and not be alone. It would have been nice if Manjeet had joined, but Joey would have probably gotten his thirty cousins to beat my ass if I tried anything. Something is always in the way.

We pulled up to a spacious field full of memories, fist fights, a rusted mattress, and burnt bicycles. In that roaring bonfire were 20 years of bent nails and burned palettes and a mound of ashen glass that must have weighed a thousand pounds. Three

17

generations of drunken assholes throwing beer bottles into fire as sacrifice to the teenage alcoholic gods.

Who rides a bike up here? Who brought the mattress? The lore runs deep. Surrounding the clearing was a forest of firewood. Twenty-five trucks were parked haphazardly in a circle. Guys were running across a half-burned log on top of the fire while friends cheered them on. Someone was always too drunk and fell into the fire. Everyone else would pull him out and have a good laugh over his losing an eyebrow. The group of us piled out of my truck and walked over taking in the aesthetic: a bonfire surrounded by flannel, jeans, and booze. Beside the fire was a DJ booth with massive lights powered by a generator and set to rave. Trucks loaded with thousands of dollars in power tools surrounded the party like a herd of rhinos protecting their young. A few of the guys had summer jobs bucking wood. There was always at least one chainsaw, and one truck was designated the wood truck. Someone always cut a cord of green wood to keep the fire going.

A Jeep blocked the warm glow of the bonfire, the spotlight on its roll cage manned by some dude who graduated four years ago. He was aiming it at a small patch of grass in front of us.

"What the fuck is that?" Joey asked. He leaned forward.

"Holy fuck, you don't wanna know," I said, and stared. He was on her like a dirty shirt. What an asshole. Two sixteen year olds drunk laying down on the lawn. I don't know him, and I don't know her, but he's fingering her in the grass. Mr. Fingerblaster and the chick are sloppy drunk sloppily fucking each other to the sounds of the roaring audience. Someone's grandfather was hooting at those kids. His middle aged son pulled him aside:

"You can't be watching teenagers fucking on the lawn man!" Grandpa grumbled something, then returned to smoking weed and drinking by the fire. It was fucking cold out there. I don't know how he managed to stay hard in the cold with all that booze. We walked up to the fire and sat down. Seemingly out of nowhere, Shirley sat down beside me.

18

Shirley

"Rex, hey."

"I didn't know you were going to be here tonight!"

"I know. Long time no see, stranger. Is Manjeet here with you? How has she been?"

Her straight brown hair was tied into a high ponytail. Even with the glow of the fire, her skin looked pale.

"She doesn't drink. She's going to college with us this summer.

"Good for you. It's good to see you again. It's been a long time." She was in a flannel shirt with a tight white t-shirt underneath. She was holding a lighter. A cigarette dangled from her mouth. The trucker-themed artsy nerd. I was the nerd-themed artsy nerd. It was a match made in heaven.

"So are you drinking tonight?" she asked.

"I just got here. I will be," I said and lifted up a two liter bottle of Nestle Brisk Iced Tea.

"Long island?"

"Yup."

It was the town's most popular drink. A two liter of iced tea plus a mickey of rum equals Canadian Long Island Tea.

My mind drifted. I could finally stop thinking about how bad I fucked up with Manjeet. Shirley started telling stories from our art class. I nodded and smiled. I couldn't remember any of them, but she had a good memory.

She liked me. All the girls were mean, and I liked her drawings and listened while she complained about them. I stood up and moved over.

"Where are you going?"

"Fire. It's blowing smoke. I'm moving upwind."

"Well, slow down, I've been drinking and I don't move so fast."

She plopped herself down beside me and kept talking. Occasionally, someone else made small talk, so Shirley just sat there and stared at us then continued telling me her stories. I had no plan. I was just letting her talk. She knew me a lot better than I knew her, anyways. I spent so much time moping and listening

The Dog Walker | R.A. STONE

and nodding that I hadn't even had a chance to drink yet. Always something in the way.

"Did you see the finger blasters on the lawn?" I asked.

"Yeah. Alice is in my little sister's grade. She's, like, fifteen, right? Gross."

"How old is Buddy?"

"He graduated last year, so..."

"Jesus. You know what? I don't want to know."

"I hope no one tells her boyfriend."

"Boyfriend?"

Shirley looked around behind us and grabbed my arm. She pulled me towards the clearing by the DJ table.

"Hey, c'mon, I think someone's about to fight."

Made sense. The liquor was running out. Once the party gets dry, the fights start. Mr. Fingerblaster is getting yelled at by some wiry guy I don't know. He's in a white t-shirt and has sawdust on his arms.

"So as soon as her boyfriend went to get firewood, she decides to bang some dude? How long was he gone for?" I asked.

"Steve's an idiot, and she's a fucking slut, I don't know. Oh god!"

Fingerblaster had a black eye. In his left hand, he was holding onto a chainsaw bar, a fifty-two incher. Must have been for work. The wiry dude took a swing with his fist and missed. Fingerblaster swung the bar and connected. An audible crack as the blade hit the guy in the side of the head.

"Oh, shit! Fingerblaster is fucking up Steve!" Shirley said.

"Steve is going to break his hand doing that," I said.

I learned in Tae Kwon Do class that punching a bone is a bad idea.

"He always fights here. Every weekend. Look at his hands. They're like lunch pails."

Shirley was right. His hands were so callused from constantly breaking them that they were more like lunch pails. Swollen bony masses, and Steve was learning the hard way: Don't stop hitting a guy till he stays down. Women were screaming, especially Alice. She was crying hysterically.

"He always does this! Why are you always like this?" Alice yelled. Then she starts making a sound like a hysterical mare in heat, a sound that taps straight into the monkey DNA in guys.

Steve was drunk, so he didn't know he had a skull fracture. He rolled over and sprang to his feet grabbing Fingerblaster by the neck and beating him upside the head with multiple shots. The sound of bone-on-bone was as loud as bar-on-skull. I can't tell which bone is breaking, Steve's hand or Blaster's head.

"Yeah, I can't believe someone ratted her out! I got to get out of here."

"Ratted who out? The 16 year old getting finger blasted on the lawn an hour ago?" Shirley laughed a bit. I shook my head.

"That's so mean."

"Yeah, a little. But Steve doesn't deserve that beating. She cheated on him and now she's freaking out like she's the victim."

Steve was bleeding out of the side of his head. Between the injury and the drinking, he was incoherent and couldn't keep his balance. The older guys broke them up, that middle-aged guy and his dad barking orders at the kids. "Fight's over. Get out of here! Tell her to shut up!"

Steve isn't moving. Probably out cold. Hopefully out cold.

"Rex!" That middle-aged voice cut through the crowd. "You're the only sober one here. We need you to take Steve to the hospital!"

Fuck. Every time I think I'm talking with a girl and making progress, it's like the world itself comes out of the woodwork to ruin everything. Shirley and I were hanging out, and I didn't get enough time to have a drink and just talk to her.

"Are you kidding? He's going to bleed all over my truck!" I said.

"It's OK, I'll come with and keep you company," Shirley said as she tapped me on the chest a few times.

"I'm going to get blood all over my truck and miss the party."

"It's okay. We'll figure it out."

I couldn't figure out why Shirley wanted to come along. The moment was over. That old guy fucking ruined it by throwing this mess my way. I was too busy feeling sorry for myself to notice she was holding onto my arm like a child. This was my last party before college, and there I was driving to the hospital instead of enjoying myself with my friends.

Why was she smiling?

"I just opened up my long island. It'll be flat by the time I get back."

"It'll be fine, c'mon," she said. She took me by the arm and led me to my truck. Two guys were dragging Steve. They leaned him up against my truck's box and tried to get him to sit in the cab.

Steve was bleeding pretty bad. I wouldn't have been surprised if he had broke his skull and his hand. He took off his shirt and made a bandage out of it. I looked at the clock on my stereo. 00:03. It was a fifteen-minute drive to the hospital. No more time for the party, I guessed.

Shirley was getting batted around the cab every time I drove over a ditch. She barely came up to my shoulder when we were standing. Sitting down she was almost my height. Slim, tiny little legs. The bouncing truck made short work of her.

As for Steve, he was mumbling something to himself. He was so drunk he seemed to be able to keep stable. No, that wasn't it. He was just limp and going with the flow.

"Rex, maybe slow down?" Shirley said.

"Fuck that," I said. "This guy's bleeding all over my truck."

Shirley was trying to tuck into my shoulder, but each bump was batting her away.

I looked at Steve again. I had to hand it to him. If someone had knocked me on the head with a five-foot steel bar, I wouldn't have enough left to throw hands let alone win. The seven streetlights of the town were coming up.

"You're here, man," I said. "Get out of my truck and get that looked after! Thanks for ruining my night, asshole."

Shirley

Steve mumbled something, stumbled into the hospital. He almost fell onto the street. He turned around and threw his dirty shirt into my cab. It landed on Shirley's lap and she screamed.

"Gimmie that," I said. Just as I grabbed it to throw it out the window, my head got a little dizzy. The bloody alcohol-and-sweat-soaked shirt landed on the door and hung there. I couldn't even get rid of the damned shirt! Shirley kicked it with her foot and it landed on the floorboard. Good enough. Fuck. I forgot. I'd had a few drinks before I left.

"So I probably shouldn't be driving," I announced.

"Why not? You just got to the party and had like one sip."

"Yeah, I finished off a mickey before I got there. I figured it takes twenty minutes to feel alcohol, so I'd be fine till I showed up. I didn't think I'd have to drive to the hospital."

"My uncle's house is close. We can sober up there," she said.

"Fuck, I can't believe I'm missing the party."

As usual, there were two of me that night. There was Rex. He was young, naive, stupid. He hated his stepdad and everything he did. Then there was Shirley's Rex. There was some kind of fantasy going on with her. Shirley's Rex was the brooding artist from school, and this was her last chance. It was only by dumb luck that I managed to keep my mouth shut. I was so preoccupied by the medical emergency that I didn't turn into the promise keeper who would never think of a woman sexually.

The alcohol kicked in and the memories faded. I was overtaken by the void. The sky was spinning. I could see the stars. I remember bits and pieces, like a camera shutter.

Snap: We are laughing in a hot tub.

Snap: We are in the kitchen having shots.

Snap: She's riding me on a bed.

She was right there, naked, young, enthusiastic, and I was barely paying attention. I'm interested, but distracted. What the fuck is wrong with me? Pussy has a similar effect to smelling salts. In my head, that old man was shouting at me,

"Hey, can you hear me? Paying attention? Hell yeah, boy!"

Fuck. I was just like Jon. I was on her like a dirty shirt. No,

The Dog Walker | R.A. STONE

not like Jon. This was different, I was better than that. I'm not an asshole. It's okay. It's not like I was doing coke and fucking someone's girlfriend. We were friends from school. She helped me save a life today. This wasn't the same thing as Jon. I'm better than that.

The doorknob turned, slowly. Shirley's cousin opened the door and saw the two of us fucking. She screamed and ran off. I was just about to cum, but then I went soft. The world always threw something in my way. I tossed her off and rolled over, embarassed. I don't know why. It felt like I was supposed to be embarrassed. I went with it.

"I can't finish now," I said. "I have to go."

"Are you fucking kidding me?"

"I'm sorry. I have to go."

"What? You don't have to. It's okay. She's cool."

"I…I just…I can't finish. I'm sorry."

I sat up and looked away, ashamed. She rolled over to the other side of the bed and grabbed her panties off the floor. She hopped as she put on her pants, not happy. I can't blame her. I don't want to be one of those guys who fucks her in front of an audience. I refuse to finger blast her when her family is watching like drunk rednecks under a spotlight in a field. That's just sick. I hung my head. I put on my pants and shirt and shuffled off. I was had. I got found out. I didn't even take the condom off.

But I'm not like him.

This isn't who I am.

I never do this.

I'm a good person.

♦

That was the last time I saw Shirley. I saw Manjeet every now and again in college. It was nice to have a friend who hated our childhood as much as I did. She was popular now, always surrounded by people. She got contact lenses. Her skin cleared up. She grew a few more inches and her tits got bigger. Jon would have said something about that and he wouldn't have been wrong.

Manjeet's dad had arranged her to be married at twenty-five per their custom. Manjeet must have fucked half the white guys in college by twenty-four. One day we were walking home from campus and she confided,

"Life is over once I hit twenty-five, so why not? Besides, the guy I'm marrying is probably doing the same thing."

"Hey, I guess." Must be a cultural thing, I thought.

"Well, it sucks, man," she said. "Why does everyone else get to have fun, but I'm supposed to sit at home doing nothing. I'm going to have fun and do what I want, and then I'll probably settle down and get married and have kids, and I never want to look back and think I missed out, you know?"

"Not me," I said. "I know who I am, and I have rules. I don't want to be that kind of asshole who does that to women. I figure if I ever do find a girl, she will appreciate me treating her well."

"Aww, that's sweet."

The only time she hung out with Indian dudes was when someone pissed her off. Then it's easy for her to cry to her twenty cousins so that they could fight for her honor at the bar. She wore her saree on Sundays when her dad visited. First thing Monday morning, she put on the cleavage-wear like a dirty shirt.

For me, understanding this shit with women was all about finding the patterns just like Mega Man II. I still had that shitty acrylic blanket from home. I couldn't wait to be done with school so I could afford nicer things.

3

Rose

Summer, 2008. He fucked another one. I could do it just as much except I'm not an asshole. I have my shit together.

I struck out last night, but he managed to take home some blond girl. I think she was a student. I saw them yelling at each other in the parking lot on my way home. By the time she stopped yelling, I would be in bed. She still fucked him after all that. The next morning was Saturday, and we were going out again.

He was wearing a baseball cap he picked up in Ireland. It matched his t-shirt with the green, white, and orange stripes.

"You're such a fuckup," I told him.

"Whatever. I picked up and you didn't."

"Yeah, but you don't even remember shit about it, and you spent like an hour yelling at each other like children. I know how to keep my shit together."

"Are you on about your stupid rules again? Did you jerk off to them last night?"

He had a point. My rules made me feel better about seeking the patterns I wanted to see and not seeing what existed. I wanted to go on dates, take girls out to dinner, learn about their inner beauty, and maybe see where it went, but I also had to sail half the year. Dating steadily gets difficult when those dates all end with my saying, "I had a really nice time. I have to go to work for the next three months. Can we do this again in October?"

It never happened again in October, so I had to make a choice. Either become pro at jerking off or learn to date faster. When I first met Mike at fleet school, he introduced me to this guy named Mystery and his The Annihilation Method DVD's.

It was cringe. It reminded me of Mega Man II, all about the patterns: Open like this, then build rapport. Start touching at Level 1 and work your way up to level 10 or until she says no. Seduce like this and don't worry about rejection.

I was desperate and I needed help. I would have listened to anyone at this point because everyone I knew in real life was useless when it came to dating and picking up women. They all gave the same advice. They either said, "be yourself" while they glanced over at their wives for approval, or "just talk to them" if they were guys so attractive that I'd probably fuck them, too. At least these nerds wearing T-shirts over top their dress shirts had a semblance of a plan.

But that kind mass market, cookie cutter dating was wrong. It was asshole behavior. I wasn't Jon, so I decided to remember them all. Being able to list from memory all the girls I knew meant that I cared, and, at least, trying to care made me better. Mike fucked that blond and I didn't, but I remembered her so I was better. I managed to sleep with the brunette named Sara while he slept with her roommate, but I remembered so I was better. He got that redhead, the Asian girl, and this one brunette named Alyssa. She was cute, but fuck was she annoying.

♦

I have six free weekends this year. Mike was posted to the tanker. He got to stay home and our gap widened. I had a weekend in February. Mike found a nice girl from Vancouver. I got shot down by twenty nice girls from Vancouver Island.

I had two weekends in March. We managed to meet two Calgary flight attendants in town for the weekend. I passed out after drinking a shot of Crown Royal, so he took care of both of them. He made fun of me on Monday because one of them slapped me in the face to try and wake me up, and the other one kicked me in the head later while she was riding him. Everyone had a good laugh.

My third weekend was in the bar early in the summer. Bethany was a sweet looking French girl with short hair dyed like a blue and gold Macaw. She was drunk and none of the patterns I'd learned from Mystery's DVDs were working.

"So why do they call you Rex?" she asked. "Is that like your real name?"

"It's Reginald. Rex is just what they call me at work."

"Why do they do that?"

"Because every time I wake up, I yell and swear until my feet hit the deck. My buddy Jason tells me it's like sleeping beside a T-Rex, and it just kinda stuck."

"Oh. I thought it might be like Oedipus Rex or something and you had a crush on your mom." Cheeky bitch.

"Hey, she's not my type. I don't date single moms. Besides, that's rich, coming from a girl wearing a Mackaw on her head."

"I'll have you know I used to own a parrot when I was a kid."

"Is that why your hair is blue and gold?"

"That's exactly what I was going for. I'm a hair color master!"

"Cool! Let me see." I leaned in and ran my fingers through her hair. She seemed oblivious, but not repulsed. I took that as a good sign. For all that color, her hair was very soft. My mind wandered. I could probably grab a good handful in the moment. Stay focused! Build report. Use the cube, that system works every time.

"I have this thing I learned from a friend of mine," I said. "He's a psychology major. It's kind of wild. Would you like to see?"

"What? No, let's do another shot!"
What the fuck?

29

"Hey, you're pretty fun," she said. "I'm having my birthday tomorrow. You should come!"

"Oh yeah? Where at?"

"GLO, tomorrow at six. Here's my number. I have to go. My friends are over there!"

She threw back a tequila shot while I held onto mine. I tossed a twenty dollar bill onto the counter. The bartender put the bill in the register and withdrew some coins for change, then looked at me. I shook my head. He threw it in the tip jar. When I turned back around, she was gone.

I had assumed things would go one way, and it was not the way they went. There's a pattern but I can't see it yet. Bethany turned out to be a pretty good friend. I went to her birthday and discovered she had forgotten we even met. After that, we became fast friends. She cut my hair for free for the next five years.

But the night wasn't over, yet. A small hand grabbed my shoulder. I turned around and saw a little blond girl staring at me. Behind her was Mike, laughing. I guess they had been watching me with Bethany this whole time and making bets on how it would go.

"Rex! There you are! I'm taking off. You gonna be okay?"

"Were you people-watching me again?" I asked.

"Yes. She was rooting for you, but I knew you'd screw it up. You should have seen the look on your face when she handed you the shot glass and ran off! You looked like Kermit on the muppet show mad at Ms. Piggy!"

I bet when he gets, home he's just going to be stupid and never call her the next morning. We walked outside and headed over to his truck parked across the street. The girl looked over at me and pouted, "Don't let Mike get to you. I was rooting for you. Don't worry about it. Eventually the right girl will come along."

"Story of my life," I said. "Thanks for the pep talk. You should get on her like a dirty shirt, Mike!"

She definitely heard that. "What is he talking about? Who

do you think I am?"

"Don't worry about it," said Mike. "Man talk, just look pretty, okay?"

"What the fuck!?" And with that, this girl's inner daddy issues came out.

"Hey Mike, I'm just gonna walk, I'll see you tomorrow."

"You son of a bitch," he said. When he turned around, she was giving him shit. He'll still fuck her. I was sure of it. It felt good that he has to work a little harder.

I never got the appeal of that truck. It did have the wow factor. It was a one-ton, but the locks were automatic. Girls waited for the click, opened the door themselves, and climbed up and into a Lazyboy of a car seat. They were five feet away from you. Since it was an automatic, you had no reason to even reach over to her side. My Sentra may have been a small, boring, four-door fuel-efficient sedan, but it was intimate. My only issue was getting past the dad car impression.

Two doors down is the Duke. I walk into the crowd which is blocking the sidewalk: drunk, bedazzled people hoping for a final chance at love for the night. I see Jason. It's hard to miss him. He's standing beside two blond girls with a tall, curly-haired redhead. He's talking to them like he's selling a used car or pitching a movie script.

"Jay!"

"Hey what's up man? Where's Mike?"

"He went home. What are you doing in this shithole?"

"Oh man. The Duke is great. Where were you?"

"Upstairs Cabaret."

"Yeah. Everyone there is worried about everyone else. They are just showing off. It's so much better here. No one comes here, so no one cares. You can just relax and do your thing."

The redhead put her hand on Jason's chest and tried to push him back, but he's so big she just pushed herself closer to me. I grab her shoulders and steady her.

"No way!" The redhead interrupted,

"We just like that they play metal. Everyone else just throws

31

out top forty crap and it's all cheerleaders being mean girls."

"Rex. She's just like you man. Won't shut up."

The redhead furrows her brow. The blond is laughing at the spectacle.

"Sure. Hey, don't you have a duty watch with me tomorrow?" I asked him.

"Yeah, 0730. It's the weekend though. Long as I don't have the first shift, I'll be able to get a nap in. But what are you doing here? Aren't you all Mr. Fucking Perfect?"

Jason had a point. He was a gong show. He would pass out on the brow and get yelled at by the officer of the day, then get three more duty watches for practice. Everyone loved him since he always wound up taking most of our duty watches which gave us more time off.

"So this here, the pushy loudmouth, is Julie. And this is … "

He has no idea who she is and I'm loving the awkwardness. I give it a pregnant pause then step in,

"Hi, I'm Rex."

"Rose," said the petite blonde. Your friend is so funny!"

Julie was a fiery redhead with porcelain skin. She had the same pattern of freckles as me and stood a little shorter than me. The other girl was tiny. Maybe five feet. She wore short heels that she was not altogether comfortable in. The word Rocawear was written across them. Her jeans looked painted-on and didn't go to her ankles. A white, sleeveless t-shirt with a v-neck collar that draped down like a scarf revealed a well-defined collar bone.

"Aren't those rapper shoes?" I said.

"Probably. I'm borrowing them from Julie."

"Are you borrowing the shirt too?" I laughed.

"How did you know?" She raised her hands in front of herself in mock defensiveness. Jay cut in.

"Because that shirt is made for girls to show off their boobs. Only a redhead would be fiery enough to buy it!" Julie had the same trucker sense of humor. She laughed right along with him.

3 Rose

They were made for each other. He was always a great wingman. Now, I get to be the good cop.

"Yeah, he does that when he is drunk."

"It's okay. It was funny, and it is her shirt."

"That makes sense. He's got a thing for redheads anyways, so you're safe. What are you two up to tonight?"

"We have an after party we got invited to. Some guy says he's a DJ. You guys should come!"

Julie elbowed Rose. I started thinking that I was meant to cover the grenade, or whatever it is that girls call it.

That was it? No opener. I didn't need to ask a question that had a time constraint or that was sexually-charged as the Mystery DVDs taught. I didn't have to start with a forearm touch. I didn't need to do anything. Just say hi, ask for her name, and follow her to a party. Or a mugging. I wasn't sure yet.

"Where is it?"

"Five blocks up. Government Street, I think. We don't come downtown often."

"I'm guessing someone's parents are out of town this weekend. That's the rich part of town. No one who DJs owns a place there."

"I don't know," she said. "You coming or what?"

And with that we were off. I didn't have to do much talking. Jason did enough for both of us. Julie showed him something, a pill maybe? He ate it before anyone could react. She looked back at Rose and I.

"You guys want molly?" she asked. Rose grabbed one.

"Naw man, I'm good," I said. "Knock yourself out."

Jon used to love cocaine. When work dried up, he switched to crack. He used to invite girls over to the cement plant to do coke in the office. But I was better than that. Rose must had seen the look on my face. There was no way she wasn't judging right now.

"You're not a molly guy, are you."

"Not my style," I said.

"What, are you Mormon?"

"Don't tell anyone. I'm doing missionary work"

"On a Saturday? At the bar? While drinking? I think you're making things up."

I didn't know what she actually thought I was. All she knew was that I'm not a Mormon at this point, so I double-down.

"Scout's honor! Do you know our lord and savior, Joseph Smith?"

"Shut up, really?"

"No. Fuck no. But, I do have a secret."

"Oh?"

"I have this thing I learned from a friend of mine. He's a psychology major. It's kind of wild. Would you like to see?"

"Sure, but hey, there's the place, I think."

Once again, I didn't get to run the Cube. It was like the world conspired to put things in my way. This is the street, it turned out. It's a quiet neighborhood. No street lights, just moonlight and a few porch lights. A quiet rhythmic bass thumped in the distance. I saw strobe lights on a roof pointed at the lawn. As we got closer, we saw someone lying on the grass.

"What the hell!?" Rose ran up and laughed. "I think this is it!"

Those tequila shots from earlier were taking effect. The world started to spin. Rose ran back and pulled me over to show me some guy with a pacifier in his mouth passed out on the lawn. She tripped and fell over him onto the grass and got a grass stain on her hem.

"Oh shit. Julie is gonna be pissed!"

I picked her up. Even half-drunk, it wasn't difficult. She was light.

"It's fine," I said. "Could be worse. Just keep that away from me. I'm allergic to grass."

"What do you mean? Like deadly allergic?" I grabbed Rose by the waist. The world didn't get dark, but I couldn't focus on any of it. The sky was spinning and the grass was slippery. What time was it? Next thing I remember, Rose was holding my hand

3 Rose

and we were walking back to the waterfront and the bars. I have no idea how much time had passed. I checked my watch. 4:30 AM. I had sixty minutes. Twenty minutes to walk to the base from here. Fifteen minutes to get to F jetty. Ten minutes to shave and get dressed. Tons of time.

We ended up at a hotel. What time is it? 5:15 AM. Twenty minutes to walk to the base from here. Fifteen minutes to get to F jetty. Ten minutes to shave and get dressed. Tons of time.

"Julie and I grabbed a room because we knew we were going to be too drunk to get home tonight."

"Well aren't you two all responsible?" I said.

She twisted her finger into her cheek like one of those anime girls and giggled.

I lived five minutes away from the bar and had never seen this hotel before. It was nice. Marble walls and floors. Brass fixtures and a beige couch against the wall. It was like being in the eighties. We got on the elevator.

"So I never told you, Rex. I'm getting married next month."

I grabbed her by the waist and pulled her into me. I looked up and saw a little black dome. I wonder if the camera is on? I gave her a kiss. She went limp and I almost dropped her. She made a sound. Half moan and half laugh. Her head fell back, and she started breathing in and out like she was blowing out a balloon.

"Oh, congratulations!" She fumbled in her pocket for her key card. She was trying to put it into the door but was too tipsy. She drops the card on the ground. I leaned her up against the wall and pointed at her. "Stay here," I said. "I got it."

I grabbed the card, opened the door, and we spilled inside. The room was small but nice. The bed was three feet from the door. She stumbled and fell onto it then took off her shirt.

"Oh, this is never going to come out," she said, examining the stain. "Julie is going to kill me."

I saw a rose tattoo popping out from her low rise jeans.

"A rose? I get it."

"Yeah. You like that?"

35

I must be sobering up. She's almost naked. I'm almost naked. Normally, I would be all about the experience, but all I can think about now is time. Hours, minutes, seconds. We are both naked except for the Omega Seamaster on my wrist. She's sloppily kissing me and all I could do was get anxious about the time. Numbers and time and a chief yelling at me and three weekends of duty watches and that smell. The smell of diesel and body odor and shaving with a cold face, so I barely noticed that we were already in the bed. She was having a blast. I couldn't tell if it was me or the molly. It's got to be the molly, I thought. I'm not really here. And she wouldn't shut up about her fiance.

"He's great. I'm so happy. I'm the luckiest girl in the world."

I mustered a small grunt. The conversation was weird. What time is it now? I bought the watch in Dubai. Steel and blue. No income tax when sailing and you don't buy food or anything while at sea, so the watch is more about the memory than it is a toy. It was now 6 AM. It took twenty minutes to walk to the base. Fifteen minutes to get to F jetty. Ten minutes to shave and get dressed. I was running out of time. Rose was still talking while we fucked. Her fiance sounded great.

She was thin, very thin. This rose had a thorn. I could feel her pubic bone. It didn't hurt, but I knew that when I sobered up, it would, like when I used to spar and I would slip up and kick someone's elbow. The stem of the rose went all the way down to her lips. It looked kind of cool. Her eyes were closed and her fiance was still great, and all I could picture was her thinking about floral arrangements or dinner seating or whether she wanted to wear a white wedding dress or whether she was going to Mexico for her honeymoon or keep it lowkey and hide on some remote island. I never did catch the guy's name. What did it matter? This is probably ruining their life together.

I should care, though, because Jon wouldn't care. I didn't really care, but it was different because I was different. Jon would get off on the thrill of conquest. I wasn't like that. I had to work in the morning, so it was different. I had to be there by 0730.

3 Rose

That would be ten minutes to get dressed. Fifteen more to get to F jetty. I was counting backwards. Why did they always park at the furthest fucking jetty? I bet the captain's parking spot was right there. I'd have to run. It's only five kilometers except I'm wearing Chelsea boots. Twenty-seven minutes in running shoes, I can do it as long as I leave here by 0630. What time is it?

0615.

"I just love him so much. He's the best guy I've ever met. Keep going, that feels so good."

"I'll bet you like it hard like this," I said. I wish I had been aggressive and lustful, but I wasn't, not really. I said it mostly because I felt I had to say something.

I hurried up because I was running out of time, thrusting like somehow forcing it will make everything work out. It didn't matter. I'm in the middle of it and all I can hear is the second hand of that Omega Seamaster ticking at me like an unimpressed coworker. I felt the mechanics tapping my wrist winding every time I shift back and forth. I was going to be late.

I was going to get charged. I just knew it. I was going to be given at least three duty watches, maybe even confined to ship. Never mind that my relief was going to be pissed. He just wants to go home, and he's stuck til I get there. Rose is still talking about her soon to be marriage and soon to be husband and how he's the greatest man in the world. Neither of us were there. We were going through the motions. If I don't finish, it doesn't count.

0629. Fuck. I don't even get to enjoy the release.

"I have to go. I have to run to work."

"Right now?"

"Yes! I was supposed to leave ten minutes ago! My chief is going to have my ass."

"I already have that ass."

"Oh shush. Where's my pants?"

My pants were crumpled up on the other side of the bed. She passed them over then crawled under the sheets.

"Just tell him, something more important came up?" she

37

said.

She was giggling. I was having a panic attack. Chelseas? One boot in the corner. Another by the door. Socks.

"Where's my shirt?"

Rose held the blankets up to her chest, a little bit of modesty for the bride. I found my shirt and put it on. It was way too tight and there's a stain on it. I couldn't even pull it down. I sneezed.

"That's my shirt," she said. " Here!"

She gave mine a sniff and tossed it towards me. It had been camouflaged in the sheets. I threw hers back to her. It landed on her head, the grass stain staring at me like a green eye patch. She laid back, enjoying the glow of molly and sex and the post sex show as the door closed behind me.

The elevator took forever. I had to run. I hated running. Every stride hurt more than the last. My heels are wood. The ground is cement. My shins shook with every step. I tasted blood with every breath.

0720.

There isn't going to be any time for hot water. No time to iron my uniform. Throw a jacket over top and hope no one notices. What the hell is she going to tell her fiance? Will he believe her? How exactly do those talks play out? I had no idea. I couldn't think about that right then. I was coughing and tasted blood. Just one more hill, then I would be at the brow.

0729.

I stopped in the brow and saluted the ensign staff. Flag wasn't up yet. Jason was holding it. He was in uniform already and was laughing. He looked like death. He looked over and tapped the officer of the day. The officer of the watch was standing there and looks over. He started laughing, too. I ran below decks.

0732.

No time for hot water. Shaving raw. Every stroke felt like pain. My pelvis was burning. My face was burning. My shins were throbbing. I grabbed the bosun call.

0745.

The officer of the day was standing at attention.

"Colors!" I put the bosun call to my lips and made the general call and stood at attention. My balls were on fire. Jason hoisted the ensign. This was the longest minute of my life.

"Play the carry on." I piped the carry on.

"Dismissed." Thank fuck.

"Was she worth it?"

"I don't know yet sir."

"Awkward!" said Jason.

"Relax. Just tell me the details when you've fixed your face. You look like hell."

"Yes, Sir!"

♦

Midnight watch. I walked up to relieve Jason. He had gotten less sleep than me but bounced back well. Rose, I said to myself. Married. Number 23. Don't forget. Jon would forget, but you're better than that. When I got to Jason, he was sleeping.

"Wake up! Chief's coming!" I said. He jolted awake and sat up.

"Fucking guy."

Jason leaned back against the bulkhead and laughed.

"Hey, man, you're looking rough," I said. "I can still hear those speakers in my head. It's throbbing."

"Yeah. We saw you running to the jetty in your bar clothes from last night. I told the LT about the girls. He started laughing, said he wished his wife would do that."

"Yeah. At least his shins aren't throbbing. Dude, I think she gave me an STD."

"What, really? It takes more than a day."

"I don't know. She was skinny and I was clacking our pelvic bones together. Hurts like hell. Did you end up with Julie?"

"Yeah. She's crazy, man. She watched me sleep and I think she's still at my house!"

"Redheads. You know my girl was engaged?"

"What, the blond one?"

"Rose. Yeah. The worst part. I've been reading up on how to flirt better with girls. There's this one routine I wanted to do but I never got a chance."

"That sucks, Rex. Guess you'll have to settle for getting laid and having fun then."

"Yeah."

4

Sara

"Who is that trailer park bitch you brought home last night?" Mike asked.
"That was Matt Webber's wife."
"Oh, Sara? Right on man. I hate that guy. I'd have done her, too."

I was monitoring comms in the control room when Webber tapped me on the shoulder. He was a wiry twenty-nine year old man with the face of a fourteen year old who sounds like he is chewing his own face when he talks. Jason was standing beside us. He smelled like cigarettes and old coffee. I didn't know Webber well, but everyone who did couldn't stand the guy. I don't think he knew. He was just one of those guys. He walked in between Jason and I.

"Don't forget, Jason. I'm getting married. You have to take me out and show me a good time!"

"We know. You haven't shut up about it all week."

I looked at Jay. He looked at me. Does this guy know how abrasive he can be?

"I'm just saying. We are getting married next month. Finally going to be one of the old hairy bags who gets to leave his wife six months out of the year."

Jason was good. He played it straight. I wished I had his

patience with people. Nothing ever annoys him.

"What was her name again?" I asked.

"Sara."

Jason laughed.

"Yeah. They met at the Duke."

It made sense now. Jason would take me there whenever a ship deployed. It transformed over time from a gothic heavy metal bar with cave paintings on the wall and black and leather as far as the eye could see into a middle class suburb inhabited by bored, underfucked soccer moms dressed in the finest bar clothing you could find at an outlet mall. The only place I thought was worse was the strip club in Tijuana where the ship docked once. They'd had a donkey outside painted like a zebra waiting for drunken tourists. Ride the Zebra™! Five bucks USD per trip!

My mind wandered back to the present. Webber was still talking. It was just noise. I hadn't missed much.

"Yeah. Her friend Erin took her there. She doesn't go out much. Anyways, we were at her parents place. I bought them a car so they could come to the wedding." He had this smug grin, like he had won the lottery. Finally, a good man with a good job. Feels good to be needed.

"Wait, you bought your inlaws a car?"

"No. Technically, I bought the car but Sara needed it. Then she lent it to her parents for a month because we were going to be sailing and I didn't need it."

"Sounds like she has you wrapped around her finger, dude." Jason prodding him kept me entertained. I'd never seen someone so excited and enthusiastic about talking about nothing. I had a mini panic attack. Everything I was terrified of happening to me if I settled down was what he was taking a victory lap about.

I could just picture how it had happened to him. Webber, slowly blinking, taking a piss in a stainless steel trough. Looking up and seeing five hundred magazine clippings of pussy wrapped in leather stapled to a cork board behind scratched

42

Sara

plexiglass. No paper towels. Just air dryers. A dance floor full of aged out shack rats. At a table across the way would be two lone white women. A red-headed goddess, Sara. Three gray stripes of hair from some vaccination, a bride of Frankenstein hair-do. Webber looking over and thinking "she must be saving herself for just the right man." Her wingwoman, a thick, rugby-inspired girl. Built for churning butter or popping out farmhands. Love at first sight.

He was still talking about the fucking car?

"No no. I'm going to be a good husband. Why wouldn't I take care of everyone? Her dad is between jobs right now, and I wasn't using it anyways, so why not?"

"Do you have to pick them up for the wedding or will they have their own ride?" Jason asked. Webber must be able to see him laughing. He just doesn't seem to care.

"Ha ha, very funny. No, I don't have to pick them up for the wedding."

"So are you having a big ceremony? Friends from back home?" I asked. I was being earnest. I was trying.

"No, I don't have a lot of friends back home, and it's like a four hour flight, so it'll mostly be her folks and some of her friends here."

"Don't worry then, Webbs. We got you, man. If you can't trust your shipmates, then who can you trust? We got a plan."

"We do?" I said. Jason slapped me in the chest.

"I do. I'll tell you about it at standeasy."

A beep started going off on the console. I excused myself to look. It was a military grade server rack. The monitor was welded into a steel cage and sported a retractable keyboard built out of heavy duty rubber, plastic, and aluminum. Across the top, a foil label read SECRET, 5-eyes (FVEY) only in metallic red.

A new message was incoming. Routine priority. CONFIDENTIAL. It was the Operations Schedule for the winter. Captain will want it in the morning. Nothing requiring immediate action.

Was Webber still talking about the inlaws?

43

"So we are actually kind of kinky," he said.

"Wait, what?" I said. Oh god. He's talking about his sex life now. Goddamned Jason. I never wanted a terrorist threat more in my life. I stood there, staring at his pale skin, his cigarette stained teeth, those boyish ... looks. The last thing I wanted to picture was him naked, hunched over, lanky and horny.

"Everyone's kinky man, whatever." Jason said, baiting him again and loving it. So was Webber. I thought we must had been the first people in his life who were aware he'd had sex before, and he had been dying to get it out.

"No, they're not. Not like this. We usually have fun with others, where we…"

I tapped him on his chest. "You mean like swingers? I said. "Key parties and shit? You?"

"Yeah."

"Wait, I thought you said Sara was a virgin," Jason said.

Now I know why Jason was baiting. He already knows all this. He knew I didn't know. I thought he was baiting Webber. He was actually baiting me. I glared at him, that son of a bitch. He can't hold it in any longer. He's laughing hard.

"When we met, yeah, she was. What can I say? I have that effect on women."

"No, you don't."

"If you don't believe me. Last weekend, do you know Candus?"

"The clerk?"

"Yeah, her. She and her boyfriend."

"She's seeing someone?"

"Aaron, on the tanker. He works with Mike. You know Aaron."

"He is so quiet. Makes sense. Doesn't want to tell everyone how he's into that stuff." A shaved head, thick hipster glasses, wiry, but strong. He didn't drink and never came out to party. I got it, now.

"So we were hanging out, and then started fooling around. Candus and Sara thought it would be fun if I got up and took pictures. At the foot of the bed. It was awesome, man."

"Where was Aaron?"

"He was there, too."

"So you sat there and took pictures of the two of them sleeping with your wife?"

"Fiance. Yeah." I stood corrected, feeling duped. I needed an excuse to get out of there.

"Here. I'm falling asleep. Can you watch comms for a bit? Want a coffee?" I didn't even wait for an answer.

"Sure, thanks Rex."

My ears were ringing. The chillers were running at a hundred decibels assaulted my ears. Have to keep the servers cold. Tinnitus is a small price to pay for emails. My ears were ringing. Maybe more from Webber's visuals than the chillers. I walked over to the ops room ladder. I turned to face away from it, grabbed the rail, and slid down like a kid on a slip and slide. Six Halon tanks were there to break your fall if you slipped. I turned and there was the burnt smell of cheap coffee. They couldn't spend the extra three cents a pound for better coffee, but it was still a small price to pay to not have to hear about Webber's dick any more. I grabbed two cups and filled them with a tarlike fluid that they swore was coffee. I added a pinch of salt. It made shit coffee bearable but will never make bearable coffee good. Five minutes earlier I would have complained, but now this cup was the most important thing in the world. It was burnt salvation. Jason ducked under the hatch combing and joined me.

"Must suck being too tall for the office," I said.

"Won't be my first scar."

"So yeah, hey, you set me up, you dick. Did Webber just admit, no, did he just brag about taking photos of people railing his wife?"

Jason grabbed a cup.

"Dude, I can't even. I figured you would like that. I had to hear it so now you have to."

"So what are we doing this weekend, then? There's a plan?"

The sugar is too wet, it's clumped and I can't pour it. I jam a fork into the jar to dislodge it.

"Well, I'm not taking molly, thats for sure," Jason said. "Do you know that chick was outside my house hiding in the bushes, and she called my house yesterday?"

"What, Julie?"

"Yeah. Man she's great in bed, but she's crazy. She already knows my sailing schedule. She emailed me some topless photos on the network. I'll show you later."

"Jesus. Yeah, I don't want to have another one of those weekends for a while. So, the plan?"

"Yeah. Way I see it, Webber barely ever drinks. I figure we get him to my place and start feeding him Rusty Nails. We drive to the bar, and I give the bouncer a fifty. We get Webbs to the bar, and then he'll get so drunk that whatever we do, he won't remember. Besides, I kind of feel bad for him."

"Because they railed his wife?"

"No. I don't think he has a lot of friends. I figure we should be good shipmates."

"Why give the bouncer the fifty?"

"Hey, I know what I'm doing here. Webber is going to be drunk, and he'll probably get kicked out. You always tip the door guy in those situations so that we don't get kicked out, too. And if I get too drunk, instead of the bouncer dropping my head on the pavement, he'll be more likely to hail me a cab. It's insurance, man."

"You've really thought this out, haven't you?"

A pregnant pause. Jason took a sip and looked back and forth. Everyone else was busy doing their own thing. He leaned in and spoke softly, "Besides, Sara is kind of a looker," he said, "in a redneck sort of way." He nods his head as if that revelation changes things.

"If you say so. Is Candus on board today?"

"I think so. What, you're going to ask her!? No way man."

"I gotta know."

"Well, good luck with that. I wouldn't tell a living soul if I let some coworkers rail my wife, let alone provide photographic evidence, but whatever."

I handed Webber's cup to Jason and he went back up the ladder duck footing it, hands-free.

I headed forward, stopping at the clerk's office. Three sailors were sitting by the door lollygagging. I stuck my head through the window, "Candus, it's standeasy. You busy?"

"Hey!" She looks at the clock. 1450 zulu time. "It's only 0950. Besides, I don't like seafood."

Maritimers hate seafood. To them, lobster is for the poors. I was a prairie boy, so I thought the same thing about beef. I'm also not a fan of railing someone else's wife. We all have our burdens to bear.

"It's Thursday. It'll be curry carrot," I said. "C'mon, it's not like you're working."

She logged off her workstation and we went for soup.

♦

The carrots were sickly sweet. The cooks had roasted them last night for supper and saved a few bucks by blending the leftovers with curry spice and called it a soup. I never liked it. Sweet and slightly burnt. The coffee was burnt. The soup was burnt. The only thing that wasn't burnt was the bacon. It's always undercooked. I ate a spoonful. It's like bad karma. I had to know what the hell was going on.

"You really love the curry, don't you?"

Candus stared at her bowl. She didn't miss a beat.

"It's better than cooking."

"I'll never get what's with you chicks. Not a single girl on board knows how to cook."

"What about O'Connor?" Candus gave a nod to the kitchen. O'Connor was standing there working the grill, burning something, I didn't know what. I stared. Candus looked back. She nodded. Fair enough.

"So how was Webber's wife?" I said. It startled her. She slammed her spoon into her soup and looks up.

"Is that what you brought me to soup for? For fuck sakes, Dude!"

She slapped me on the arm. I was laughing too hard to feel it.

"I'm just fucking with ya. I hear Sara is kind of a looker though. Good for you!"

"Yeah, she's all right. Kind of has that trailer park look to her, you know?"

"I've been there."

"You too?"

"No. I mean I understand."

"But Webber. Damn, Webber is such a dweeb. Don't tell anyone this by the way."

"Naw. The last thing I want to do is tell everyone about Matt's dick."

"Oh he didn't get naked. I kicked him out of bed and told him to take pictures. Aaron and I wanted to fool around with Sara, but I wasn't letting him touch me."

"Harsh, lady. Harsh."

"Well, I'm not going to let that guy's dick anywhere near me."

"I get it, but damn."

"Yeah, don't tell him. They come over now and again and it makes Aaron happy. Why did you want to know anyways?"

"His bachelor party is tomorrow. Jason and I are hosting it. I have to figure out what to do."

"Oh that's easy. He can't drink for shit. Just get him drunk then tell him the next day how much fun he had."

"That's what Jason said!" Candus took our bowls to the dishwasher, loaded them onto the rack, turned around and shook her head. She gave me the stare. I got it. Don't tell anyone. Get him drunk. Become a hero.

♦

The lounge area at the club had these great white leather

sofas. They inspired me to buy mine. Jason and I sat down. He gave me the nod that meant, We did good, right? I felt a tap on my shoulder. I turned around and saw the door man, a three hundred pound black dude, looking at us. At least he was smiling.

"Hey man," he said. "It's a good thing you put your friend in a cab. I was just about to kick you all out of here."

He gave Jason a pat on the back, and we went back upstairs to continue dancing and drinking. Jason looked at me like he just discovered fire.

"Now that is why you tip," he said.

I gotta hand it to the guy. There's a method.

"I got this round," I said. I stood up and pointed at his bottle. He nodded. "Matt really can't handle his liquor, can he?"

The bartender looked over. He leaned in and I yell, "Four tequila shots and two Molson." I dropped a five into the tip jar. He nodded and went to the fridge. Someone threw an arm around me. I tensed up.

"Rex!" Squeaky voice. False alarm. Red hair. Three patches of white.

"Sara?" We've met briefly, once at a Christmas party for all of three minutes, but she was looking at me like it was a reunion.

"Yeah! We heard you guys were taking Matt out for his bachelor party, and we happened to be out drinking and thought we'd come by and say hi."

"We?"

"Yeah. This is my friend, Erin. This is Rex."

"Hey."

She wasn't fat, but she definitely had the look of a professional butter churner, or a rugby player. She had a wide face with deep dimples and freckles like a Jackson Pollock and the hindquarters of a horse girl on the farm. Not my type, but cute. She looked sober. Sara's eyes were lit up like a Christmas tree. I wondered if she had the same bachelorette plan as we did?

"Nice to meet you," I said to Erin, then turned back to Sara.

The Dog Walker | R.A. STONE

"You looking for Matt?"

Sara nodded and looked around the room.

"Well, you just missed him. He blacked out and we had to throw him in a cab."

Bartender pushed four tequila shots towards me while opening two bottles. I set a pair of twenty dollar bills on the table and wave off the change.

"For us?"

"I guess so, now. Ugh, congrats?"

I looked over to wave Jason in but he was already behind us. He grabbed a bottle with his other hand and almost dropped his shot on my neck. We headed back to the sofa and started chatting. I sat back, looked up, and took a deep breath. The world started to spin.

♦

How long had it been? I looked at the Seamaster. 3 AM, not that long. I was still sitting on the sofa. The ass end of a pair of acid washed jeans was rubbing up and down my belt buckle. Erin was sitting on Jason's lap beside me. He was biting his tongue and laughing.

"See? I told you I have better booty than other white girls!" The jeans spoke! They turned around and I caught a strand of hair in the face. Gray. Sara sat down on my lap and brought a drink up to my lips. This one's not my fault. I didn't do anything. At least, I don't remember doing anything. I never walked up to her. She walked up to me. She reminds me of Shriley a bit. Hair was straight, and she had it in a high ponytail. She barely came up to my shoulders when we were standing. When I was sitting down and she had her ass in my face, she towered over me.

"I stand corrected."

I remembered that thing Mystery's DVDs said you're supposed to do: Tell a girl she's not good at something and she'll correct you. They can't help it. They just have to tell a man he's

4 Sara

full of shit, like it's instinct. I must have told her she was stiff on the dance floor. Suddenly, the music stopped and the lights turned on. Time for the Cube. I looked over at Sara.

"I have this thing I learned from a friend of mine," I said. "He's a psychology major, it's kind of—"

Sara took her palm and placed it over my face. She leaned over to yell at Erin. Her breasts are in my neck. She's skinny and they are kind of small but still feel soft. I have no idea what she was yelling, but Erin didn't look happy with her.

Jason leaned back to face me and said, "It's like 0330 comes earlier every weekend, man. We don't have to go home but we cant, stay, here."

I hated that song, but Jason sang it every single time.

My ears had been compensating for the loud music for the last few hours. A loud tone pretending to be silence snapped me sober.

We all got up and headed down the stairs and out to the sidewalk. A crowd of fifty people have formed spilling onto the street. Three cabs sat just outside the mob, and competing groups of people were talking amongst each other. A drunk blond girl stumbled over her words while negotiating for a cab. A couple dove into the back seat while she poked some guy in the chest. Sara and Erin shivered in the cold night air. I yelled like we were still inside.

"C'mon. The cabs will take an hour to get here. My house is five minutes away. We can wait for the rush to finish then call it from there." Sara lit up, looked over to Erin.

"Erin, sound good?"

Erin had a neutral expression. Jason had his arm around her back, resting on her hip.

"I'm sober. I can drive," said Erin.

She pulled out a set of keys, a Nissan logo on the keychain. My kind of girl. She pointed across the street at a black sedan. Nissan Altima, nicer than my Sentra. She pushes a button and the car winks at us. Jason and I open the back doors. I get in first. Sara shoves Jason over to the front seat and jumps into the

51

back with me. She lays on my lap, reaching behind her for the seatbelt.

"Get on the bridge. Take your first right. Look for the street Dingley Dell"

"Dingley Dell?" Erin said. "You're making that up."

Sara starts laughing.

"I know. I didn't name it. A Dell is like a cul de sac but no circle at the end of the street."

We pulled in and I pointed Erin to visitor parking. I guided the gang to my door. I motioned for quiet so as not to wake the neighbours. Sara giggled as I turned the key and opened the door. Erin walked in and noticed my mini bar. It sported an imitation leather front and a lacquered wood top. It was filled to the brim with every kind of cheap booze. Every sail, we smuggled back ten bottles, tax free, and I've had five sails this year.

♦

"You have a bar in your house?" Erin said, mildly impressed

"You expected a milk crate for a TV stand?" Just wait till she finds out about my fancy linens. I had forgotten that my duvet cover was ruined from another experience, so my top spread was just an exposed duvet, no cover. Naked. At least the bed's made.

"Well, you're not the first sailor I've met, so yeah." Jason was already behind the bar coming up with another one of his great ideas. He smacked the bar to get our attention.

"Hey hey hey! Here, I'm making flaming Sambucas. Blow it out before you drink."

Girls were easy to impress. Just use fire. It was catnip. I noticed Erin swaying. She was not sober. She looked so convincing as a wet blanket that she was either faking it or ... Smash! Sara dropped her highball glass. It was expensive, too.

"I'm sorry!" she yelled. "Don't step on it!"

Sara's laughing.

"It's tempered. It breaks into chunks so you don't cut yourself. I'll clean it up later."

The set of six is down to three. Sara continued sprinkling herself around the house like a fairy in a chocolate factory. She couldn't focus on anything but noticed everything.

"Is that a butcher block kitchen counter? Wow! And all your bathroom towels match? Who are you?" she walked over to the second bedroom. It was locked.

Oh shit, I forgot. Mike was in there sleeping, or was he sailing?

"That's my roommate. It's off limits, Sara."

She forgot about it instantly and ran over to my bedroom.

"Your bed is made? Are you sure you're not gay?"

"Not yet!" I said.

"And why do you have a duvet with no cover? Did you ruin your other sheets? Some bitch?"

Of course she noticed that.

"Long story, trust me, you don't want to know," I said, but she wasn't even listening. She was in her own little world.

"Erin! I'm dizzy! The room is spinning! We should just stay here tonight!" She spun in a circle like some acid washed trailer park princess fairy. The more I sobered up, the louder my tinnitus rang my ears. It was at six on the way to eleven. Sara stopped spinning, raised her arms in a t shape, then fell back onto my bed with a small bounce as she got consumed by the goose feather fluffiness of the duvet. I half expected her to talk about how great her fiance was, but she didn't.

I would have gone in there and done her. Jason was staring at me. Erin was staring at me. She took Jason's hand off her lap, set her drink down, and stumbled into the bedroom.

"Okay," she said. "I think that's enough. Time to go." My night was over. I didn't know whether to cuss Erin out or thank her. Jason stood up.

"Hey, can you drop me off on the way?"

"Yeah, just hop in the back seat."

Sara went limp. Erin tried to pick her up from the bed like a sack of rice. She managed to roll her onto the edge and hold

53

her up enough to get moving. Once everyone had shuffled out the door, I walked over and turned the deadbolt, then went back to the living room and sat down on that great sofa, alone. Inside my head is like an air raid going off. My ears throb from the EDM residue. I would have been on Sara like a dirty shirt. It was different though. I knew her name. I knew her fiance. No one at work liked him. He'd already passed his wife around for the stories. Yeah, they were swingers, after all. It's not like I was doing coke at the cement plant with a coworker's wife or anything. Mike would probably have fucked Erin and no one would have said anything the next day, and this night would have gone very differently.

Thankfully I'm not that kind of guy. I'm not like Jon. I'm better than that. I took a deep breath, then blew it out like I was extinguishing that bass rhythm in my head. I didn't even take off my socks. I just went to the bedroom, opened my arms, and fell back onto my bed.

♦

It was 630 AM. My phone's alarm was going off. The music was from Air Man's stage in Mega Man II. Pleasant, but with a sense of urgency. I loved that game. Awake, I tasted ashtray. It was sticky and dry. My uniform was hanging on the bedroom door. Everything was ready, prepared the night before. I just put it on and walked. If I'd had to think and make decisions, the morning would be chaos. My legs tingled. I should have taken my socks off last night. I need a coffee.

I walked out of my room and saw that Mike's door was open. He was home after all.

"Dude, who was that trailer park bitch you brought home last night?" he asked.

He shoved a coffee into my hands while he drank his, shaking his head like a disappointed father. He grabbed the remote and turned on the TV, changing the channel to Sports Net.

"Sorry, I thought you were sailing yesterday."

4 Sara

"I was supposed to. They cancelled for some last minute maintenance. So who was that chick anyway? She sounded annoying as fuck."

"Yeah, that was Sara,"

"Webbers wife?"

"Yeah, you know her?"

"Sara? Ha ha ha. No shit! I'd have done her too man. I fucking hate that guy. He's such a dweeb."

"I didn't fuck her! I think she tried though."

"Sure man. I'm going to tell everyone you did. Who do you think is going to believe you?"

The caffeine was starting to mute the throbbing still going on in my head. My ears heard just a gentle hum now. I took a shower and a shave. I grabbed my uniform off the door and got dressed for work. My work jacket was in the coat closet. I opened the door and reached inside. A small leather jacked was in there beside my coat.

"Mike! Hey, what is this?"

Mike walked over. "Is this yours?" He burst into laughter.

"Little small for me. Wait, is that Sara's coat? Oh man, that's good."

Yeah, a real knee-slapper. We headed out the door and started walking toward the base. I'm never going to hear the end of this. Mike couldn't stop laughing. After a few minutes, I'd had enough.

"That's not funny man. What the hell am I gonna do about that? I have to go work with him today. And I'm going to say what? Hey man, had fun with your fiance last night. Here, she forgot this."

"Just give it to Webber. What the fuck do you think he's even gonna do? Like you said, you didn't do anything, right?"

As the boat came into view, I began dreading the next eight hours.

So I stood on the brow. Saluted the ensign. Grabbed a coffee. Went to the control room. Checked morning messages. Nothing urgent. I puttered about the mundane activities of a ship alongside. My mouth still tasted like tobacco and tar. Soon, a pipe sounded across the intercom. The general call. Ten already?

Standeasy.

Fish soup. Candus didn't show up. She hated fish. Jason wasn't there either. I wondered if he'd even made it into work. No rumors about his getting charged. He was probably sleeping it off in his rack. When he drank hard he would usually just sleep on ship. Can't be AWOL when you're here. We set our mess to be cold, which Jason liked. Matt never ate soup. It got in the way of kissing our chief's ass. He had to work on the bridge that day, so I hid away in the control room. I couldn't even bear to look at the guy.

Mike was probably on that tanker telling everyone about me banging Webber's wife. Someone would be over there to drop off a message or something, someone would tell him what they heard, and in an hour our entire ship would be talking about it. Word of my exploits would be disseminated fleet-wide by 1600. Say what you will about the navy, it was efficient. My supervisor came in, coffee in hand. Laz. He was a tall Polish guy who was recently posted to our ship after spending a few years at the shore office in Naples, Italy. I thought he was gay, but you'd never know it to talk to him. He was the saltiest man I have ever met. When he sees me, he smiles from ear to ear, gives me a nod, and in his cigarette-burned voice says, "So you slept with Webber's fiance, huh?"

"I really didn't, PO." Technically, I could just call him Laz, but I was hoping that by calling him by his rank, he would change the subject to the professional instead of the personal. No such luck. It doesn't even phase him.

"Come on. What are people going to believe? That you brought her to your place at three in the fucking morning and nothing happened? No one is going to believe that."

Then the phone rang. Thank god, work.

"Petty officer Lazaroff," he answered.

I quickly exited and slipped below decks. I set a record for how fast I took that ladder. I almost kissed the Halon tanks at the bottom.

I felt like shit. I barely slept and my mouth tasted like an ashtray and the world didn't have enough shitty burnt coffee to turn off the hum in my head, and, now, my fucking boss was laughing at me for fucking my crewmate's fiance during his bachelor party when I hadn't even done it. But I haven't seen Webber, so at least there's that. The PA turned on, another general call:

"Clear up decks. Return gear. All personnel are to …" Thank god. Almost in the clear. I don't know why I thought I was in the clear. We had another three years of daily contact. But I just felt if I could wait a few days, it would all blow over. I almost made it. That whole day I didn't have to see Matt. I didn't have to talk to Matt. I could just go home, lie down, and then figure out what to do next, or just wait and see. I went into the mess and grabbed Jason. He had the blanket pattern on his face.

"Time to go home. I can't believe you slept all day and no one came to get you."

"I know man, thanks. I feel like death. Oh, so you had a good night, eh?"

"Not talking about it. Come on, we can walk to my place and I'll drive you home. Jason put on the clothes from last night. He smelled like sour tequila and ash. I moved upwind so as not to get sick.

"Did you know Sara left her jacket at my place last night?"

"Oh dude! You should give it to Webber!" He started laughing through his migraine. I could see his eye twitching. I grumbled as we opened up the hatch and entered the quarterdeck. As I stepped out of the hanger, I stopped.

A chill ran up my spine.

This was exactly what I didn't want to happen.

I had gone the whole day.

The entire day.

And managed to not.

And now I'm here.

And right there.
Fucking Webber.
And he sees me.
And it's so much worse than I thought it would be.
Sara is there beside him.
She's laughing and smiling.
And four older people beside him.
Is that his parents?
Are those her parents?
Now they are all staring at me.
And Jason is staring at me.
"Let's get this over with."

We walked over to the brow. Matt walked up and put one hand on my shoulder and the other one on Jason's. He leans in.

"Hey man. Thanks for taking me out last night. I had a blast. Also, I appreciate you taking care of Sara. She said she would have never made it home if it wasn't for you guys. I'm glad you were there to make sure everything was ok."

That's it? Maybe I didn't need to catastrophize? We walked to the brow, and just before I was in the clear he stopped. Everyone stared at us.

"Oh, by the way. Sara said she left her jacket at your place. Do you mind if we come over and pick it up? Did you walk? We can give you a ride, or can just follow you if it's easier."

Wut.

"Sure. We walked," I said. Just go with it. I must have fucked that pause in the conversation because it was pregnant. I looked over at Jason, but he was already gone, saluting on the brow. Once he lowered his hand, he looked at us and belted out, "Awkward!" and walked off leaving me there. Alone. This would have been a great premise for a sitcom if it weren't so weird. I didn't like Matt. He was such a dweeb.

I sat in the back of Matt's car. Sara was in the front seat while Webber drove. His parents were in their car and her parents were with them.

"Just this way. Take a left before the bridge. Turn onto Dingley Dell."

"Dingley Dell? That's hilarious."

"I know. I didn't name it. A dell is like a cul de sac but no circle at the end of the street."

I pointed to the same parking spot Erin had used the night before, and everyone collected in the parking lot.

I walked into my building and everyone quietly followed behind me. I opened my door and invited them in. Webber went first, then the parents, then Sara. As she closed the door behind her and walked forward, she stepped on a piece of glass. It crunched, but no one said anything. I walked to the closet and slid the door open.

"Here, man." I grabbed the jacket out of the closet and handed it to Webber. Without even looking, he passed it back and Sara grabbed it from him and started talking to her mom. The two of us never make eye contact. You'd never think it by looking at her, that she has a better ass than other white girls. I wonder if I should mention that to Webber.

"Thanks. See you Monday!" And like that, everyone was gone and I was alone in my house. My head was clearer. I still tasted ashtray, and I was tired. I should lay down, I thought. I needed a nap, then I had to go buy that new duvet cover. First, I need to piss.

I didn't get it. If he had punched me, I could understand. But nothing. I probably deserved it, and I'd have let him. That's only fair. Had he asked me what was up, I'd have been honest with him and told him what had happened. But he didn't. He wasn't going to. He never asked. He never even thought to ask. Not a look of suspicion in his eye. Not a sound of curiosity in his voice. His parents hadn't thought to mention it, not that I knew of. Her parents hadn't said anything, not that they would. No, he one hundred percent trusted this woman, and whatever she told him sounded like Leave it to Beaver or Donna Reed or Everyone Trusts Raymond. He trusted her implicitly. I wished I was as trusting as Webber, but I wasn't. I would have gotten mad. I would have had questions. I sure as hell wouldn't

59

have invited my in-laws and my parents to watch it unfold.

I washed my hands and looked into the mirror. I looked like I'd been hit in the face with a shovel, but I felt fine. Soon, the adrenaline of sleep deprivation would wear off. I saw a guy in that mirror who was burning the candle at both ends, and he didn't seem to be enjoying it.

I probably would have punched him. He deserved it. What a dweeb.

"I didn't know what to think about it all. But you know who did."

It's okay. You don't have to pretend. I know you better than you know you. You wanted to fuck that trailer park trash, and you wanted Webber to fight you so you wouldn't feel bad afterwards.

"That's a stretch, don't you think?"

I don't think it is. You never hated him till he liked you. You acted just like Jon and he didn't care. Sara didn't care either. Everyone was doing their thing and being happy and carefree about it.

"Carefree about random people raw dogging his wife?"

Fiance.

"Of all the details, that's the one you're nitpicking?"

I mean it's a choice dude. He figures that she is the best he can do. She figures that he's an easy mark. It's weird, but they are both just fucked up enough to make it work. Or not. Either way, that's not your problem.

"You're not making me feel any better."

Your feelings are stupid and you should feel stupid for having them. You aren't the first guy, and you weren't going to be the last guy to do it. She was basically throwing herself at you. The only reason you didn't was because you didn't sort out that mother hen.

"Erin? She wasn't a mother hen."

Sure she was. If Jason was a better wingman, she would have fooled around with him and left you two alone. But he screwed something up, and then it became a game of, If she can't have fun, no one can.

"That's not the point."

It should have been the point. Instead, you're crying about your rules and your morals, but you're not the one engaged or married, and you didn't even do anything. Oh, and thanks for that. I was going to have fun, then you fucked it up for the both of us.

"I didn't do anything!"

Then why are you here talking yourself through some existential crisis? Why not get a nap and buy your fucking duvet cover that makes all the difference?

I hate that guy, but he's got a point. What exactly did I do wrong here?

5

Melissa

My sofa was sticky and uncomfortable and annoying but it cost seven grand and was fine Italian leather. I must not be used to fine things. I was sitting in my living room, reading, but would have to go out soon. I remembered how sticky my ass felt when I was having sex on the chaise lounge. It hurt my skin, so I bought a throw to keep from ripping my skin off again. I had Conan the Barbarian on my television mounted in my tetris-inspired bamboo bookshelf. Nothing got me riled up for a night out quite like Conan. I was also reading Bruce Lee's book The Tao of Jeet Kune Do for the twentieth time. Every chapter starts with a quote. I was on chapter four where Bruce opines:

When I didn't know the art, a punch was just a punch and a kick was just a kick.

Then when I studied the art, a punch was no longer a punch and a kick was no longer a kick.

Now that I have mastered the art, a punch is just a punch and a kick is just a kick.

I liked reading it every six months. I would forget parts then read them again as a reminder. This was my third time reading it that year. Eventually, I'd have it memorized. Things take a while to stick.

I looked at my Seamaster. It was almost time. I turned everything off. I put everything away. I looked in my closet for my best untucked dress shirt with gold stitching on the sleeve that looked like a dragon tattoo. Dark jeans. A spritz of Prada, Amber Pour Homme. Zirconia rocks for earrings. I didn't wear them for the look per se. I wore them because the military said not to. The navy may have made me work on Christmas, but I drew the line at getting dressed to go clubbing. I got in the Nissan and drove to the base. There was Darcy's pub. There was the civilian dockyard, then military housing. Military housing was hard to get. You had to be either an officer or a new family to get on the shortlist. They preferred people to live "on the economy" as it was cheaper for the queen. I showed my ID to the guard at the gate then pulled up to the Fleet Club.

Mike was already there. It was the base's bar for the enlisted men. It was a large concrete cube built to be a bomb shelter in case the Germans got uppity. It blocked the view of the rest of the base. No one likes to drink while staring at their office. Mike was in front of the screen. UFC was on. I used to love the sport back when it was a 150- pound kickboxer smacking a 300-pound sumo wrestler in the face with his mushy broken hand. Everyone who watched it was an amateur something and there were barely enough fighters to fill a Street Fighter character select screen. There were no patterns. There was only chaos and violence.

Why does everyone have to systematize everything? If they had just let shit happen and lean in on the chaos, it would have been a much better sport.

Beside us is a sonar operator wearing a hoodie with Tap Out printed across the torso and stretched out by his massive gut.

"I can't believe this shit! Couture, it's a fucking arm bar, just escape that shit!" he yelled. Eventually, he stopped combining his knowledge of mixed martial arts technique names in new and interesting ways long enough to finish off a pitcher of Keith's. Foam fell onto the p in Tap Out. I was angry. Who else was here? In the corner was a little blond girl not more than five foot three. She had a shoulder length bob and eyes large enough for anime. She was also thin. How novel. Looked civilian.

I walked over and sat down. "You don't look military," I said.

"Because of my hair?" She had a thick, maritime accent. Not Newfoundland. New Brunswick, maybe?"

"Well, I was going to say because you were thin, but your accent gave it away."

"Awww shucks. You're some cute, bai."

"That's the dumbest thing I've ever heard," I said.

She giggled. I don't know why they speak English but in French. It's always some far, some awesome, some cute. She's some trouble.

"Why did you think I was a civvie?"

"Because most women I meet join for one of three reasons. They're either looking for a man, looking to get away from a man, or because their dad was in."

"You don't know Lieutenant Lavesque?" she asked.

I sure did. She was the bitch in charge at the orderly room. She had power over our paychecks.

"Fair," I said. Women who are looking to get a man know the process. Find someone who is either a chief or an officer. Forget to use birth control. Retire.

"My buddy Mike and I are headed out after this. You should come with." I point to Mike as he walked towards the table with a pair of beers.

"Well, I'm here with a friend." Melissa pointed to a woman sitting at the bar. She was dark skinned with jet black hair, thin, easy on the eyes. Native? She had rather large, almond-shaped eyes, well-defined clavicles, and arms longer than what seemed natural. Bronze skin, a statuesque frame. On any other night, I'd have been on her like a dirty shirt. Mike sets the drinks down with a solid thud, then says,

"What are we talking about?"

"I was inviting Melissa out with us, but she says she has to take care of her friend."

"Bring her too!" Mike didn't care so long as he got laid. Plus, he was dating that Alyssa chick. If he didn't like the friend, he would just help me out like a good wingman then call her on his way home.

We all got in Mike's one ton, a Dodge 3500 in jet black. It was the vehicular equivalent to shoving a sock down your pants. I had the Sentra.

"Mike, let's go to the Duke," said Melissa.

The Duke was the place to go if you didn't want attention. It was four blocks away from the Upstairs Cabaret. Everyone went to the Upstairs, and that was the problem. Everyone saw everyone else. Everyone knew who was doing what and with whom. The Duke was where you went when you want to have fun and avoid that walk of shame that you'd have to talk about at work while drinking what the navy considered coffee.

The walls at The Duke were covered in oil paintings of twenty thousand year old Lasceaux cave paintings. The regulars were dressed in their finest heavy metal wear. You'd see them in their black clothes, chrome piercings, and pale makeup followed by four people dressed like a Gap commercial. The music was so loud you had to pantomime a conversation. Everyone is more interesting when you can imagine what they are talking about instead of actually hearing it.

When I looked over at Mike, he had that look in his eye. I knew that look. He was either going to roast me in front of everyone, or he was going to leave so he could fuck the long-armed friend.

"Hey man I gotta jet," he said. "I have work in the morning. Just make sure to tell her about your STD." Melissa looked at me quizzically. "Your what?" she asked.

"He's fucking with you," I said. "I don't have an STD."

"Riiight." Melissa rolled her eyes. Mike was laughing, hard. I was hoping she was in on the joke. If not, I was fucked as far as getting laid went.

Her friend interrupted. "Hey, do you mind if I get a ride with you?," she asked Mike. "I have to get home soon. I have work early, too."

It was a great performance on her part. Mike seemed pleased. "Yeah, hop in," he said. "Later Rex."

I never caught the girl's name. She turned around at the door and gave me a look. Then she looked at Melissa, who nodded. Then she and Mike were off, and I was on my own.

"Let's go out for a smoke," I said. I took Mel by the hand and led her out the back door.

Focus, I told myself.. Remember what Mystery said on the DVD. Keep it light, flirty. Tell three stories that show you have high value. Look for three indicators of interest from her. Reciprocate with three of your own. Escalate physical touch. Start with the forearm, move onto the leg, then pause. I looked at the Seamaster. Five minutes for the cigarette, fifteen for the story. Plenty of time.

I was on fire. Every line was effortless. Every story got a laugh. I hadn't even taken the cigarette out from behind my ear while she sat there puffing away. I have a smile from ear to ear. I had put in a year of effort to get this good. Melissa grabbed me by the arm, blew a lungful of smoke to the side, moved a tuft of her hair out of her face and said, "Rex, it's okay. You don't have to try so hard."

And with that, a year of working on fucking got fucked. I had great ice breakers. They were called openers. I had great stories that made me interesting. They were called rapport builders. I had mastered the art of breaking the touch barrier. It takes a lot of work to look casual, incidental. Hundreds of hours, multiple rejections, and a few successes. Now that I finally had it, I didn't have to try so hard.

The rest of the night went quick. We drank. We smoked. We made out. We left around eleven. I wasn't trying hard so I didn't really pay attention which was why I started doing it this way. Build a routine to be in the moment.

"Taxis take like an hour to get here. I live just across the water. Let's walk. You can call your friend on the way if she's worried about you."

"Yeah, I bring her along just in case I need help. She doesn't actually like going out very much. Besides, she says she likes people-watching."

"Ah. A temporary wingman. That's Mike."

"I think that's you," she said.

"What?"

"Never mind. Let's go."

Ten minutes later, we were naked on the couch. I bought this leather couch because it looks sexy, but it's not sexy. It's sticky, makes noises, and you're better off putting a throw onto it as a buffer if you're going to use it. Throws are what your grandmother uses, but that's not sexy. I tried really hard to stay still and not make the leather squeak. Not that it mattered. I gave up and picked her up by her hips and slid the throw underneath. It's the Nissan Sentra of sofa accessories.

Not less than two minutes later, Melissa was having what I thought was a seizure even though we had barely started. She pushed me up with both hands.

"What's wrong?"

"Wait, wait. Don't touch me," she said.

I assumed it was some sort of play to slow things down, like, Wait, we should stop, or something. Nope. As quickly as everything started, it was over. I didn't know how to process this. I preferred to believe that I was just that awesome. What guy wouldn't prefer to believe he's packing death, destroyer of worlds? A minute of preamble then five minutes of post-game analysis. Afterwards, she grabbed her bra and unceremoniously snapped it in place.

"Do you always cum that hard?" I asked.

"I have anemia. It's low iron in my blood. It's one of the side effects."

"Well, what about me? I'm not done yet."

"Well, finish yourself off, bai?"

She laughed. I don't know why I laughed. I got the Sentra and drove her home. I asked for directions and realized we were headed towards the base. Closer and closer. She lived in the barracks? No. Worse. The military housing just outside. She's a mom. That's the only way a young sailor gets one of those. Is her husband home. Is that why she's stopping me this far from her door?

"Drop me off on the corner here, okay?" she said. "Come by next weekend, you can take me out." Melissa kissed me on the cheek, then a noise, not so much a giggle as a hrmph. She checked both neighbors' houses for signs of life, then opened her door to go home. This is why I can beat Mike when I try. A Dodge would announce your arrival to the neighborhood. The Sentra is a four cylinder; quiet as a mouse. Why start drama? I prefer a simple life. On the drive home, I glanced at the rear view mirror. That guy looked pleased with himself, but I was so horny and blue-balled that I wanted to smack that shit-eating grin off his face

"Yeah. I'm proud of you bud. You may have gotten blue-balled, but at least you didn't fuck yourself this time."

I'm sure it was a one time thing. This girl should be fun. I probably should stop listening to the guys at work who tell me not to date military chicks. She wasn't bad, was she?

"If you say so." I made it home and threw the keys on the counter.

I grabbed the remote off the coffee table and turned on the TV. Threw on porn. College fuck fest. Tanned, slightly orange skin chick with dark hair and great tits. I finished myself off. I wouldn't try so hard next time.

♦

I had an uneventful week. Worked, came home, ate, worked out, repeat. Then it was Melissa's weekend. I pulled up to her place to take her out clubbing. I knocked on the door and she answered, she paused, looked left and right. She was scanning for the neighbors' watchful eyes. I heard high-pitched crying coming from her house. Satisfied that the coast was clear, she walked out and got in my car. She wore a denim jacket, a beige skirt, and a mean mug.

"Was that a kid crying?" I asked.

"That's Kaya. She's mine."

"Where's her dad?"

"Who fucking knows. He's an abusive asshole. Mom's watching her"

"You mean the lieutenant?"

"Fuck off. Sorry. She's just pissing me off right now. Let's go."

We had the same night as we did last week. She was nothing if not consistent. I pantomimed conversation while she smoked and got drunk. Then we walked back to my place. We made out for a few minutes, and she'd jerk me a bit then we fucked for few minutes and it was over. One night, we were drunk and she kicked over a hundred dollar martini glass I had ordered special. It had the Rossi logo and everything.

A week later, the only difference was that I had been sailing, so I still smelled like the ship when we went out. That time, she kicked my onyx chessboard when she came. She shattered it. I got that thing during the day of the dead celebration in Ensenada. At this point, I calculated my cost per bang. She was expensive, yet insufficient.

It was our third session. Once she stopped convulsing, I took a minute to daydream. King Midas, every pussy he touches turns to orgasm. How tragic. I look back at Melissa and her panties were back on. She was looking for her shirt.

"Here, it's on the night stand," I said. I threw it at her. "Are you free Saturday?"

"Actually, I've been meaning to tell you. I have to sail a bunch this month so I probably won't be around."

"Gotcha. Want me to take you home?"

"No thanks. My roommate is coming to pick me up. I guess my mom is annoying the shit out of her and she needed out of the house anyways."

"She doesn't want to come in does she? I haven't cleaned."

"I'll tell her to meet me outside."

Sailing. Bullshit. She didn't know I was one of the secret

squirrels in the communications room. I had access to the fleet's sailing schedule. I knew she was on the tanker, and it wasn't heading out for another three months.

At this rate, I would make it through every episode of College Fuck Fest by November. The next morning, I started up a pot of coffee. I walked into my bedroom. Staring back at me was my set of sateen sheets in ivory, my old duvet cover in navy blue. A deep red fist-sized stain in the middle of the sheets.

"Fucking anemic! Those are custom fucking made!" Sateen. Egyptian cotton. 300 thread count. A navy and ivory set, soft as silk. The navy gave us blue and white prison sheets and a scratchy wool fire blanket. At home, I wanted to sleep in luxury. Another petty rebellion. I grabbed the phone and called my mom. She used to be a seamstress. She would know if I could fix this.

"Can you get blood out of Sateen?"

"No, that's pretty much it."

"I don't know what to do then. I guess get rid of them."

"Well, if they are stained you can't do much about it. Just send them to me. I'll make them into pillow cases or something."

"No, you don't want them"

"It's fine. They are just sheets."

"Trust me. I don't think you want them"

"Nonsense. It'll be fine. I'll just cut them up and–"

"Mom, trust me. You do not want them."

There was a long pause as she did the math. "Oh. okay."

I'm out one duvet cover, one onyx chess board, one hundred dollar martini glass, and I've had to jerk off more with her than without. I really didn't need to work this hard. It was getting expensive. At that time, she was the worst fuck of my life. That was until the ship decided to run laps around the island for six months.

♦

My place looked the same when I got back. I was getting ready for my new posting soon, and it was a shore posting. I would finally be at home indefinitely after completing the worst sailing tempo in the history of boats. I had been home so little that my house felt like someone else's when I did make it home. Driving my car felt like I was test driving it at the dealership. I had forgotten everything, but it came back quickly.

And I loved all of it. I had been throwing up for months. Drinking horrible salted coffee, eating undercooked instant bacon, and sleeping under sheets that were made for convicted felons. My captain loved to sail the straits of Juan de Fuca. The island we lived on became a NASCAR track for 189 days out of the year. All the pain of a deployment sailing schedule, none of the benefits of foreign ports, foreign women, or smuggled liquor for the mini bar at home. It was one of the more difficult navigations in the world.

The waters were calm going south. The island kept us calm. On the northern trips, we had the pacific ocean to our side. The waves would hit us starboard to port. It was the worst way to keep the ship from rocking. The ocean kept me sick. I was a lightweight. I threw up more at work than I ever had when drinking. I had some kind of ear thing and one of the side effects is constant sea sickness. The skin on my neck was raw from wearing seasickness patches.

My first night back, I was exhausted. I wanted a drink before sleep, so I stopped at the fleet club for a drink or six. Randy Couture was fighting again on the big screen. There were twenty guys wearing Tap Out hoodies and t-shirts, and not a single one of them looked like they had come from the gym. Tons of arguments over who was an idiot for not doing some simple move or another. Everything was the same as it had been, only bigger. More. Over at the pool table I saw her again. She, too, was the same, but different. More.

"Melissa?" I said.

"Rex! Haven't seen you in a while."

"Same. You look different."

"Oh, you mean these?"

She popped open her denim jacket to show off her new implants. She had okay tits before, small but shaped well. Now she looked Irish. She was proud of them. She arched her back to make sure I could see.

"I meant you grew your hair out, but now that you mention it…" I said. I laughed at her. She casually looked me up and down. I wasn't trying. I was tired. I had almost forgotten about her. I also hadn't seen a woman in six months. I'd also never fucked a woman with fake tits before. I didn't have to try that hard.

"So, what do you think?"

"Money well spent."

They looked great but felt all wrong. She hadn't changed. I was an idiot. I shouldn't try so hard. Two minutes later it was over. She's vibrating beside me with a death grip on my wrist so it doesn't touch her while she sorts her shit out. I'm fucking her on my bed. I have no duvet cover. I have several small scratches on my body from the feathers' little quills. I didn't even bother jerking off afterward I was so tired.

The next day she had me over to hang out at her place, still in the military housing.

"I was so tired that I passed out right after you came."

"Yeah. I tried to wake you, but you were out like a light. It's fine though. I called my girl and she picked me up. Kaya was sleeping, so it wasn't a big deal."

"You're still living with that girl. Is she here?"

"She's watching Kaya in her room. Come on, let's go upstairs."

It was even worse this time. Those tits looked even better when I was sober. I avoided fucking her right away. I could stretch this moment and almost feel satisfaction.

"Give them a squeeze"

"I already have"

"Yeah, but you were so worried about wrecking them last night that you didn't really. I mean a hard squeeze. Leave a mark."

I squeezed a bit harder. She furrowed her brow.

"Come on, don't be a pussy. You won't break them."

I grabbed them, hard. Harder than I wanted to. A little revenge for such a dead lay. Melissa is expensive. Costly. She's false advertising. It was like they weren't even sexy to her. They were a new purse. A pair of new shoes, an accessory. A trap for some poor unsuspecting second husband with no options. She was killing my joy of the game.

Yet, I was there and had not left.

I put up with the worst sex because I wanted to know more about fake tits.

It was embarrassing.

But I still didn't leave.

At least, this time she had the courtesy to blow me a bit first. I'm filled with so much resentment I didn't even enjoy it.

But I'll take it.

And just like that, it's over. I looked at her. Her tits were pointing straight up while she was laying down flat on her back on her shitty flannel sheets in pale green. A great visual. Look but don't touch. I could see why the father was an asshole. I must know more.

"So how much do those things cost?" I asked.

"Cheap tits make an incision under the breast or at the nipple," she said, "but the scars show and it kills the nerves so it's harder to feel anything. So if you don't want to lose all the sensitivity, you have to do a small cut under the armpit. The implants squeeze in under the muscle. That way they look natural and feel more natural, but are just — more."

Heaven forbid she loses any sexual sensitivity.

A lot of money and a lot of effort went into everything but her performance, enthusiasm, or stamina. She was so worried about looking perfect and being sensitive that she became the worst fuck on earth. I hoped I never ended up with someone like that. The synthetic sheets make my skin tingle, and not in a good way.

"What's the matter, Rex?"

"Nothing," I said. "Your sheets feel weird."

"What are you talking about?"

"It's hard to explain. You wouldn't understand."

"Okay. Whatever. You want something to drink?" She donned a silky bathrobe and stood over me, scanning me up and down.

"If you're getting something, sure."

Melissa left the room. I heard clinking in the kitchen. She came back with two glasses of water and sat down in front of me at the edge of the bed, handed me a water.

"Thanks," I said.

"I hear you've been dating a bunch since I saw you last."

I sipped some water.

"I wanted to see if I could still snag you," she confessed.

I should have listened to Laz when he told me: Never date sailors.

"Dating? You mean Sara?"

"And Sara, yes."

"I never did sleep with her."

"Oh? So she was just over at your place at 3 a.m. and nothing happened?"

"Yeah, well you got me now."

"To be fair, you're easy. It wasn't that hard."

It looks like plastic surgeons can increase anything: Tits. Attitude. Dysfunction. She will make a good wife to someone, someday, again.

"What can I say? I've been sailing a lot. Haven't seen a real woman in a while."

"Yeah, I've been sailing a lot myself."

I had not, in fact, been dating much, and she hadn't been sailing at all. I had been sailing. I should have been dating girls who I didn't already know were the worst lay. Neither one of us were better than this. I should've been listening to what she was saying, but all I could think about was the pain in my balls.

Why was I even here? Because I didn't have anything better

to do and neither did she. There had to be a better way. I needed to figure out how I could get off in sixty seconds. Maybe I'll try staying sober? Maybe if I didn't wear a condom? I'm sure that's what Kaya's dad thought. She's going off, again. I'm turning into a sounding board for her mommy issues.

"And mom's getting married this month."

"Huh? Congrats."

"No, not congrats. She's the CO of the Orderly Room. Get this. She saw this officer, Dan. He showed up from Halifax and she pulled his financials. She saw he had a few houses and investments, so she stopped acting like a bitch and suckered the guy into marrying her. She's gonna do what she always does. Stick around till she gets what she wants, then she's going to leave and take what she can."

"Isn't that illegal?"

"Well who do you think handles those cases? She just drops it when it hits her desk. God. I never want to be like that woman. I'm better than that. I am better than that, aren't I, Rex?"

"Sure." I wonder if her mom lasts more than 2 minutes. I hear a door closing. Was someone listening in?

"What was that?" I asked.

"That must be Kaya getting up. You should probably go. I've left my roommate in her room all day, and I feel kind of bad."

"I think she was watching us."

"I don't fucking care."

♦

It's been a long year.

A lot had changed. I finally got my new posting. I was a teacher now. Fleet School, alongside. I woke up in a new set of sheets. Like silk. I made a coffee, sat down and played a little XBOX before work. My new girl was sleeping in the bedroom. She didn't have work till 0930. I had to be in my office earlier than usual. They started a new course for me, and I required the personnel awaiting training to submit twenty different security clearances.

The drive to work was pleasant. I beat the morning rush. I walked in through the doors, coffee in hand. Students were running about holding clipboards and reading lights. I ducked so as not to obscure their view,

"Morning, Master Seaman!" Matthew was waiting at the staff door.

"How long have you been here?" I asked. "It's 0740! Don't you have anything better to do?"

"Five minutes maybe. And nope. How's my security clearance? Am I on course?"

"Don't worry. You're on it. The CO has your leave request on his desk. Your wedding will be approved. They won't be sending you to sea for a while. Come back in ten minutes and we'll finish."

I sat in the staff lounge. There were twenty of us former deployeds in there. Freshly promoted, sitting around and bantering. Five years and this was the first any of us have had to enjoy a home life. Matt sat down. I went through his checklist. Age, date of birth, hometown, etc.

"Do you have any foreign assets in the following countries?"

"No"

"Do you have references from your home town who can vouch for your character?"

"Yes, here."

Matthew pulled out two sheets of paper, one with the name of his high school teacher, and one from his childhood neighbor.

"And spouse," I said. "By the time this goes through, you'll be married, so we will enter it in now. What's her name?"

"Lavesque."

"No shit? That's crazy. I used to date a girl named Lavesque."

"Oh, you mean Melissa? Me too!" chimed Maxime, a thin and wiry frenchman who was in there working across the room.

77

The office erupted.

"Oh, Melissa? Yeah, she's awesome man."

Marty too? He's a bit on the fatter side, and married. Doesn't matter. Everyone had a story, our first common bond outside of work since being posted. Steve poked his head out from behind his desk. That shiny bald head of his made him look like a light bulb going off.

"Oh Mel? Yeah, she's great!" said Steve. "We knew each other back on our training qualifier level 3 course. (TQ3) She was so much fun to hang with." I looked over and Matt, a timid, Asian man, was staring at us all, quietly.

"You're quieter than usual, Matt," someone said.

"Yeah," he said. "That's her."

The air got sucked out of the room. I heard a mouse click from twenty-nine feet away. Steve ducked back behind his monitor. Maxime left the room. One of the other kids was standing at attention outside, waiting to get charged. Maxime loved to make them wait before chewing them out. It was more about the theater of law than the actual law that keeps everyone in check.

"Follow me, ordinary seaman. I had to waste my whole fucking morning on you already." The kid marched off with him. The rest of the school would know by noon. All it took was one ear. Just like with Sara. The course was six months long. It was otherwise uneventful. We never spoke about Melissa again.

♦

We had a tradition. Upon course completion, the instructor took the class to the strip club and paid for drinks while everyone got one no-topic-off-limits bitch session that we would never talk about again. It was their introduction to mess culture before getting posted to the fleet. These courses and their traditions were the most rewarding experiences in my career. One of the girls in the course, also named Sara, sat with us in the meat seats in the front row. The latest girl had just finished her set.

UFC played on the television while we waited for the next girl. Sara number two slid into the seat next to me and said, "So you know how you fucked Matthew's wife, right?"

"You guys know about that?"

"Oh fuck, everyone knows. We used to razz him every time you left the room. How does it feel to know that Master Seaman railed your wife? He would get so pissed!"

"You guys are fucking savage."

"Oh, whatever. I just want to know. Are you happy for him or sad for him? He never brought her around, ever. I think this will be the first time we get to meet her."

"She's fine. Same as you. Loud, sweet, likes to drink. She has a kid though."

"Wait, Matt's getting an insta-family?"

Sara's eye lit up like she had gotten the juiciest gossip.

"Okay," I said. "I think I've said too much. I'm out. You should lay off the guy. He's a good kid. And he scored higher than you so he might be your boss soon. I'm getting a round. Grab a table for us and I'll meet you all there."

A few of the students' girlfriends arrived. Some they knew. Some they were meeting for the first time. Everyone was there but Matthew. He was in the bathroom. A little blond girl was sitting in his seat. She was a bit thick. Cute, but she definitely had a few too many pounds stuffed into that small red dress. If I were on a dry spell, and she weren't with one of my students, I would be on her like a dirty shirt. A great rack though. Such a waste. They really need a way to make girls stay thin if they are getting their tits done. I should have recognized her.

"How are you doing, bai? You've been some busy these last few years!"

"Mel? Holy shit. I haven't seen you in a while. You changed your hair. I didn't recognize you."

She stopped trying so hard. Her blond bob was closer to a pixie cut now. I couldn't believe she let herself go like this. All that time and effort into the perfect sales pitch. Guess she didn't need it anymore. I played it cool.

"Yeah. Getting married now. Gonna move out of the PMQs pretty soon."

"I heard. Congratulations. But yeah. Just working for me. Sailing constantly. I just got home and they put me in fleet school. How's Kaya?"

"Mom's watching her."

"So I take it you don't have a roommate anymore?"

"Yeah. It would be weird to have her around. She moved out a while back."

Matthew came out of the bathroom and joined us. I wondered if I was going to have another Webber situation on my hands. I looked him in the eye. He looked me in the eye. I couldn't read him at all.

"Hey, I'm in your seat. It's all yours."

"Thanks, Master Seaman."

"Just call me Rex. We aren't at work"

He pulled me aside, out of earshot of the class.

"Thanks Rex, for, for not making things awkward. They razzed me a lot all course."

"It's only professional. But hey. I was going to ask, but, actually…Never mind. Grab a drink," I said.

I looked at him and he looked back. Now I'm getting a read. He nods, takes a deep breath, then puts on a forced smile. I kind of did ask. He kind of answered.

I called it early and went home. The next morning, I grabbed a haircut. Bethany was out of town this week. She was at some seminar about dye or color in Montreal, so I had to go to the barber by the base. He looked like he came right out of the 1950s. Crop top, slightly grey, glasses.

"I'll be with you once I finish up. Have a seat and relax."

"Sounds good," I said.

They had Playboy magazines stacked on the table. I opened one. November 1985, The Women of MENSA, America's smartest female nude. I pretended to read an article. She had great tits on the cover, no scarring at all. Must be the underarm insertion.

"I'll be about four minutes, ok?" the barber said.

He was giving a four year old girl a haircut. Her grandmother stood beside them giving commands. She looked familiar, the grandma. The girl was getting a bob. Grandma walked to the till, purse in hand. The little girl was kicking her legs in the chair. Then it hit me. Of course, that's Lieutenant Levesque! Which meant…

"Hey Kaya, that's a nice haircut you got!" I said.

"Thanks," she said. "It looks like my mom."

Grandma looked at me, scowled, and grabbed her granddaughter's arm and rushed out of the shop. I didn't care. I just hated that I was going to look like a jarhead that weekend. I sat down in the chair and stared at the mirror. I'm looking at a guy who figured out that a punch is just a punch and a kick is just a kick, and I'm starting to like that guy.

But his buzz cut looks horrible.

Kelly

There's nothing in my way now. All around me are rows of linen, bolts of fabric, sets of sheets. There had to be a duvet cover somewhere in there. I don't want that woman at the counter to think I'm some sort of bed sheet fanatic or homosexual, but I need new sheets. She looked maybe twenty-three, twenty-four at most. Olive skin, Asiatic eyes, a short and punky haircut. She looked sort of boyish except for the top bun. Her jet black hair was straight as an arrow.

But fuck that. I had to focus. A duvet cover.

They always put the damned comic prints in the front. Fucking comics. fucking dinosaurs. White sheets covered with paw prints. I hate them. One hundred fifty thread count. Too scratchy. Six hundred thread count. Liars. They crumble once the chemicals wash the rayon out. The only good they would be was if I could just treat them like shit and throw them away when they got dirty. I don't care about cost. I'd rather pay for what I want a thousand times than settle. I was very young but remember dad, my real dad, giving me the only piece of fatherly advice he ever gave me:

Don't settle. If you want something, get it or go without. You can always hawk it later.

I saw why mom left him. I spied a set in flannel: red and black. They call it campfire plaid. No, they won't work. The fabric

83

would stretch and pill and I'd itch too much and sweat in bed. The only good thing about them is they could get dirty as hell and I wouldn't have to worry about stains.

I'd rather do the laundry than worry about laying down in filth like that. If my previous sheets had been like this I'd be laying in — I don't want to think about it.

Halfway in the aisle were the pastels. Rose colored. French teal with a maritime texture. Espresso. Fucking espresso. Espresso and beige are the sheets a wife would buy to spruce up the place and kill the joy. I can see some former prostitute thinking they looked bland and unassuming enough that they could trick a guy into thinking she's the girl next door, the one to settle down with and pop out 2.2 children. A ton of pillows were piled up at the end of the aisle. Who doesn't love a pillow fort? How intimate. It's trench warfare-inspired linens. No man's land for a dead bedroom. I didn't notice when the counter girl walked up. How long had I been daydreaming for? How long had she been looking?

"Need help looking for something?" she said.

"Yeah, actually. I need a new duvet cover. Queen set."

"Well if you follow me we can take a look."

She doesn't have a sway, or a swagger. She's thin and walks all androgynous. Big horn-rimmed glasses in black lacquer. She must have been blind because her eyes looked larger through the glass. She had a slight buck tooth; her upper lip curled up to expose it.

"I have to get home soon, so I only have a bit. I have a question: If you were on a date with a guy, and he had three hundred thread count sateen sheets, what would you think?"

"Honestly? I'd wonder if he was married or gay."

"Why is that?" I asked. I made a limp motion with my wrist. She smiled.

"Because no guy buys expensive sheets. No guy even knows what a duvet is, let alone sateen."

"My mom was a seamstress. She stitched it into my head."

"Sounds like she's a good woman."

"She's the best. She told me that you can't trust women to do anything, not to make so much as a sandwich for you, so you may as well learn to do it yourself. So now I'm buying a duvet cover."

She pretended to be offended but her smile gave her away. She had dimples. Nice. A thin black choker. I wondered if the rumors about chokers are true. Are they a signal that she sucks dick? Are they some kind of body ownership dominatrix thing?

"Well, I'm not like other girls. I don't cook. Mom never taught me. She said she never wanted me to end up like her."

"Is she divorced?"

"No. She's been married thirty years now. She hated cooking is all. I bet I could teach you something about good sheets though."

"Ok then. I'm game. I want three hundred thread count, but I also need them to be easy to wash, so I don't want the six hundred or that bamboo junk they add."

"Just how often do you mess up your sheets?"

"Not as much as I'd like. I work at the dockyard, so I sweat often and like to be comfortable at home."

"You're in the navy?"

"Yeah, but don't tell anyone."

"Why not?"

"Because there's two types of women," I said. "The first kind hate the military. They think you're a baby killer and won't give you the time of day."

"And the other?" She leaned onto the shelf, knocking over a few bags. The espresso sheets roll onto the floor. She fronts them as I continue.

"The other absolutely love it, but then they start asking about all the guys you work with and if you know them. They scare me."

"I'll bet that's awkward," she said with a smile. Smiles are good especially when you're telling her a story. That's part of my mental checklist: Tell a story. Make sure she knows I have a job and am not broke. Establish a little world we are a part of. Establish rapport. She was facing me at that point, looking me in the eye. You can always tell because people switch between left eye and right eye when they are looking in your eyes. The wobble gives it away. Don't get too clingy or familiar until she looks interested. Wait for the hook.

"You don't know the half of it! So I guess you're not like the other girls." I brush my hand against her arm. I'm trying to break the touch barrier, but all I get is a finger full of sweater. The door chime goes off. Another customer. Why does the world always put obstacles in my way?

"I have to go for a minute," she said.

I looked at the pillar at the end of the aisle. Why did they need a mirror? Were people trying on the fucking bedsheets? I looked shorter in this mirror. I was wearing a grey henley and blue jeans with work boots looking like the kind of guy who talks about linens with his boyfriend. I've gotta get out of here. I go to the till. She was standing there helping some old woman with a package of pins.

"Hey. I just realized I have to go. I'm going to be late for a thing. What's your name?"

"Kelly."

"Kelly. Thanks."

"But you didn't get any sheets?" I'm desperate. I have nothing left. Fuck it.

"Yeah, but I'm not in a rush, I still have another set. But I'd kill myself if I didn't ask something. I am tired and I'm still wearing work boots and I feel like hell. My hair isn't washed and I didn't expect to run into anyone interesting today. Give me your number, I want to take you out for a coffee, maybe a drink and get to know you better."

"Just like that?" she asked.

An old lady was meandering about the bobbins and the sewing accessories, oblivious to everything else. Is Kelly bored? Is she testing me? She has a killer poker face.

"Well, if I'm keeping you from the exciting hustle and bustle of the textile industry…" I joked.

Kelly

She laughed. She was testing me.

"Ha, fair," she said.

"Here's my phone. I've already put your name in there, Kelly. Put your number here and I'll call you tonight, and we can hang when you're free."

"You spelled it right the first time! Most people add an e. I'm off at five. You can call me after six."

Thank god. There's already a Kelley in there, and that would be awkward. I got in the Sentra and sped home. I glanced at the Seamaster. Thirty-nine minutes to wash my ratty old sheets. Forty-five minutes to dry. Ten minutes to change them. Ten minutes to get ready. Plenty of time. Maybe I can get those blood stains out of the cover? No, then she would assume I didn't need a duvet cover and I'm just creeping around looking for women in the sheets section.

I'd bring her to GLO. Home turf always helped. Hopefully Jasmine was on shift. I could use the boost.

♦

The picture windows faced the harbor. It was late, the magic hour made the entire bar glow in a golden glow. I get now why they called it GLO. I need to start bringing girls here earlier. There's no good reason not to start drinking in the late afternoon. Kelly finishes her question,

"So then, what are you?"

"I'm Mostly English, but something like a quarter black, what about you? Are you Chinese or Korean or what?"

"Native."

I flinched. No, wait. I'm not like Jon. I'm better than him. Jon thought he did some good work by teaching me the slurs when I was eight. She was a chug, a squah. I can hear him saying it now. But I'm not like him. I don't think that way. Still, a part of me liked her a bit less, and I hated myself for it.

I'd never had a chance to practice my opener on her, that polished ice breaker. I wasn't ready, and she was working. It had

87

felt rushed. Something always gets in the way. I was amazed that I got as far as I had.

It was busy at GLO for a late afternoon. A group of guys at the other end of the bar were enjoying a few drinks after work. A guy and a girl sat in a booth. They were dressed nicely. They might be on a date. An old man was reading a book by himself while nursing a beer. I guided Kelly to the bar, my hand lightly touching the small of her back. She hopped onto the stool like a toddler. The TV was tuned to women's tennis.

"I didn't think you'd come," I said. "I didn't know my in depth knowledge of thread count would have been a turn-on." Is she interested, or bored? Is this a free drink or a chance at love? For once, I have nothing to do tomorrow. I glance at my Seamaster out of habit. Plenty of time.

"Yeah, I usually don't do much. I work at the store and read at home. You are the most interesting guy I've seen in a while so I figured, why not?"

"High praise."

"Not really. I'm just bored." She chuckled.

I can work with this. Is she nervous? Fidgety? I couldn't tell. She's adjusting herself on the chair again. She still has her hair up in that bun. It's long enough to hold a shape but short enough that it still pokes out in places. Artfully disheveled. She puts her hand on the bar. I place my hand on her wrist. She doesn't flinch. I give it a 3 count then pull back.

"Well, I can't promise much, but I can promise that I can be more interesting than an old lady buying push pins."

"So you're in the military? Like a soldier or something?"

"It's the navy. It's more like an office on the water. I work in communications. If I hadn't told you, you might not have even known."

"I suspected you were. It's the haircut. No one else gets a buzz cut unless they have to."

I want to run my hands through my hair, but I'm just rubbing my scalp.

"Yeah. I actually have a friend of mine who is a professional stylist. She's at some conference so I had to get my haircut at the base. I usually don't look like this."

"Navy, eh? That must mean you travel a lot."

"Actually, yes. I almost never get to be at home. I was just in San Diego for a month, and I'm leaving soon for Seattle. Then I'll be in Hawaii and possibly Guam at the end of the year."

"That's exciting! Why do you sound so annoyed? I would love to travel that much." She leaned in and rested her head in her hand.

"You'd think so, but after a while it's just hectic. I miss Canada. I've only been home for four weekends this year, and I miss people, you know? Building a real connection. Finding a gem in a fabric store. You can't do that when you travel."

I was building a world, a little world with only the two of us in it. Us versus everyone else.

"I get it. Still, I would love to be out and about more. It's so boring here, and I feel trapped."

"Well we are on an adventure of our own, right now."

"Oh are we?"

Of course, we are. It's us vs them.

"Yeah. Like look over there. You see that table? The well dressed couple there. Do you think they are on a date or do you think they have been in a relationship for a while?"

"I don't know. It could be anything."

"It's not about that," I told her. "Take a guess. I want to know what you think. I'll go first. I think they just met. I think she's into him, but he's not sure yet."

"No way. They are probably married. Why do you think they are on a first date?"

"Well, you notice how he's sitting?"

"He's just sitting."

"Not just sitting. Look closer. He's sitting like he's not sure yet, but he is curious. If they were a couple he wouldn't be facing her like that. He wouldn't have one leg pointing at her and one leg pointing away from the table. He's leaning in with his body but his legs aren't.

"But you're sitting like that."

"Am I?"

"So what, you're not sure if you're interested in me?"

"I don't know you. That's why we're here. Besides, we are talking about them, not us."

"And she's just going to start impressing him, or their date's over?"

She was catching on. It was on me to fumble it or not.

"Well what about her?"

"So I think they have been dating a while. They've been going out for a while but she's getting bored with him. She's not sure if she wants to keep going."

She leaned forward again, a smirk on her face.

"What makes you say that?"

"She has her phone on the table. She's hoping it does something so that she can have something more interesting to do. She put it between them."

I looked down. Her phone was face-up on the bar. She pushed it to the side to make room for her elbow.

"Interesting. What do you think the guy did to bore her?"

"I think it was fun at first, but as soon as they started having to deal with real life, he got distant. I think it was just some fling that she can't end."

I want to tell her about how I own my own condo. Most guys my age still live with their parents. I could talk about my university degree in fine art, all kinds of interesting things, my passions and loves and desires. I have to fight against that instinct with everything inside of me. I could make her a coffee in a cup I bought just for her or make her an omelet. But she doesn't want my me. She won't love my me. She was there for her me, and her me is not me. He's that fucking asshole, the one trying to take over. He's what she wants in me. He's the guy she wants to fuck. All I can do is ruin that with my me.

Stick to the plan, I tell myself. Time to role play.

"I don't think he did anything. I think that's the problem. He's just there, and thinks that being there is enough."

Kelly

"Eww. Do guys really think that?"

"I have no idea. He would be doing a lot better if he were having fun, though. You have to be pretty boring when a cell phone is more interesting than you are."

I reach over to Kelly's phone and flip it facing down. She looks down, then back.

"Do you think you are interesting?"

"Me? I'm just some guy. I'd be that guy you meet. The guy that you maybe hit it off with and maybe you don't. I'm hopeless. I'd be the guy you have a fun date with, but then I am out to sea for a few weeks while you think about how it went. Maybe it was so fun you want to do it again. But it's been weeks and the feeling fades. I come home and you either want to pick things up where we left off or you don't. It'll be like no time had elapsed at all. Or we never see each other again. Who knows?"

Jon would have been on her like a dirty shirt, but I wasn't like that. I was different. I don't lie. I'm entertaining. She got dressed up. She did her hair. She put on makeup. She wore a lacy tank top with spaghetti straps. She put on a skirt. At the store, she was dressed in cargo pants and a hoodie.

"You make it sound romantic," she said. "Is it lonely?"

"Sometimes. That's why I like people watching. You are pretty good at it, too."

"Well, like I said. It's more interesting than my life."

"Is it lonely?"

"Sometimes. I used to have someone, but it didn't work out."

"Too boring?"

"Too immature."

"So he's not the kind of guy you would go shopping for a duvet cover with?"

"Ha, no. I don't want to talk about him right now. I want to talk about that girl."

"What about her?"

"She looks stressed like she has a lot of stuff on the go. She looks like she wanted to come out and have some fun. Look at her shoes."

"What about them?"

"They are Louboutins."

"Is that good?"

"Yeah, that's really good. They are expensive. No woman wears expensive shoes to have a beer and talk about the dishes. She wanted to be wooed. All he had to do was tell her she was pretty, to pay attention. He's just ... there."

"That's funny. His problem is he's there, but not present. My problem is I'm present, but not there."

"Yeah, but that's romantic. A man who is stuck in the middle of nowhere. He can't think about anyone else because there is no one else. Waiting for the opportunity, you know?"

"I do know. It's like being able to do all the boring stuff in life, then pausing it every now and again for some fun. A chance to forget who you are for a while."

"Yeah."

I'd been holding onto her forearm for the last few minutes. She moved back so that our hands were touching. She hasn't looked at her phone this entire time.

"I'll be right back," I said. "I have to go to the bathroom. When the bartender comes back, have him get us another round. Give him my card so he can start a tab."

I was halfway to the bathroom when I glanced back. She was looking at my card like she was fishing for details.

♦

I washed my hands and zipped up. I looked in the mirror. Messy hair with just a touch of shine. Omega Seamaster on the wrist. I smelled like Prada. My hands were cold. I washed them for a minute longer than I should have. The water should help. The water burned a bit and my skin turned red. I ran through a mental checklist:

Three stories with three declarations of value. Us versus the world. Keep building rapport. When I come back, look to see what she's drinking. If she's got a club soda, it's over. I couldn't see the drinks. She was blocking the bar. She still had not touched her phone. As I get closer, I can see it. Rum and Cokes, doubles.

"I got you a double. Hope you don't mind."

"Not at all," I said. "Cheers."

"So hey, Rex. What do we do now. Do we go over to that table and ask them if we were close?"

"Oh god no, are you crazy?"

"Well, we've made up an entire story about them. Aren't you the least bit curious if you were right?"

"Well, I know we were right."

I grabbed her hands. Mine were still warm from the water. They stung, but she can't feel that.

"I did that once, and you know what happened?" I asked.

"No, what?"

"It's never as fun. Right now the guy used to be exciting, but now he's immature. She's bored and put on her nicest shoes because she wanted to be the center of his world for a bit, and now she's hoping her phone saves her. All he had to do was look her in the eye, tell her a story, hold her hand, and enjoy the moment, but he's screwing it up. But if we go there."

"But?"

"If we go there, then it's not honest. People always change how they act when they think someone is watching. She doesn't want to hurt his feelings and so she will say it's actually going well. He doesn't want to be boring so he will start trying to entertain us, and that will just piss her off. Then she knows he could be interesting, but chose not to be."

"So we would probably break them up?"

"We could. Or maybe they are both just tired and this is their one time out this month. They are so happy and comfortable with each other they can just sit there and be with each other."

"So you're either wrong, or you'll embarrass them?"

"It's more that people lie when you ask them," I said. "They are so worried about stuff that doesn't matter, and worried about what people think about them, so they lie. It's not like you and me. We already know what they are really like. She thinks he's boring and she just wants to be excited. He's interested in her but not sure if she's the one for him, so they sit there and just look at each other. Not like us."

"Like us?"

"Yeah. You're not bored and I'm not unsure."

"You sound confident."

"I've never met a girl who I could people watch with who could talk about people this well."

"Well, what else are we able to talk about?"

Now's my chance!

"Funny you mention that. I have a friend who's a psychology major at the university. He showed me this crazy thing they do with patients. It's like mind reading. He made me promise never to tell anyone because you have to sign a waiver or something and it's possibly dangerous. Would you like me to show you?"

I felt like I rushed it.

"No, I'd just lie to you anyways," she said.

Smirking bitch. I leaned in and kissed her. She closed her eyes.

"Cheers, to the lie and to being exciting."

She giggled and tapped her glass against mine. I told another story while she fidgeted in her chair.

♦

I drove her home. She held onto my arm like a child in a crowd. I pulled away from her to shift gears. At her place, I walked in like I was supposed to be there. She didn't stop me. It wasn't a nice apartment. The walls were stucco. The beige carpets had not been updated since the nineties. The whole place smelled like shuffleboard wax and looked like an old folks home, but I didn't mind. After smelling nothing but diesel and body odor for weeks, this place may as well have been a palace covered in rose petals.

There were some toy cars on the ground.

As soon as she entered I pushed her against the wall and kissed her. I held her hands above her head. She didn't resist. She was still holding her keys, and they were jabbing into my palm. I grabbed them, threw them on the floor. She closed her eyes and let me guide her.

I took her down to the carpet and laid on my back with her on top. She was enjoying herself, but I wasn't into it as much as I could have been. The carpet itched my back. She knocked over her purse with her foot. Her phone tumbled out and landed face down beside the sofa. I saw a light blinking on it, but she was in the moment and didn't notice. I cupped her breasts with my hands. She moaned and started grinding harder. I squeezed harder, and she moaned harder. They really do just feel better without the augmentation. Softer. She's getting into it and, finally, I'm starting to get into it. I twisted her nipples. Suddenly, something's off, wrong. My face got warm, and there was a taste in my mouth. My eye started stinging. The taste was sweet, familiar, but also different. I looked up and saw a dribble of milk on my thumb.

"Oh no! Are you OK?" she said. She fell forward, laughing. She took her hands and wiped something off my face, but it just smudged more than anything.

"What are you stopping for?" Kelly asked as she grabbed my face and held it up against hers. We stared at each other while laughing. She started grinding again.

"I'm sorry."

She wouldn't stop apologizing and fussing. I flipped her over.

"Stop talking," I said. My skin tingled from the carpet scratching my back. It still itched but blended with the tingles of sex. Kelly closed her eyes, back in her moment. The Rex she imagined was doing great. He was exciting enough and not immature. He was in the moment and knew that just being there isn't enough. He was performing like a boss and she was enjoying herself.

My Rex, however, was secretly freaking out. Where in the hell is the kid? Is she married? Is dad coming home? What time is it? I looked at my Seamaster: 10:34. It felt like we have been here forever. Nothing but time. She's moaning, and moaning, and moaning, then nothing. No noise. No knocking on the door. No crying. It started and then over and that was that. She pulled away and leaned against the sofa.

"I'm so sorry. I've never done that before." Her legs were crossed. Her leg was covering most of her torso.

"It's funny. I haven't either. You're not married, are you?" I pretended to be nonplussed. Her look of embarrassment fadeed.

"Oh god no! Why would you think that?"

I gave her a blank look.

"Oh. Right. No. I'm single. I have a little boy. He's almost one. His dad was a deadbeat and a loser. I kicked him out long ago and now it's just the two of us here."

"He's here now?"

"No, he's at my mothers place. I asked her to take my little guy last minute because I had a date."

"Oh, my bad. I didn't know you had a date tonight. Do you want me to go so you can spruce up?"

She slapped me on the arm.

"Shut up! It was you, silly."

"I know. I'm just goofing around. I had to ask. It's happened before."

"What, you're a homewrecker or something?"

"I didn't want to be. The girl didn't tell me until during."

"That must have been awkward."

"I was in the moment. I never gave it much thought."

"Well you don't have to worry about me."

"Why would I?"

"I'm not looking for a dad. It's just annoying sometimes, you know?"

"I get that."

I did not get that.

"Like, I can be a mom just fine. I have my family to help me when I need to. I have a job and my own place. And sometimes, I just want to do…something. You know what I mean?"

"Yeah. I know."

I did not know.

"And then you come around and tell me about how you're traveling all over the world and you're barely ever home, and I couldn't do that. I don't want to do that. But, it's nice to kind of do it, a little bit. Thanks, this was fun."

We sat there quietly. I absorbed the moment. She wanted me to be on her like a dirty shirt, and I had been.

She walked over to the kitchen and opened a cupboard. She grabbed a glass and turned on the sink,

"So hey, I don't mean to be that girl, but…"

"You're kicking me out?"

"Oh no, not right away. But my mom's coming back in an hour, and I have to work in the morning. Want a glass of water?"

"Sure, thanks."

She grabbed a second glass. I grabbed my underwear.

I'm a homewrecker. No, wait, she is. I'm a cheater. No, wait, they broke up a while ago. I don't even know what I did wrong, so why do I feel horrible? The kid's not even one year old. How do you fuck up the first year? She was telling me something, but I wasn't even listening. I didn't even want water, but every time I take a sip is a moment when I don't have to say anything.

"So you're off to sail the world then?"

"I'm home until Friday, then I leave for two weeks. I'll give you a call. If we can make it work, we can make it work. If not, well I won't blame you."

"It's all good. I get it. Call me. You can come over tomorrow. I have wine in the fridge and we can hang, talk about bed sheets or whatever gay stuff you're into."

"Sure. Gay stuff," I said. I buttoned my pants. "Have you seen my shirt?"

Kelly grabbed it from the sofa and tossed it to me.

97

"Do me a favor, though. For when you sail."
"What is it?"
"When you get back, bring me something."
"What would you like?"
"I don't care, just make it exciting."
"I can do that."

♦

I slept over the next day, and once again on Wednesday. Then Friday came and I was back to smelling diesel and body odor and grease steam. Laz put me on the bridge that sail. I got to smell the sweet smell of salt air and enjoy the weather. But it was fall which meant it was wet, cold, and windy with no excitement or magic anywhere. I was surrounded by other sailors but felt alone. I looked at my Seamaster. I ate breakfast at 0700. I started work at 730. I broke for standeasy at 1000 and ate dinner at 1230. Then I worked out and had a nap. Supper was at 1730. I cleaned the toilets and the floors til 1800. I started my evening watch 1830 and was off at 2330 then slept till 0700. Repeat.

We were given two days in Seattle, but I had a duty watch for the first day so all I had to myself was a Sunday. There was nothing to do and no one to talk to. I walked around Pike Street like a tourist. The first Starbucks opened here. You'd think it would be something important, the Millenial mecca. I wondered if they would have a museum and a coffee table book. I assumed it was built up to be a flagship store like something you'd see in Times Square to show off the brand.

It was plain and boring. I'm an idiot.

The first Starbucks was just a store in a nook on the street. It didn't have any of the perks I was used to back home. No seating area. No wifi. They didn't have the fancy clover brewer or the nitrous coffee or even shelves with bags of overcooked beans for the authentic branded experience. No cookies or egg bites or lemon cakes.

6 Kelly

There was nothing.

A desk, some coffee, and a queue. I grabbed a cup off the counter. It's plain, white, with the old seventies mermaid logo on the front. The only difference between it and every other Starbucks cup was that this logo wasn't censored. The mermaid had her legs up and wide apart. The only modesty was your thumb covering her clam. Coffee is coffee, I suppose. I don't know why I needed it to be exciting, or why I wanted to be so enthusiastic about it. It's just coffee and cream and sugar. The line to order is long but moving quickly. The whole back of the bar is a mirror. I have bags under my eyes. I look like a guy who is bored and tired at work, looking forward to seeing a single mom who needs to scratch an itch. I look at that guy and I don't like him very much.

Just tell yourself the mermaid makes it taste better, you dumbass.

"I'm not in the mood."

Oh it's fine. At least you listened to Melissa and aren't acting like you'll break them when you squeeze them.

"Yeah. I wasn't ready for the milk. That was new."

"Wait. You want no milk?" someone else said, someone not me or the other me. The barista was holding my cup and staring at me.

"No. I mean yes, please. I do want milk." I don't even like milk. I only ordered it because it was different than the shitty black, salted coffee I'd been drinking the last few weeks.

Keep it down, that other me said. *People are going to think you're crazy.*

I shouldn't have gone to Pike Street. It was better when I thought it was some kind of amusement park, some adventureland for coffee addicts. Now I know it's just some shitty coffee stop before going to work and throwing up.

I arrived at the register, a thin guy with a septum piercing and blue hair grabbed my coffee and handed it to me.

"Just the coffee?"

"And this mug. Do you guys have any sort of gift bag or

anything?"

"No. Sorry," he said. "Just the normal bags."

He puts the mug into the brown paper back with the Starbucks logo on the front. He adds some brown paper for protection. As I walk out the store, I look back at the mirror. One foot pointing at the counter, the other foot pointing at the doorway.

Look at you. Got a gift for her and everything. A Starbucks mug. How exciting.

It was good enough. She was into me, but I just wasn't sure yet.

I was already sick as hell and we had to circle around to the open ocean before we went home the next day. We were sailing mostly in the open Pacific. Without the island to protect us, it was a constant battering by the waves. Sea state six. Twenty-foot swells directly against the side of the ship. The entire sail. I was either vomiting or I was sleeping.

I forgot to buy more Gravol. I broke my record. I threw up eight times on a single shift. My stomach was so weak by the end I could just delay it long enough to run to the heads. Eventually, I gave up and went to the MIR for seasickness patches. I wore them all day. My neck developed a rash by the time we pulled in.

I pulled garbage duty. Government decided it was a good look to have this floating hundred million dollar weapon of war have a recycling policy and so we built a recycling facility on board. No reason not to make it sailor-friendly.

The aluminum cans go in the shredder and dumped overboard. The cardboard too. Plastic was a whole other beast. We needed to melt it into disk shaped pucks and dispose of it when we pulled into port. Space was at a premium. The bosuns had a great idea for morale: they would leave porn mags in the space and you were required to curate your own pornographic topper for each one. You would then be judged by the crew when they carried the pucks to the garbage on your pornographic sophistication.

You couldn't phone it in either. Sometimes they would put

ladyboys, or chicks with dicks in there so if you used whatever was in the space and grabbed the wrong picture you'd never hear the end of it. Morale had never been higher.

Thankfully, there was nothing left for me here but porn pucks and a mug with a boring looking mermaid with her clam on the side. Oh, and customs.

We anchored a mile away from the jetty all evening while customs scheduled their duties officer for Monday morning. Jason lived on the waterfront. He could see his house through binoculars. The ships engineers, affectionately called Stokers were alcoholics. Unless an engine went out they had a lax schedule so they partied all night. Candus was drinking with them and having a blast. I just wanted my coffee and to sit quietly until my shift.

Jason came up to the bridge. We sat there staring at the lights along the coast.

"I've never seen you so sick on a sail before," he said.

"Yeah. I forgot Gravol this trip. I'm wearing the patch, but it's itchy."

"Oh, yeah, dude. Be careful with those. I took a shower with one last trip and I felt drunk. I'm pretty sure those things give you cancer or something. You got plans when you get back?"

"I'm seeing someone, sort of. You still fooling around with Julie?"

"My roommate emailed me. He got home after work and she was in my house. She told him I said it was okay. Hell of it is, I don't know how she got in. I never gave her a key."

"Yeah, that's kind of crazy."

"Meh. I haven't seen a woman in two weeks. I'm gonna finish in like a minute. I'll just tell her the first ones for me. I'll get her next time."

"I'm glad you can just get past all the red flag stuff and focus on what matters."

"Ah whatever. She knows I'm not looking to settle down. I'm getting laid so it's good enough."

"Just be careful man," I said. "You never know what she's

got planned."

"I'm sure she's on birth control, and I would be surprised if all these radar dishes we work under mean that we aren't just shooting blanks already."

"Ha. At least you got that. I don't know if I like this one very much though. She's a native girl. She's got a kid. And she's kind of boring."

"In bed?"

"Yeah, in bed."

"Oh, the dead fish. Just laying there. I hate that, man. I don't know what to tell ya."

"I just hope it gets better than this."

"Don't even worry about that. Just get yours and don't worry about this other stuff. You overthink things."

"If you say so. My biggest fear is that I accidentally knock one of these girls up and then that's it."

"Yeah. My dad was like that. My mom left him when I was, like, three years old. I promised myself that I would never do that if I had a kid, but that won't be for a while. Until then, it doesn't matter. Besides, you don't have to care. Just get laid."

♦

We secured the lines then the real work began. Everyone was motivated to shut down the ship and get the fuck home. We had the comms work: a technical mess of server shutdowns and unpatching cables. Locking up tape disks and hard drives. Jason and I stowed all the cryptography and the laptops for storage in the safe.

"PO. Why can't we do this during mids watch? We wouldn't have to be the last department on board and go home."

Laz shouted back, "Because you never know if you need them up until the last minute. I've been on sails where the captain gets a call and we turn around at the last minute. And if we aren't ready with his secure comms then I have to be the one grabbing my ankles in his office. So just fucking do it when I tell you."

Jason patted me on the chest.

"Yes PO. Dude, go do the pucks. I'll finish up in here."

The garbage space was stuffed with cardboard and plastic. Garbage from two hundred fifty people for two weeks being compressed and compacted and melted and pucked and shredded. A line up of the remaining crew formed a chain passing the pucks down the line. We all got covered in melted plastic and trash. When Candus and the other women on board had to carry the porn pucks, everyone laughed.

Then, the brow was stood up, the ensign was raised, and the alongside watch took the brow. We arrived at dawn just in time to sit in afternoon traffic. Every time I got home, it felt like I was driving a new car for the first few minutes.

Once I was home, I stripped down and started a hot shower. I stood underneath and rubbed the small rash on my neck from the Scopolamine, a sea-sickness patch. I forgot I had it on and forgot to take it off like Jason warned me.

The drug and the warm water interacted. I still had my sea legs so it was already like the world was spinning, but now my legs feel like lead. I could think clearly and focus, but I felt drunk. I knew where everything was in my house, and I knew how to shower, but all of a sudden my place seemed like someone else's, and dangerous. I almost slipped and cracked my head on the toilet. I sat down until the room quit spinning.

My clothes still smelled like garbage and plastic and porn. I almost fell asleep in the shower. I couldn't just sit there and enjoy it. Nod off while I used up all the hot water in the building. How long would that even take? Probably a few hours. I got up and fell straight into bed. I was naked and wet on my same old sheets that I still haven't replaced. I looked at my Seamaster. I had a few hours before Kelly was expecting me. I could get a little shuteye. Plenty of time. I closed my eyes. I breathed deep. I was out in seconds.

The phone rang.

I could sleep through a fucking cannon firing, or a one ton

anchor scraping across the deck, but a curtain opening or a small beep on my phone and I was up like the Manchurian candidate. I threw the blankets back until I could see my pants and grab the phone out of the back pocket. It was Kelly.

My duffel was on the floor, half open. The mug was still wrapped in brown paper in that branded brown bag. I saw half of the logo: a mermaid leg and a hint of a green vagina.

"Hello?"

"Rex! I thought you said you were coming home this afternoon."

"I think I fell asleep after my shower. Why, what time is it?" I had no idea where I left the Seamaster. I felt naked without it, no idea what was going on. I grabbed my wrist. I still had it on.

"It's nine. You know I was thinking about you."

"I was thinking about you, too. I actually got you something."

"Oh did you?"

"Well, don't get too excited. I originally tried to bring some fireworks and a handgun home, but customs said, No."

"You didn't!"

I heard her laughing. She sounded excited. Or was it frustrated? Bored? I was still groggy and it was hard enough to feel someone out on the phone.

"No. Of course not." My head throbbed. Something was wrong. Am I dehydrated? My neck was itchier than before.

"Well. I have a surprise," she said. "Are you busy?"

You'd expect someone to sound surprised. It was more like she found time in between appointments. Clinical. Almost banal.

"Why?"

"Well, my baby daddy is out of town today. You should come over."

"Wait. I thought you two were separated."

My head was pounding harder, my right eye twitching to the beat of the throbbing. It's like being outside a nightclub after a hard night of drinking. Scopolamine is worse than alcohol. I swear I'd be better off with the vomit.

"Well, we are, technically. Mostly. He stays in the other room sometimes. But he's out of town this weekend. So I have the place all to myself!"

"I can't. I think I came down with something."

I'm not Jon. I'm better than him. My uniform is dirty. I need to wash it. The garbage smell is making me sick.

"Aww. Are you sure?"

I'm better than that.

"Yeah. I have to go to bed. I'll talk to you later?"

This didn't count.

"OK. Feel better."

I made a promise. I was the better person. I won't fuck her. You're welcome. I looked in the bathroom mirror. I was scowling at myself. Fuck, that guy is an idiot.

I felt my cheek. I had a new scratch from my duvet. I still needed to buy a duvet cover. My sheets were filthy. I was down to my last pair, and everytime I thought to get more, I did something stupid and ended up with the same crappy sheets I started with as well as no cover for the duvet. I laid back in bed. The throbbing in my head kept me up for what felt like hours. I drifted off, eventually.

I woke up again. The lights were off. It was dark outside. What time was it? I was buck naked except for my Seamaster. Thank god. I felt naked without it. 0432. Even for the morning shift, I was up early. Had I stayed up and slept with Kelly, I wouldn't have gone to sleep til midnight and would have gotten up at a reasonable hour. I grabbed my robe. I hadn't felt cotton in weeks. I walked to the kitchen. On the way, I grabbed that coffee mug out of my duffel. I removed all the packing paper, and the crumpled mess dropped to the floor. I looked down at that green mermaid opening her legs for me. I set it down and started water for coffee using my Lagustina aluminum-core stainless steel kettle. The set cost almost a grand. I couldn't stand ship food. It was all deep fried, and the cooks were always stressed out. They didn't even cook instant bacon all the way

105

through. It was always ready and all you had to do was point to it and they'd give it to you, but I liked doing it myself. The kettle whistled.

I poured it into my French press. La Creuset. Stoneware. I would never drink coffee at home that needed salt. I refused to eat shitty food. I now had a coffee mug with a green vagina staring at me. I put my thumb over it for modesty and started to drink. Milk and a pump of Hazelnut. My neck was dry and itchy. At least, after a good night's sleep I didn't feel sick anymore, but my head still hurt. The fucking Scopolamine refused to let me have peace. I poured a second cup. It tasted bitter, acerbic.

I wanted to like having milk in my coffee. I couldn't. It just made me sick and felt acidic. Even with the sweetener, I didn't like it. As I got older, I could appreciate the simplicity of simple coffee, made well, with no complications. I just never knew what good coffee was when I was young. It took me a lot of shitty coffee to train myself to know the difference. Yet here I am, still trying to train myself to have it with milk hoping that I can get used to it.

I shouldn't have poured that last cup. Brown sludge waited for me at the bottom. I felt the grit in my teeth and on my tongue. That last sip was bitter and then it was in my teeth. I stepped down on the garbage bin pedal. The lid opened up. I dropped the cup in the trash. In the dark, I could barely see my sofa. I loved that white, Italian leather. A pile of dirty sheets sat crumpled up on the chaise lounge. I sat down, grabbed a controller and turned on the XBOX.

Waiting for players...

7

Kate

I got laid with the help of the best stackable washer and dryer that money could buy, and it was all made possible because that chick knew how to cook. I threw the fitted and flat sheets and pillowcases into the wash. I was down to my last set, so the bed was just laying there, naked and unprepared.

I've never met a woman who could even make a sandwich; I just haven't seen the point of a girlfriend. Every new girl was one more broken glass, one more ruined sheet. I needed to buy a cheap set for fucking because this was getting expensive.

The washer lid dropped with a hollow metal thud. I started the heavy cycle. The timer ticked away. I checked the Seamaster. Thirty minutes. I sat down at the computer to check my email and saw a new message notification.

I'd been on that site for a year. Mike swore that online dating was like shooting fish in a barrel. I sat on it for months and…nothing. I had tried OKCupid. I had tried PlentyOfFish. I was now on hi5 and Facebook. I read the blogs on how to make a good photo. I had a shirtless selfie in a cowboy hat, an action shot of me dodging a tackle for a naval football game. A third picture of me on a date at GLO with Jasmine at the bar artfully cropped so all you saw was some hair and an arm. I checked all the charts and the statistics and the graphs. The developers were trying to help. This was the first time I caught

The Dog Walker | R.A.STONE

anything:

Subj: Kate messaged you: You're kind of cu...

Mike had been right! It was like Logan's Run, he said. Blowjobs on speed dial, he said.

I clicked the link.

I guess if I just waited and lived life, one day I get an email and a notification and there she was. Was she real? Was this a catfish? I clicked her photo album. A lot of girls liked to crop it tight so you see a set of titties and a smile while hiding a shit locker or a dump truck behind that camera angle. There were a dozen photos wearing nothing but panties and bra. Blond hair, straightened and flat. She had bright green eyes. She looked attainably thin, maybe a bit moreso. Each photo caught the green and magenta artifacts from her digital camera in the low light of her bedroom.

It said she was online, so I typed,

"Hey, got your message."

... Kate is typing

"Hello."

I had no idea how to type to someone I wanted to take out. I couldn't exactly run an opener. As far as I knew, she was in Timbuktu. It feels weird. Do I do it all at once, or do I send a message for every sentence? How the fuck is this supposed to work? At least it gives you a second to think. I don't want to immediately comment on her photos. She's almost naked and it looks needy. I don't want to ask her how she's doing. That's just stalling. Fuck it, I go with blunt honesty

... Rex is typing

I'm not going to lie. I've never actually used this account before. I have no idea how you're supposed to start a conversation online. Normally I would have met you outside, or at the bar and it would be easy

... Kate is typing

Oh thank god. Me neither. I dumped my boyfriend and got drunk and made this account months ago. I was bored and messaged you. I figure it was weird but whatever.

… Rex is typing

Ha ha ha. You're too cute. If I saw you outside, I would have walked up and gotten your phone number, gone out for drinks, then would have learned whether we were a good match

… Kate is typing

Do I look that easy?

… Rex is typing

You don't look anything. I've never met you. But you don't see many girls with green eyes. Do you remember that movie Big Trouble in Little China with Kurt Russell

… Kate is typing

Oh yeah! The girl with eyes of creamy jade!

I liked Kate's bubbly personality and, even better, she knew the movie. Big Trouble in Little China came out in like eighty-six. Either she loves good movies, or she's a lot older than she looks in those photos. It feels weird to have so much time between responses. I can't tell if I'm being charming or creepy or what. How do you just ask if her photos are current?

… Rex is typing

Don't you seem a little young to be watching movies from the eighties

… Kate is typing

My dad loved it. He used to make me watch it with him when I was a kid.

I smiled. I was getting the hang of this. Now how the hell do I go from typing to a meeting?

… Rex is typing

Tell you what. If you promise to wear more clothes than you do in your pictures, I'll take you out for some drinks. There's a new lounge around my place called GLO and I know the DJ who is playing this weekend."

… Kate is typing

I've heard about that place. Is it any good?

… Rex is typing

It's my favorite. You'd love it. A DJ plays there every weekend

... Kate is typing

OOoooohhh.

... Rex is typing

What's your number? I'll call you and we can check it out tomorrow

She actually sent it. Man. If I was a murderer this would be like shooting fish in a barrel. I put the number into my phone and sent a text to confirm. I'm not stupid. I remembered in college, Manjeet used to brag about sending random numbers to guys who hit on her and laugh at whoever they tried to call the next day.

I heard a ding. The wash was done.

I typed a message to her: "The future from the 1960's is now. Scanning a few pictures, sending a few lines of text then meeting up for drinks."

I read it back, then deleted it. It sounded like I was looking for dial-a-lay. I've got the number. She's game. Don't fuck it up by saying anything more.

I grabbed my sheets. They were wrapped around the washing basin and weighed an extra twenty pounds damp. I fed them into the dryer and started the timer. Forty-five minutes.

I went over a checklist. By tomorrow, I'll have clean sheets, the clothes, the cologne, the strategy. It's just me. Mike wasn't here. Jason wasn't here. As far as I can tell she's no one's wife or fiance. I sat back on the computer and zoomed-in on her photo album, looking for clues.

She's got no stretch marks. That's a plus. I don't think she's a mom. She said she's nineteen, but she knows eighties movies. Her account was two months old. I zoomed in on her front shot. She looked Irish. It's a handful; it's not wasteful. She was crawling across her bed. Was someone taking that shot, or was it on a timer? I'd rather not think about it. The only thing I was missing to make this perfect was a damned duvet cover. It'll be fine, right? By the time she's here, I doubt it will be a deal breaker. Mike was sailing, so he won't be here. I still had two highball glasses, for now. I put on the pick up DVD for a refresher. A man named Mystery, wearing a feather top hat and leather aviator glasses, walks me through openers, rapport building, and the Cube.

The Cube.

"It's a great way to really get inside someone's head," he said. "To be in the moment. To play a game and have fun. You have to already be doing well or else it's just weird. If she doesn't want to play, that means you haven't built enough attraction yet."

"You tell her it's dangerous. Tell her some psychologist you know taught it to you. Build it up like it's magic. You want interest."

"You ask her to define the cube."

"You ask her about the ladder."

"You ask about the flowers."

"You ask about the horse. This is important. Look for yourself in the horse."

"You ask about the storm."

I tried this with Sara, but she didn't bite. I tried it with Melissa, but she didn't take the bait, either. I tried it with Rose. I tried it with Kelly. I've tried it twenty times with twenty different girls, and I've failed all twenty times. I wanted to see it work, just once. Just once to have the world not put things in my way.

I was pumped. Let's do this.

♦

It was time. I checked the Seamaster. 1500. I wondered how much time I had.

I don't like talking or texting or messaging. Half of the fun for me was the anxiety of approaching a girl and just not knowing. Gadgets got in the way, made it feel scripted.

I called.

"Hello?"

"Hey, it's me"

"Me? Me who?"

"Rex, silly."

"Oh, hey you! So what's your plan?"

"Easy. Parking is a bitch, but I live only a few minutes away so you can park your car here then we can take mine to GLO."

"Then what?"

"We see if we connect, then figure it out from there."

"Well, that's mighty presumptuous of you."

"I think you really underestimate how much I love John Carpenter movies. I need you and your green eyes to make Lo Pan mortal again. I figure if you can get here for seven-ish, we can take off from here and not fuck around with parking."

"Oh, good. I live like forty-five minutes out of town and don't want to drive anymore than I have to. So where am I going?"

If I can get past the description of my street, I think this can work.

"Easy. Take the Bay street bridge, drive down until you see Dingley Dell, then take a right. It's right there."

"Dingley Dell? That's hilarious."

"I know. I didn't name it. A Dell is like a cul de sac but no circle at the end of the street."

"I'm going on a date with a guy who lives in Dingley Dell! Are the rest of the lollipop guild coming, or is it just us?"

Shit testing me with a sense of humor. This will be fun.

"Yeah, so that attitude will not get you a golden ticket to my chocolate factory."

"Oh. I love chocolate. Fine, I'll be there in an hour or two, but you promised a chocolate factory so don't disappoint me."

"Sweet. Call when you're here and I'll meet you outside."

I pushed play and resumed the Mystery DVDs. I was on hour three of seven. I went over my notes.

Sell it hard.

Get her buy-in.

Ask about the Cube, the ladder, the flowers, the horse, the storm. If she nods, say "and," then continue. If she shakes her head, say "but" and say the opposite. Whatever she says about the horse make it about me. I got this. In the video, Mystery

Kate

takes off his aviator shades and looks at the crowd of guys on that cool white italian leather sofa.

"Remember. Women are up for hot fun with a cool guy, but are hyper-sensitive about being thought of as slutty. Don't judge. Go with it, and keep it light. Most of the time you are ruining your love life because of unforced errors. Just don't be judgy."

He then discusses establishing your home as a safe place:

"Tell her you have to feed your fish or something at home quickly. She gets to come in your house, see that you're not a serial killer and have a clean place, then you leave. When you want to go back later, she's not walking into the unknown. And clean your bathroom. They always look at the state of your bathroom."

I had it all covered except for the quality of my linens. If she cares about linens, I'm fucked.

The phone rang.

I had set the ringtone to the Imperial March from the Star Wars soundtrack which made it more ominous than it had any right being. Why did I do that?

"I'm a minute away. Do I park in visitor?"

"Yup. I'm coming out now."

I was meeting my first online girl offline. She was driving a blue Bronco II. Speckles of rust on the black bumper and on the spare tire storage bar. That brought back memories. I almost forgot to get a look at her as she hopped out. Her photos were one-hundred percent accurate. She walked towards me in a lavender long-sleeved shirt and a short white skirt, walking with confidence while wearing white shoes with thick high heels. She was still shorter than me even with the heels. Her skin was fashionably dark with that hint of orange from the tanning booth. Her hair looked exactly like it did in the photos. Her eyes were the color of creamy jade. She had a big smile.

"I'm here! So you're not going to rape me, are you?"

"That's a stupid question."

"That's not a no."

"Too funny. Here, come in for a second. I have to grab my

keys and turn off the washer, then we can go, okay?" I have the keys in my hand already but she doesn't seem to notice. I should have bought a dog or some fish or something to feed. She came in and looked around.

"Nice place. What kind of plants are on your patio?"
"Orchids."
"You garden?"
"Yeah. Work is stressful. It helps me unwind."
"That's cool. So do you own or are you renting?"
"Oh, it's my place."
"Wow, you pay your bills? I'm impressed."

I'll never understand what impresses women. It's always the silliest stuff.

"That sofa is huge, too."
"Italian leather. It was my first designer purchase since moving in. It's my baby. Anyways, I'm good to go. My car was the Sentra beside yours."
"The four door?"
"What can I say? Bitches love a man with fuel efficiency."
"Well at least I know you're not a rapist. They never worry about fuel efficiency."
"Oh hush. Hop in."

I felt like a poor, but Kate made me feel like an aristocrat. The doors were manual. The windows were manual. The stereo was cheap, aftermarket. But it did have one benefit. Everything was tactile. I had to go to her side to open her door, so I could touch her on the small of the back and guide her in. Mike's truck used to be very impressive for the girls, but the Sentra was a better experience and my favorite wingwoman. I shifted into first and drove towards the bridge. Kate rolled down her window and waves out the door.

"Bye, Dingley Dell!"
"Killing me, Kate."

She laughed then adjusted her shirt. She saw me laugh. She laughed harder.

"Proud of yourself?"

7 Kate

"I'm just excited. I need a drink."

I got past the bridge and hit downtown. I shifted gears at the light, tapped her on the leg then pointed out the window. I didn't forget Mystery's advice about breaking the touch barrier. She looked down at her leg, then looked over.

"So you've never been here before? It's just down here. Most people never come here because the Duke is that way, but GLO is a gem in the rough. You can't really see it from the street."

"I never have. Though I've never been to the Duke either, that's probably why."

"Yeah. We came here by accident. My friend Jason and I go golfing sometimes on the weekend, and he introduced me to the place. I've been hooked ever since. He orders Kahlua and lime juice."

"Eww. What the hell?"

"I thought it was weird too, but it kind of works in the summer. I can't explain it. When I take you golfing, you'll see."

"Yeah, okay grandpa. Let's just golf and talk about the stock market."

♦

The bar looked great, a white, lacquered circular bar with the bartenders on the inside. Tables well-spaced. They could pack it out, but it would lose its feel and probably its popularity. The lack of noise was what gave it intimacy. I pointed to the far side of the bar and sit down.

"Don't you want to sit closer to the DJ booth? I thought you knew the guy?"

"It's better on the other side of the bar. You can still see the DJ, but you see that table over there?" I pointed to a long table in front of the booth. On either side are eight high chairs.

"Yeah."

"Well, that's the single girl birthday table. There's always sixteen chicks sitting there screaming and taking pictures of each other. It's really loud and they'll make your ears ring."

115

"How thoughtful."

Jasmine walked up. She was a tall Australian with long blond hair. She leaned onto the front of the bar and tucked her elbows just far enough to show that she's packing heat. She knows her craft well. I stayed at eye level.

"Rex. Good to see you again. The usual?"

She used to have a thicker accent. Over the years, it's diluted, I could almost understand her now.

"Jas, hey! Yes, please. Oh and this is Kate, she'll have …"

Kate paused thinking, Who is this woman? Why does she know this guy by name? How many girls does he bring here? She must have questions. They always do.

"Chocolate martini?" Kate finally says.

"Oh right, Wonka factory. I almost forgot. So hey Jas, is Shelby working tonight?"

"Not tonight. She was asking about you though."

Jasmine popped up, spun around, and walked to the liquor rack behind the bar. She grabbed a shaker, jigger, some random tools and a few bottles off the shelf. Kate had a curious look on her face and said, "Well, aren't you popular. Who is Shelby?"

"Friend of mine. She manages the place and sometimes has afterparties here."

"And the blond?"

"Oh, that's just Jasmine."

"She's tall." Kate gave her a once over, then looked back at me. "She's like six feet tall, and that's before she put on the heels. She's gorgeous."

"She's a good bartender, too. Aussies know how to drink."

She was wearing a long-sleeved shirt similar to Kate's but in blood red, and a black pencil skirt with the hem above the knee.

"I'll bet they do."

"Remember when I said my friend and I used to golf on the weekends? Well, turns out she moved here from Australia a year or two ago and this was her first job. She got the early Saturday shifts which were usually dead. Jason and I were the first guys she met in Canada."

Of course, we always tipped her very well.

"And Shelby. Are you and her dating or something?"

She had her hand on my arm like she was holding me in place. I was so busy doing my thing I hadn't noticed what she was doing. How long had her hand been there? Why am I talking about other girls? Is she jealous? Curious? I was in the zone going down the checklists. I had to remember: Pay attention. Be in the moment. For the first time in my dating life, everything was lining up and I didn't need to screw it up by drifting.

I didn't need an opener. I wasn't trying too hard. The situation happened to include rapport-building stories already, so I didn't need mine. A tall, busty blond with an Aussie accent shined on me in front of my date. Can't get more valuable than pre-selected competition. I didn't talk too much. I offered a little mystery.

Oh, then the Cube. And don't forget the horse.

Jasmine set the drinks on the table. I handed her my visa, which she dropped into a jar by the register. She then placed a martini with a coffee bean, clear liquor and a drizzle of chocolate around the glass in front of Kate, and, for me, my usual.

"What is that?"

"It's called a Gibson," I said. "It's like a James Bond martini, but instead of an olive it's an onion."

"Shaken, not stirred. So you're a wannabe Bond?"

"Not yet. They call that bruising the gin. It waters it down, so you stir it and that's it."

"Oh, sorry. I didn't know it was such a science."

Kate licked chocolate off her glass.

"It was my Dad's favorite drink. It's got history. I don't remember much about him, but he always had these when he would take me to this hotel bar. I was maybe six. He was friends with the guy who owned the bar, and after my parents split up, he would take me there before we'd go hang out. He would take me to the arcade then we'd stop at the race track."

"Your dad took you drinking and gambling? I can see why

they divorced."

Kate rested her chin onto her hand and her elbow on the bar.

"No, no. I didn't drink much until I was at least nine."
"Stop."
"But yeah, my mom wasn't a fan of the gambling."
"What was your dad like?"
"Oh, everyone loved him. He had a way with words, a silver tongue. You know those old shows in the seventies where the guys wore white leisure suits and had those red tinted aviator shades and big gold rings?"
"Yeah, like Telly Savalas?"

Dear god. She's referencing stuff I barely know.

"Yeah, that was him. I didn't get to see him that much. We left to live on a ranch. So it's one of the few good memories I have of the guy."
"So you're a cowboy, then?"
"I was a cowboy. I haven't gone back to the ranch in over a decade. I'm done with dirt. Cheers."

I tapped glasses and sipped. Tastes slightly sweet, with that astringent citrus gin taste. I felt like a professional. The liquor didn't burn anymore.

Dad sounded like he would have been cool to know as an adult. I wonder what I could have learned from the guy if he were still around. My mom would tell me stories about how he was a charmer, how he picked her up when she was working at the race track, how she used to drive his Corvette around town, and how he had to get out of the military when he busted his knee parachuting.

I was drifting again. Pay the fuck attention.

Stepping outside of myself when I should be paying attention to the girl who's right in front of me. I could see that other guy sitting at the bar talking to this girl. He's smiling. She's smiling. They are drinking and having fun. She's hanging on his every word. Meanwhile, I'm sitting here inventing a history of my father who I barely know. That guy could have been me. I could have been as good as he was. Don't forget the horse.

"I have this thing I learned from a friend of mine," I began. "He's a psychology major. It's kind of wild. Would you like to see?"

"Oh, fancy. OK. What is it?"

"It's called the Cube. He says it's something they develop to learn about people's darkest secrets. You have to promise that you won't tell anyone if I show you. He could get in a lot of trouble."

"Oh my god, you are going to rape me, aren't you?" she said. "Fine. I won't tell anyone."

Jasmine doesn't look up but shakes her head while laughing quietly.

"Okay. Close your eyes. I want you to picture a plain room. Inside the room is a cube. Take a second. Notice everything important about it. Wait a second. Okay, you ready?

She nodded.

"Now open your eyes, take a beat, and tell me about your cube."

"Well, it's small," she said. "It's on the ground, and it's shiny."

"Is the front of the cube facing you or away from you?"

"It's facing me directly. What does that mean?"

"The cube is how you see yourself. You're small, shy, reserved."

I watched. Her head made a small, shaking motion. That's a negative. "But, you're an extrovert once you get to know someone, and you can trust them and you're always gleaming."

"Wow, that's pretty accurate."

"I told you it was crazy. Now, close your eyes again. Next to the cube is a ladder. Picture it, wait a beat … now open your eyes."

"The ladder is leaning on the cube. It's like a stepladder. What is that?"

"The ladder is your career. You have a good, stable job and small ambition. You don't want to be a billionaire but you never want to have to go without either."

She shook her head again.

"But that doesn't mean you don't like nice things. You just don't want to have to rely on someone. I guess I never asked about your job, did I."

"I work at the bank. I handle all the customer service."

"And the Bronco?"

"My friend sold it to me. She's my bestie. Okay, what's next?"

"Hold up. Next is flowers. You know the routine."

I grab her hands and place them inside of mine. I lean in so that this time when she opens them up we are looking right into each other's eyes. It startles her.

"Woah. Ummm, there's one of those clay pots, the red one, and one flower, like Charlie Browns Christmas tree. What does the flower mean? Is it my closet?"

"Nope. The flower is your friends. You don't have a lot of friends, but the ones you do have are the best friends and all you ever need." I watched her face. She doesn't know she's doing it, but she's nodding. "And since it's beside the cube, you are both like partners in crime. Peas in a pod."

"This is kind of scary. How do you know this?"

"I told you it was scary, right? Now close your eyes again."

"What is it this time? Do you want me to picture a table or something?"

"Nope. Better. This time I want you to picture a horse. Any horse, doing anything at all."

Every single time when I ran this in the past, something got in the way. Finally, this girl who basically fell into my lap is having fun, and, more importantly, everything is going smoothly, effortlessly. Jasmine looks over and holds up two fingers for more drinks. I nod. This is the make or break time. Don't forget the horse.

"Ready?"

"Oh, I'm ready."

"OK, open your eyes. What does your horse look like?"

Kate

"He's Chestnut brown. He's one of those show horses. You know, the ones that prance and dance?"

She uses her arms to mimic the trotting motion of a horse. I bust out into laughter.

"What? What is the horse?"

"You aren't going to believe this."

"Not going to believe what?"

"Are you sure you've never heard of this before?"

"No. I swear. What's the horse?"

"Well, the horse is your ideal lover." She pulls her hands out from mine.

"Shut up! That's so stupid."

She couldn't stop smiling from ear to ear. I looked down at my complexion.

"Chestnut brown, and dances." I mirror her prancing gesture. Kate was beside herself. I leaned in, she closed her eyes, and I kissed her. She was enjoying the moment. After a few seconds, she pulled away. It was the first time tonight I've seen her move slowly. A few more seconds and she snaps back to her bubbly demeanor.

"Okay, now what?"

"Ready? There's one more."

"I'm ready."

"Are you sure?"

"Stop playing with me. I'm ready."

"Outside, there's a storm. I need you to picture what it looks like, and how you can tell from inside the room what kind of storm it is." She paused, scrunched her nose, then opened her eyes.

"OK. Well, my storm is a thunderstorm. There's a really big window and I'm just sitting there with my cube and I'm watching the rain fall. I love watching the rain."

"Well, then. That's really interesting."

"How so? What is the storm?"

"The storm is your biggest fears. Turns out you're not afraid of anything. You'll try anything once."

121

The Dog Walker | R.A. STONE

I couldn't tell if she was shaking her head or if I was reading too much into it. I took a guess and go with it. "But, you have that window in the way. You don't let it into your life."

"Wow. That's really good. I've got butterflies in my stomach."

"Me too. I haven't done it before. I'm amazed. It's like I know you already."

Jasmine set down two more martinis and winked at me. I shushed her away.

♦

It had been an hour. Normally, I was focused on getting her back to my place and all the logistics, but I was having fun. I wasn't drunk. The room wasn't spinning. I barely had time to drink. The DJ was still playing some very chill EDM.

"Me neither," she was saying.

"Serious, Kate? Never?"

"Yeah, serious. I've never had a date from online before. I was so worried it was going to be horrible, but it's kind of fun actually."

"Yeah, it's weird, the online thing."

"Part of the fun for me is meeting a girl, not knowing you're going to hit it off, that little bit of anxiety, you know?"

"I was going to say."

"You did say. The rape?"

"Yeah, I figured if you could react to that without getting weird than it was probably OK."

"So what was it about me you first picked up on?"

"Well. The fact you own your own place, and you pay all your bills on time."

"That's what first intrigued you?"

"Yeah. Remember that ex I told you about? I always had to pay his bills because he would forget, such an asshole."

Not good. Change the subject.

"Oh, that's everyone. I've never met any girl who could do

122

anything. Did you know I've never had so much as a sandwich from a girl I've dated, ever? They can't cook."

Kate sat upright. She looked angry.

"Excuse me. I used to run a restaurant with my dad. I'll have you know I'm an amazing cook."

She put her hands on her hips and scowled.

"I honestly don't believe you. Really? What kind of restaurant was it, and where was it?"

"Mexican. We had one in Mexico where I grew up, and the other one was in Vancouver."

"Oh yeah? Well, if you say so."

"I tell you what. Let's go shopping, right now. You're buying. I'll show you."

I swigged the last of my drink and motioned to Jasmine.

"Can I settle up?"

Jas nodded and grabbed my Visa, ran it through the machine. She handed me the display where I entered the tip and password. I'm so preoccupied with the machine that I don't notice that Kate has been talking this entire time and I haven't been listening to a word.

Suddenly, I catch, "You just better have proper sex." I perked up.

"Wait, sex?"

Jasmine doesn't lift her head. She just laughs.

"Smooth." Kate looks at the two of us.

"No. I need a frying pan and a saucepan. The proper cooking set."

"Oh, a proper set," I said. "Yeah. My kitchen is fully stocked." Jasmine handed me my Visa and took the machine.

"You don't miss a thing, do you Jas?"

"Have a good night, Rex. I'll tell Shelby you said, Hi."

"Thanks."

Kate held my hand and walked a half-step behind me on our way to my car. I unlocked my door and guided her into her seat. Once she was settled I leaned in and gave her a kiss. I was in uncharted territory.

The Dog Walker | R.A. STONE

Normally, I'd be making flaming Sambuca shots or lighting brandy and cherries on fire before placing them into ice cream.

Normally, she would be breaking another highball glass or staining my sheets or spilling booze on the floor.

This was nice. This was new. Now Kate was in charge, and I was going to get the first home-cooked meal that wasn't made by my mom or an Indian grandmother in probably twenty years.

♦

A waft of steam came off the pot on the stove. Kate had a thick, brown sauce in the saucepan, slowly bubbling. It smelled savory, earthy with that nutty smell of chocolate. Beside it, red tomaro sauce and poblano peppers. I didn't know what they were. They looked like a cross between a jalapeno and a bell pepper. She breaded them with corn flour, stuffed them with cheese and mexican rice, and deep fried them in my cast iron pan. The hood vent was going full blast. It was louder than the lounge if we had sat beside the birthday girl's table. The smell was amazing, addictive: deep fried breading plus the home-cooked smell of the sauce.

"Hand me the tongs," said Kate.

Of course. I was a good little sous chef. She pulled out another breaded pepper and added a new one to the oil.

"So what do you call this?"

"Chiles Rellenos. It's a Mexican dish."

"I'm impressed."

"I told you, but you didn't believe me. I was actually born in Mexico. That's where my restaurant was."

I was confused. "But you're white?"

"Yeah, my parents used to spend their summers there and I just got lucky. I moved back when I was thirteen. Pass me another pepper?"

I reached into the oven and grabbed another one. It was impressive. She put them in the oven and scorched the skin, then peeled the skin off before stuffing them. I had never seen this level of effort in the kitchen in my life. It only took a half an hour to make, but it felt longer than an entire night at the bar for me.

"Now hand me the pot."

"This is?"

"It's called mole. It's a chocolate sauce, but it's not sweet."

"Willy Wonka?"

"Exactly. So you pour it over your peppers, then add some sour cream. And that's it! Let's eat."

It was hot. It was spicy. I was sweating. She didn't seem to notice. I was half way through my pepper and I set my plate on the floor. I grabbed hers. I set it down beside. She leaned back. I went in for a long, slow kiss. It burned, bad. The spice was killing me. She tasted like tomato and fire and chocolate. I unbuttoned my shirt as she put her hands on my chest. I reached down and took her shirt and lifted it above her head. Her body had a large, snake like tattoo stretching from her neckline all the way down to her back. I sat back.

"Nice ink."

"They are diamonds and stars. I have one hundred twenty-seven of them, all the way down."

"Well, this I gotta see."

I kissed the first one in the nape of her neck and slowly moved down the line. The only thing I hadn't planned for, that I couldn't have planned for was spice tolerance. I was hoping she thought I was sweating because of her and not the food.

♦

"Oh no!"

We were only laying there for a few minutes. I was relaxed and freshly fucked wearing nothing but my watch. Kate was resting between my legs. I was on my back. She was lying down with her breasts across my leg wearing nothing but her ink, but she was looking down to the floor, distraught.

"What?"

"My shirt! My skirt!"

Underneath her skirt was her plate of rellenos. The mole and the tomato covered the front of it. Beside it, one of her shirt sleeves was in my plate. Guess we forgot about that in the moment.

"Don't worry," I said. "I got this."

I pulled her clothes off the floor being careful not to spill anything. I headed into the hall and opened the closet. Beside the laundry machine was a collection of bottles of various cleaners for stains and such.

"You may be the cook, but laundry is kind of my thing."

Pulling out a brush and a bottle, I liberally sprayed the stained areas and set them in the sink.

"I just need a minute to break up the stains then I can run them on a speed load. We got it quick so it won't stain."

It must have looked ridiculous, my now flaccid dick flapping back and forth with the scrubbing motion.

"That's my favorite outfit. I hope so."

She was biting down on the nail of her index finger. Her forearms were covering her breasts.

"I have to get home soon. My mom is going to be worried."

I focused on the skirt in the sink, dabbing away the sauce and keeping the area wet.

"You live with your mom?"

"Yeah. I lived with my boyfriend, but when we broke up, I moved home. He couldn't pay the rent on his own, and I wasn't going to cover him, so…"

"It's okay. I don't need to hear the whole story about your ex. Here." I set the outfit into the washing machine, set the cycle to delicate, and started the timer. I checked my Seamaster.

"It'll be about thirty minutes to wash, then twenty minutes to speed dry. Now we have an hour to kill."

Kate sat back down on the bed as I walked in like the Roman Triumph. I wasn't sure how sexy it looked to scrub tomato stains while standing buck naked in the bathroom, but it was good enough. She put her hands under my armpits and gripped my back pulling me into her and back onto the bed, holding me in while she kissed me. It doesn't burn anymore and now she tastes like girl, not tomato.

"That was my last condom."

"It doesn't matter, I have an IUD."

"What's that?"

"It's like a permanent birth control. Shut up, I want you inside me." It was the first time I didn't wear a condom since graduation. I had no idea what an IUD was. My mind raced. What if she gets pregnant? What if I come too quickly now? I didn't even notice her pulling me inside. Suddenly, my mind went still.

Be in the moment. Enjoy yourself. Fucking idiot. God, I hate this guy. Don't forget about the horse.

♦

I checked the Seamaster. Ten more minutes til the cycle was done. Plenty of time left. Kate lay on top of me drawing circles on my chest. I lay back staring at the ceiling. We weren't saying anything.

Ding!

The dryer alarm. Kate snapped up and ran to the dryer. She grabbed her skirt and held it in the air.

"You weren't lying," she said. "You can't see anything!"

She did a little hop and shuffled her feet into the skirt, pulling it up and clipping it on. She reached into the dryer and threw on her shirt. She didn't put on her bra but tossed it haphazardly into her purse.

"I've gotta go, bye!"

I hadn't even gotten out of bed yet, and I could hear her running down the hall to her car. The Bronco started up with that eight cylinder Ford sound that took me back to childhood. And then I was alone again.

I got up and grabbed my bathrobe. I picked the condom up off the floor and threw it in the toilet and flushed. I rinsed my hands and walked into the living room, sat down on the sofa–

127

white Italian leather—and started up the XBOX.

I didn't feel like multiplayer, so I started up the campaign. No waiting for players just straight action cinematic. I looked down and noticed I had almost stepped in a plate of rellenos.

I picked up the plates and brought them into the kitchen. Looking over, I saw that guy in the mirror again I don't like that guy, but he seemed happy with himself.

"Now that I got it down to a science, I didn't have to do that anymore, wham-bam 'em like Jon. I could just be myself.'"

If you say so.

"I'm not like Jon. Even you're better than him. We did it."

You were literally on her like a dirty shirt.

"Yeah, but I fixed that too."

Look. I still don't like you. You're still a whiny, needy, validation-seeking loser and you've gotten in the way of me getting laid every fucking time. This was the one time you left me alone and everything went perfectly. No one was married. No one was a single mom, and there was no bullshit. I'm trying to help you here but you keep focusing on making mom happy.

"Don't put that on me. I'm trying to do right by everyone."

Look. You've done a lot of work. You practiced your ass off and had a really bumpy ride. But you got us here, and I'm grateful to you for that. You are Jon. You're just doing it in your own way. You took the good parts and ignored the bad parts. Let me take it from here. I see how you do things and I can do it better, and you can still be your good little boy. We can have it all. You've just got to stay out of my way and let me handle it from here.

"Fine. Mike was back from a sail that day and were going out as a group. He was bringing that girl he started seeing, and Mom had invited my cousin to come meet me. Even you shouldn't be able to fuck this up, I told him."

Four people with drinks and dinner? I can handle this. Just don't fuck it up and be a bitch.

Alyssa

I was on the phone with my mom. Her email about the biological family was confusing as hell.

"Wait," I said. "You were adopted?"

"Oh, yes. I don't talk about it. But I've been able to track down my family, and it turns out they all live on the island. You have a cousin that lives near you. I'm going to visit at some point, but I went ahead and called her and told her about you and everyone wants you two to meet."

"Oh? I don't know what to do with that."

"Well, meet her, go grab a coffee, ask her if her mom is willing to meet with me. I can't get a hold of anyone else."

"Fine. I'll see what I can do."

A notification popped up on my computer.

"Here, I'm sending you her details and some photos. Her name is Jullianne."

It made no sense. The only thing we had in common were the freckles. I was olive skinned, she was porcelain. I had dark hair and she was a fiery redhead. But she looked familiar and I can't place her. Jullie-anne. Jullie. Anne. Julie?

"Uh mom, you're not going to believe this."

"What do you mean?"

"I know this girl. We've met before. She's dating a friend of mine."

Mom was ecstatic. "Oh good! OK. You go meet her and then tell me how it went. I'm so happy."

I hung up the phone. I had been in the military for years, and this was the first close call. At least the introduction would be easier. I clicked on my contacts and found Jason.

"Hello?"

"Jay. Are you busy tonight?"

"Nope. Why? What you got planned, man?"

"I need you to come over and have a double date with me."

"What the fuck are you talking about?"

"I need you and Julie to come over."

I heard loud, distant groaning from the phone.

"Are you kidding me? I've been trying to hide from her all weekend. She's been calling me non-stop."

"Yeah, but you're not going to believe this. I mean, you're really not going to believe this."

"I already don't believe this."

"It turns out she's my cousin, and I need to ask her about her mom."

"She's your what!?"

"Dude, I know. I just found out myself. I'm looking at photos right now my mom just sent. She tracked down her biological family, and now she wants me to help broker a meeting with her sister. It's her."

"Oh man, this is too fucking funny. Imagine what would have happened if I like blonds more than redheads."

"Don't remind me. I almost had a fucking heart attack."

"Look. I'll do this, but you owe me. I won't be able to get her out of the house for like a week. I swear to god she copied my key and sneaks in while I'm gone."

"Thanks. I'll owe you one. Next time you get drunk and miss work I'll cover for you so you don't get charged, okay?"

I needed a drink. I needed a goddamned duvet cover. I reached into the cabinet and pulled out one of my two last highball glasses. I wanted a vodka. I walked to the minibar and reached to the Van Gogh. Vodka. Good vodka tastes like water, but vodka tastes like vodka. I wanted a vodka.

♦

Jason was late. Jullie was probably blowing him or murdering his pet cat. Mike showed up, handed me a bottle of black label, and in walked a brunette in a light colored summer dress and a denim jacket. She was cute. Attainably thin. No tattoos. Big eyes. She looked Irish.

Her name was Alyssa and she volunteered to walk dogs for the SPCA. She was the girl next door type. Way too good for Mike. They sat down together like a nice wholesome couple. She must have fallen for his big truck and that scruffy stubbled face. He also treated her like shit. She seemed nice enough. She probably would do better with a guy who treats her right. Very girl-next-door of her. She thought she could change him or something.

"I'm almost out of glasses. Are you two fine if I make you a drink in a mug?"

"Yeah, that's fine," Alyssa said. "It's Rex, right?"

"Yeah."

"Unusual name. Is it short for anything?"

"Reginald. Everyone just calls me Rex."

"Why do they do that?"

Mike interrupted. "Because have you ever seen this guy wake up? Every day on ship he starts screeching and howling. He's the grumpiest person in the world. It sounds like the dinosaur from Jurassic Park."

"Thanks, Mike. Now she thinks I'm a whiny asshole. So what is it you do anyways?" I asked Alyssa. "We don't meet a lot of civilians."

I grabbed a mug and made her drink.

"Well, I actually just started a new job. You know Zellers?"

"Who doesn't? A national icon!"

"I know, right? Well, they hired me to run their marketing department."

"I didn't even know their headquarters was here. I figure it would be in Toronto or Montreal."

"Yeah. I guess they started here and decided to keep it in the city."

"So you just started? What was it you used to do?"

"Oh, you're not going to believe this. I used to work for a company that set up bachelor parties."

"There's companies for that? I thought it was just something the best man did."

"No. That's not what I mean. We hired college girls who needed money and bouncers who wanted some extra cash. We made poker chips and then sent them over to parties while the girls deal topless."

"Wait, so like the bunnies in the Playboy mansion?"

"Yes, just like that. The guy runs security to keep the girls safe, but he mostly acts like a bartender and a bouncer. It makes the guys feel special. The girl then gets naked and the guys feel special for a night. Plus, since a lot of guys have jealous wives, they get told it's poker night with the boys and so no one stresses out."

"That's actually a pretty sweet idea. I'm surprised you quit. You guys must make a fortune!"

"Well, it gets old fast. Plus, the girls are a huge pain in the ass, so you're always having to source new ones. After a few months, they either start doing drugs and missing shifts or they marry one of the clients and quit. Half the time they got so annoying I would just stop calling them for jobs."

"Guys are marrying strippers?"

"They aren't strippers. They are table girls. I'd much rather market bicycles and snow shovels to soccer moms than market ass to frat boys."

"Fair enough. Want ice?"

"Yes, thank you."

She was easy on the ears. She speaks in tune like she's singing. How the fuck did Mike find this one? She's not like his usual girl. She's more like the kind of girl I would go for. I bring in two whiskey and cokes, refill my vodka on ice. The good stuff. I want the vodka to taste like water.

"So this friend of yours. Let me get this straight. You picked up her friend and now she's dating Jason?"

"Yeah, it's funny how small a world we live in."

"So you mean, if Jason had been into blondes and not redheads …" Alyssa smirked, proud of herself. I scowled, not impressed. Mike pretended he wasn't paying attention.

"I know, lucky, right?"

"I'll say. Well, it all worked out in the end, right Rex?"

A knock at the door. Jason and Julie. Jullie wore a good poker face. She looked at me like we were just meeting for the first time. Doesn't she know we were a cunt's hair away from accidental incest? Maybe she didn't care, or didn't care to think about it. Maybe she was drunk and forgot who I was. I didn't get how anyone could get so drunk that they forget a whole damned person. Sounds like something Jon would do. Thank god I'm not that fucking guy.

I took their coats. We all do the greetings. Once everyone was seated we started drinks and chit chat.

Alyssa asked Julie, "So how do you and Jason know each other?"

"Actually, it's a funny story. I had met Jason a while back. We were on a date and I was with a friend of mine. Rex happened to be walking by. It was a complete accident. I wouldn't have thought twice about it, but finding out we are family was wild. Stars aligning, fates doing what they do. Nothing much happened. We talked some and then he had to go to work or something and honestly I had forgotten about the whole day until Jason told me." She certainly had a way with trickling the truth.

Mike looked at Julie and laughed along with her story. Alyssa looked at Mike and crossed her arms, sucked in her cheeks. Her cheekbones were protruding. Her eyes were slanting. She's tapping her foot. She's waiting for a moment.

"Isn't it crazy. You met Jason and him, and if you had just

The Dog Walker | R.A. STONE

had different taste in men this could have been the weirdest meet ever, like redneck cousins."

Alyssa raised her eyebrow. She laughed, but her eyes haven't moved. I took a deep breath and looked at her. That's one.

Mike broke the silence. "Awkward!"

Everyone laughed.

I continued. "Thank god. For a minute there, Alyssa, I thought you were going to make this shit weird." I looked at Julie. She was laughing. She thought it was hilarious. There's no way she wasn't getting irritated. She was just playing nice. That's okay. It was my house. I'll be the honest one here.

Julie continued to smooth things over.

"I know right? Flipper babies and banjos. I think you can just tell though. Something in your soul."

Maybe we are related? A girl making a Deliverance reference? Mike put his arm around Julie. The two of them fed off each other. He laughed harder and so she laughed harder. Alyssa stopped laughing and glared.

"Here, I need a minute, gotta talk with my cousin. Julie, do you smoke?"

I opened the patio door. She grabbed a pack of cigarettes from her purse. We grabbed our drinks and closed the door behind us. The air was crisp. The evening was cool, just warm enough that our breath didn't fog.

Julie looked at me. "Look, Rex. I want to make sure we are on the same page. I'm really good friends with Rose and ..."

"Relax. I don't know what you're talking about. Rose went home or her hotel or wherever and had to get to work that morning. That's it."

"Yeah, that's what she said. Nothing happened."

"Nope. Scout's honor. I walked her home and had to run to the base. I had an early shift."

"Good. Right. Exactly"

"Yup."

"That's what Jason said, too. So you and I are family huh? You look a little ... different. I would have expected you to have lighter hair."

"You mean the tan?" I held my forearm next to hers. They are a similar shade. How the hell does that work? She had goosebumps from the chill. A similar splattering of freckles on our arms.

"Yeah, the tan. So where are you from anyways?"

"Originally, I'm from Edmonton."

She looks at me for a second and rephrased. "No, I mean where was your grandfather from?"

"Well, I don't know him well because of the adoption and all that, but I'm told he's from Saskatchewan."

I loved this game. I enjoyed watching people squirm.

She thought for a second, then said, "No, I don't mean that. I mean originally."

She was trying her best. I could tell she hates to delve into the topic. She's stewed enough.

"Oh. You mean why am I brown?"

"Yes," she said. "Why are you so dark?"

"Well, it's because I'm part Irish."

She slapped me on the arm.

"Why do you have to make this so hard?"

"Ha! Honestly, I don't know. You're the first family I've actually met from my mom's side. My dad was as pale as you. Freckles. Redheaded. If anything, I should be a pale redhead with blue eyes and freckles." Mike slid the door open, cigarette in hand. I handed him my lighter and went for the door.

"I need another drink. Julie, when I get back, can I talk to you about your mom?"

She nodded. I went back inside while Mike slid the door shut behind him. Alyssa was with me beside the mini bar making that sucked-in face again. I turned back and saw Mike laughing with Julie.

Alyssa looked at me and said, "I need a fucking drink."

"Sure, come on over," I said. "I got everything."

I grabbed her mug and rummaged through the bottles.

"I wonder what the fuck those two are joking about," she

said.

"Probably laughing at me. I'll probably call it a night pretty soon. Jason has to take Julie home. He's got a duty watch in the morning. Thanks for coming down. It was nice finally meeting you."

"Thank god," she said. "I guess that whore will have to find someplace better to be."

"What did you say?"

"What? I just mean she can be somewhere else instead of here acting like a whore."

I set the bottle onto the counter. That was twice.

"Hey. That's enough of that. She's family," I said.

I didn't know why I was getting so protective. I didn't know either of these girls a few hours ago. Jon fucked whores and hated his family, but I was better than him. I wasn't going to put up with this shit even if she was new.

"Whaat!? I didn't say anything. I just called her a whore. Oh, come on, you barely know her. What do you care?"

"You're drunk," I said. "Cut that shit out."

I looked her in the eye. Her eyes were glazed over. She looked defiant. She wasn't even looking at me. She was side-eyeing the two of them on the patio. Jason was looking through my XBOX games giving zero fucks about any of this.

"Look, it's not my fault if you have a whore for a cousi …"

I don't think anyone ever told Alyssa "No" before. I don't think she had ever seen a guy who wouldn't put up with her attitude. I don't think she was ready to get thrown out of my house, either.

I wasn't Mike. I wasn't fucking her. I didn't care.

I grabbed her by the arm and dragged her to the door. She wasn't ready. She lost her balance while stumbling over the parade of shoes. Her sun dress was bouncing off each leg on each step as she scrambled to catch her footing. In any other moment, it would have been a nice view, very wholesome. But it's too late. I let go of her and opened the door. I placed my hand on the small of her back and shoved her, hard.

She stubbed her toe on the door jam and landed in the hallway on all fours. She turned her head back to say something but flinched as I threw her shoes at her. They bounced off her ass and fell to the ground. Mike came running in. He laughed while field stripping his cigarette,

"What just happened, man?"

"She called Julie a whore. I'm not putting up with that shit, sorry man."

Mike shook his head and grabbed his boots.

"I get it man. Don't worry, I'll talk to her."

I could barely make out what he was saying. He was laughing so hard.

"I don't care what you do with that dog walking bitch. She just ain't coming back in here."

Alyssa collected herself. When she bent over to pick up her shoes, I tossed her purse into her backside.

"I know I know. Here, I'm staying at her place tonight anyways. Have a good one man."

Julie came inside. Jason whispered to her what had happened.

♦

I had been fucking the Dog Walker for a few months. Go figure. It had been three days and she still wasn't returning my messages or my calls. It was the story of my life. Refuse to learn the lesson, segue into my second lowest point. Mike had his last box of clothes and was walking out the door. The Dog Walker called him after I was an idiot and expressed my feelings. She wanted to get back together with him. I guess he was the better asshole after all.

"Just stop. She told me everything. I can't believe you."

"I figured you already knew. You sure you don't need a hand?"

He didn't look up.

"No, that's fine. I don't want you fucking any of my stuff if

I let it near you."

"Are you fucking kidding me? Why are you being such a bitch about this. You don't care. You never cared before."

He was walking into the hall. I followed behind.

"Dude, I was dating her. You don't fuck another mans woman!"

He threw the box and it landed with a thud.

"She's not your woman. You're fucking like three other girls right now."

"I don't care man. You don't cut another man's grass."

"I don't get it. We go out all the time. You fuck everyone and everything. Every girl we meet, you're on them like a dirty shirt. Even my cousin when she and Jason came over. I saw you make a move on her. None of this would have happened if you weren't trying to fuck her."

"Oh fuck off. You only knew you were related by accident. You're just being a baby because you got all offended that Alissa made that joke about cousin-fucking. You're talking like you were changing her diapers as a kid. It's a rule. You don't fuck another man's girls."

"You've never cared about this before," I said. "You never had any rules. I'm the one who had rules, and you've made fun of me for them every fucking time."

"Because your rules are stupid. You fuck girls and dump them the same as I do except you do it a hell of a lot less because you're so bad at it. You act like a homo half the time."

"I do not."

"Sure you do. You keep bringing up your stupid fucking stepdad every time some chick throws a whiff in your face then you do something stupid to ruin it."

"That's not it at all. I just don't want to be a piece of shit like you is all."

"But you are a piece of shit. You've been fucking married women, single moms. I have never slept with a sailor before and you've fucked three. You couldn't even fuck Webber's wife, and everyone has fucked Webber's wife."

"How did you know that?"

"Everyone knows that. She's fucked every sad fuck sailor out there and that's why Webber was the only one who would marry her. You keep thinking you're not a piece of shit, but you're just as bad as me. Except you're worse because you're not even any good at it."

"Apparently, I am. Alyssa preferred fucking me."

Mike shoved me into the wall. I got right in his face.

"What, you're going to fight me over some chick?"

I shoved Mike, but he was ready and didn't budge.

"Yeah, fucking enjoy it," I said. "I'll be right there when she gets bored of your ass."

"I hope she pegs you. You deserve it."

"Wait, what? Pegging? Did she peg you?"

Mike stopped glaring and turned away shaking his head.

"No. Fuck are you talking about?"

"I know she's into kinky shit. I've seen the whip. I've seen the leather. I wouldn't be surprised if she had a strap on. Did she peg you?"

"Fuck off she did. I don't know about that shit."

I was laughing while Mike got angrier.

"She didn't peg me, for fuck sakes!"

"Because I wouldn't care if she did. You know I don't judge."

"I'm going to peg you here in a second."

Mike threw his arm over my head and pulled me into a headlock. We fell to the ground. I pushed against his face but his arm was locked. He lifted his knee and drove it into my ass. He was too high up to hit my asshole, but I felt it right in the small of my back. It shocked like lighting.

"Fuck off Mike. That hurts!"

He was mad and I couldn't stop laughing. He drove his knee into my back a few more times before I slipped under his arm. I grabbed the collar of his shirt and tried to pull it over his head. For a few minutes, neither one of us can get any clean hits. It was just a mess of arms and skin and headlocks and rolling around. I caught someone's door in my back. I was rubbing

The Dog Walker | R.A. STONE

Mike's face into the carpet when I saw my neighbor standing above us. She was a forty-five year old divorced woman. She had a bat in her hand. She was wearing pajamas

"Rex, Mike, what the fuck are you doing? Do I have to call the cops on you two?"

Mike and I released, let go, stood up. My shirt was ripped. Mike pulled his shirt back over his body.

I apologized while Mike grabbed his box and walked to his truck. There's no way she didn't peg him. I'm not into that shit. I may be a piece of shit like Jon, but at least I'm not so desperate to be wanted that I'm willing to let a girl shove something in my ass. Destroy my sheets if you want. Break my glasses. Ruin my life if it suits you. But stay out of my ass.

I'm better than Mike. I could have fucked more women than him, but I'll be damned if I'm going to get pegged by some whore.

Charli

Jason was standing at attention. Laz was not happy.

"Look, we have no fucking bandwidth at sea. I don't care what you're doing when you're at home, but don't be having your girl sending pictures and jamming the god damned MTP queue. We have fucking traffic coming in and I'm not about to sit in front of the captain and grab my ankles over this shit!"

"PO, I keep telling her no," he said. "She's fucking stalking me. Last time we got home, she was waiting for me in my house. She was making dinner. She's crazy man. I don't know what more I can do."

I was told Julie's tits were nice. I wasn't about to monitor the servers knowing my family tits were on there. Laz agreed to let me work on the bridge. I had picked an interesting time to go down and see how communications was going.

Both watches loved it. They gawked and enjoyed and roasted Jason over the only interesting thing to happen in weeks. I wanted to joke with Webber and ask his wife to send hers, but Laz was turning red and not in the mood. Maybe later. I pretend not to listen to Jason getting dressed down while I check my email. One message:

Subj: New Message, from Charli.

I clicked it.

"So call me when you get home. I have some vacation coming up and I want to come see you. Once I get there we can go linen shopping. I think I know the perfect place for you to get some new sheets."

This online dating thing was great. You just put a few photos up and made sure you're shirtless and doing something cool and they just messaged you. I had been talking to Charli for the last month. It started in an internet cafe in Seattle. She had messaged me first. I checked out the photos on her profile. She was thin. She had long, straight brown hair. She looked like the girl next door eight hours away. She lived in some small town on the mainland. I was sailing so it may as well have been Mars. She looked as good as Kate, maybe a little better.

Maybe too perfect.

She emailed while I was sailing. When I landed in port, I would go to a cafe and she would chat or talk on video. When I grabbed a hotel in Ensenada, Mexico, she called me for phone sex. It was fifteen minutes of telling a girl what you want and what you want to do to her, then she gets to tell you how much she liked it. Then she makes some moaning sounds while you jerk off to a photo of her.

True love.

It's not hot and it's not sexy, but when you've been at sea for a solid month doing nothing but work, sleep, eat, throwing up, and sometimes working out, it's good enough. It was the best way to spend my one Sunday I had off before two more weeks of sea sickness. After that I would be home. I kept reading her messages.

"Hey baby. I have all this vacation and I don't know what to do with it. I already have Christmas booked, but I want to see the island so I'm booking a week off and I'm going to catch the Greyhound and come down. Are you going to be home? TTYS LYB."

"We arrive home Sunday," I responded. "I'll be home after four. Just text me when you're arriving, and I'll pick you up at the station. It'll be nice to finally have you over. I'm so happy. Love you."

Send.

Laz left the office and Jason looked over.

"Dude. I should have never brought her over to your place. Ever since she came on that date, she's been crazy."

"You mean the nudes? I don't want to see that shit. Those are family tits."

"Not just the nudes. She's doesn't know how computers work, so they are huge files that take more traffic than anything else and they are jamming up our network. She tells my roommates that I told her she could stay there. She calls the house while waiting in the bushes to see if I answer and walk in front of the window. I'm fucked."

"I'm just glad I wasn't the one who found them. That would have been weird."

"Do you want to see?"

"You sick bastard. No."

"Oh, come on, it's fine. You only found out about her like two weeks ago."

"Yeah. I'm good. I think I'm gonna make that my line. No looking at the family nudes."

"They are nice, though. Real too."

The general call plays over the PA system:

"All hands, docking stations, docking stations. Return all gear. Man your stations."

"Jay. I gotta go. I'm on garbage. Good luck with those tits. I swear to god if you show me I'm going to kick you in the nuts."

I don't want to see my cousin's tits. I want to show Charli off at the Christmas party. I want everyone to tell me that they can't believe I landed a girl like that. She's thin. She's hot. She's not a trailer park bitch I brought home last night. She's got no kids, no baby daddy, and no bitch mom to watch them. It's nothing that I don't want.

I went to man the garbage stores. Beside the puck machine is a half torn copy of Penthouse. Candus is in there with me. She's shredding boxes.

She stops and says, "You're on the pucks. I don't feel like

porn right now. I'm sure you'll just be happy you're not related to them."

"You heard about that, did you?"

"Laz was talking about it yesterday. You have plans when we get back?"

"I met a girl."

"You met a girl?"

"Well, technically, she met me. Have you tried this dating online thing?"

"No, I'm not a nerd, Rex."

"I used to think so too, but I've met my second girl on there already. Good looking too."

"So who is this one?"

"Her name is Charli."

"Does Charli have a last name?"

"Cappadonna. She's coming to see me after we land."

I pushed the button and pressed the hammer down. Pucks are just like making pancakes, only with porn and the stench of hot plastic.

"Wait, Cappadonna? She's Italian?"

"I don't know, maybe."

"Well, that sounds fun. I'm happy for you. What's she like?"

"Oh, she's perfect. She's not like any other girl I've ever dated."

I grabbed the puck out of the machine and placed it on the stack. Twenty pucks with the collection of photos from this month's Penthouse Pet.

"Aww, I've never seen you like this."

"I know, right? She loved hearing about me. Not just the fun stuff, either. She liked hearing everything. She already knows what I like in my perfect woman. She knows I have the Christmas party coming up. She wants me to show her off, make me look good. She even loves how much I care about my bed sheets. She knows I used to love those old sixties flight attendant outfits."

"Sounds like she is perfect."

"I'd say so. I've talked about some of the crappy girls I used to date."

"What, like Sara?"

"Very fucking funny. Actually, yes. She agreed that going out during your fiance's stag was trashy. She said her mom used to be like that. Get bored then do something stupid and ruin relationships. She never got to know her dad."

"She sounds exactly like what you've always wanted."

"Oh she is. Hey, do you think I should go with the bent over ass shot for this puck, or the one with her legs in the air and showing off her clam?"

"Eww, Rex. Keep this up and I'll put your cousin's tits on one of them."

"You bitch."

"Seriously, though. Why do the bosun insist that we do this?"

"Tradition, and they get irritable if you don't. They get so bored at sea since all they have to do is rounds and overboard watches. For them this is the highlight of their week. Plus, if you don't, they tell everyone you're gay. Just be careful, cause the chief sneaks magazines of ladyboys. If you throw them into a puck without paying attention then they get to roast you for a whole sail."

"Guys are fucking retarded, Rex. Tell me more about Charli."

"I can see myself making her an omelet in the morning. All I've ever wanted is someone I can have breakfast and a coffee with."

"Aaron always makes me coffee in the mornings. I get it."

I placed the last puck in the pile. A wholesome girl next door was being shipped in just for me. My current moment consisted of a hard working military man, the perfect woman on her way, the smell of burnt plastic, and the sight of leather clad ass. I think I'm in love.

The chief bosun's mate yelled into the garbage stores and broke my reverie.

"Start handing the gash. Lets go!"

♦

I'm gone. As I get to my car I get a text. It's Charli.
I'll be there in 30 minutes.
I didn't want to be late, so I drove like a madman. I looked at my Seamaster and turned the outside dial til the 35 on the dial aligned with the minute hand. Five minutes to get home. Ten minutes to shower and get dressed. Ten minutes to get to the station. Plenty of time.

I hopped in the shower and scrubbed off the scent of porn laminated garbage. My arms were red, almost raw. I scrubbed until the water ran clear. I don't want to meet Charli for the first time with her smelling diesel or the sweat of a warship. I didn't want her to smell burnt plastic porn and bad decisions. This needed to be perfect. I imagine she smells neutral, normal, clean. No baby powder or lactation surprise. Maybe the scent of a home cooked meal? I picked the same clothes I would have worn out with Mike and Jason. Dress shirt, designer jeans, Chelsea boots. I check the Seamaster again. Ten more minutes to get to the station. Plenty of time.

The streetlights were red every other day. I have to wait every other day. Not this time. Everything was green. Traffic was gone. All the sailors who usually jam up the roads wanted to go home. No one wanted to stay in town. Nothing in my way. Everything was prepared. Everything was perfect.

I checked my watch. I still had ten minutes. I saw the station ahead. A few cars in the parking lot. I must not be the only one who is finally meeting their crush. I sat in the lounge and waited.

The bus was late. Then it was here and Charli came through the door. A rush of cold winter air followed her. Fresh and crisp air gave me a chill. I shook it off. There's a few girls there. That girl on the left looked like the photos. Probably her. I looked over. If she looks back and smiles, then I'd know for sure. I tried to keep my cool, but I looked as excited as I did when I got Megaman II on Christmas. She looked up. It was her.

"Rex!" She lifts her hands up in the air. Her duffel fell to the ground. I ran. Her plaid, woolen jacket was scratchy and cold. I grabbed her shoulders and felt her body. A thin, solid girl underneath. My arms itched. I ignored it. She reached under my arms for a hug.

"Oh my god, Charli! How long was the ride?"

"Oh, only like nine hours. My legs are almost asleep!"

She pretended to pass out. I wasn't ready for it. She almost fell over. I grabbed a fist full of jacket to hold her up.

"Well, come on. I've been back long enough to get out of my uniform. Let's get you home."

"Not right away. I just got here. Where can we grab a drink?"

"This early? Probably the Shark Club. You a hockey fan?"

"Ha, nope."

"Me neither."

"Where's your car?"

"Right there. The Sentra."

"Four-door sedan? My favorite. Bitches love a man who cares about fuel efficiency."

I gave that joke out a month ago. A throwaway line. She had a Rolodex of my life for every occasion. I've never seen anyone care this much about me. It was honest. Refreshing. Authentic.

"Oh shut up, get in."

I unlocked her door. She didn't wait for me to guide her. She hopped in and shoved her duffel over the console into the back seat. I ran around to my side and she had already reclined her seat.

"You do the pedals. I'll do the stick," she said.

I didn't think I'd ever seen a girl who wanted to take charge let alone drive a manual. The first few times the gears were grinding upon each attempt. After the third shift, she got my rhythm down.

"Oh my god, the ride down was so boring. They had me next to some guy who smelled like weed. He wouldn't shut up about it. He wanted my number, said he knew some places to party."

"Oh, you mean party?" I tapped my nose.

"Yeah. I used to date a guy who was into that stuff. He was such an abusive asshole. He was always trying to control me, to manipulate me. I told him I wasn't like that anymore. Thankfully, my ex moved away six months ago. I told him I was headed to the island to see the greatest guy in the world. He's such a nice guy, and he's so comfortable, so great. It's just what I need."

"You told him all that? You should have told him we were engaged."

"I almost did. He was having a hard time accepting no for an answer. It's all good though. Is this the place?"

No one in the Shark Club was under fifty. Twenty TV's were spread around: behind the bar, beside the pool table, in the bathroom. Every channel was playing the Canucks game. Charlie grabbed her cell phone and dropped her jacket onto a stool.

"Grab me whatever you're having," she said. "I'll be back in a second."

I motioned to the bartender.

"Two Guiness."

He nodded. I wanted to take her home and fuck her. I'd made so much progress with her so far and was hoping nothing got in my way like it usually did. I couldn't tell if it was the sailing or the messages and phone calls that built more anticipation. Not that I cared. I was getting to be the guy who figured out the patterns and finished the game for once. If I hadn't worked so hard for this it would have felt too good to be true. Every fantasy I had. Every preference. Every dream and desire. She had it all. It was too good to be true.

The bartender returned with the drinks. Charli joined shortly after. She hopped onto the stool and sat with her legs spread apart, both hands in between. She leaned in and the back legs of her stool lifted an inch.

"I've been waiting to finally see you for weeks now," she said.

I touched her cheek and put my other hand on her leg to keep her stable. We briefly kissed. I held for a second, then opened my eyes. Was she looking at me or were her eyes closed too? They were closed. I quickly closed mine and wondered, How long can I hold it here? After what felt like not enough time, she popped up and started drinking. I had to sprint to finish mine before she put her glass down.

"I got this round," she said. "Grab us a pool table!"

A single empty table sat in the middle of the club. I put a loonie into the machine and the balls dropped with a clack. Charli walked over with two drinks in her hand while I racked. She looked like a waitress. A black v-neck t-shirt and dark, skin tight blue jeans. Her smile stretched from ear to ear. She had a small mole on her left cheek. It reminded me of Cindy Crawford. Charli's hair was not quite blond but not quite brunette, either. Long enough to be long, but not so long as to look like a homesteader. How did she sit on a bus for nine hours and show up with it looking great? The little hairs on her arm were standing upright. She held my glass up to my lips and I took a sip. She walked over to the rack and grabbed a cue.

"So when I was a kid, before my dad and mom divorced, my dad used to play pool. He taught me how to shoot, so don't feel bad if I beat you, chickie," I said.

"Oh? I don't really play. I just like having something to do while I'm drinking."

"That's okay. I promise to take it easy. We aren't playing for stakes."

"Oh, like for money?" she asked. "Or for blood, like in the movies?"

"Yeah, like for money. I don't think our date would go well if the loser had to get merc'd."

I broke well. I had a lot of options with a few easy choices. I decided on solids.

"The trick is consistency. Cause no one can shoot perfectly, but everyone shoots imperfectly the same way. So if I always end up hitting the pocket an inch on the right, I just aim an inch on the left to compensate. You just have to pay attention."

"Oh? That's good to know," she said.

I'm not nearly as good as I thought, and she wasn't as bad as she let on. I should have gone with stripes. It looked like such an easier set of shots. I don't know why it looked so good before. It was that one ball in the corner. I was so focused on the first shot that I forgot I had to make seven others. Lesson for me: What good is learning patterns if I'm too slow, arrogant or stupid to do anything about them?

Now that I've cleared off a ball or two, all I have left are some tricky shots, but every one I make gives her more room to work. One is blocked by her balls. The other is across the table. I don't have the skill to shoot any of this well.

"This is fun, Rex. So what do you have planned now that I'm here?" Charli took a swig of her beer, leaned across the table, and extended her arms all the way out to reach for her shot. The cue wiggled a bit in her hand. Her breasts rested firmly on the table. I focused so much on them that I didn't see how she shot. She lifted her leg for balance. She was up by three with one more ball before she could shoot the eight. She missed her next shot but set me up perfectly.

"Well, you came just in time," I told her. "It's my birthday tomorrow, and the ship is having its Christmas party the day after. I hope you brought something nice. It's a formal event."

I was distracted. I didn't hit my shot with enough force, so my ball stopped short.

"Oh, nice! I actually have to go shopping, but I want it to be a surprise. Would you be cool if I borrowed your car for a bit tomorrow?"

"Course not. Whatever you gotta do to look good, right?"

Charli put her last ball into the pocket.

"You're better than you let on."

"Well, yeah. You always hit your shots gently like you want every ball to perfectly roll in every time. I knew you would probably tap yours and it wouldn't drop. You set me up perfectly for the kill shot. Good thing you didn't play for blood. Your heart would have been mine. I'm bored. Let's do something else."

"We can talk about the party and have another drink."

"I can do that. It'll be fun to meet all the military people. I promise I'll make you look good in front of the captain."

"Oh, I already look good. But I'm sure you being there won't hurt. The event usually devolves into drunken sailors by the end of the night, so you just have to be standing at the end to impress everyone."

I grabbed her by the waist and pulled her in.

"Come on. It's cold," she said. "Finish your drink. I smell like a bus ride. Mind if I take a shower when we get home?"

"Sure."

I grabbed my keys and swigged the last of my beer.

As Charli walked into the condo, she pulled a small dopp bag from her duffel. I pointed to the bathroom door and she walked in and closed it behind her. I heard the bathroom fan start and she called out, "Hey, make us something to drink. I have to shave my legs."

I set her duffel bag down by the laundry room. The machine hadn't been run in weeks. In my bedroom was my duffel full of uniforms and socks and underwear. It smelled like burnt plastic and porn. I took my last two glasses from the mini bar and rinsed them in the sink. The hiss of the shower drowned out my tinnitus. It sounded like a snake about to strike. I grabbed a new bottle of Jameson from the bottom of my duffel and poured two fingers into each glass. I added a touch of bitters and a maraschino cherry and a few ice cubes.

The door opened a crack.

"Hey, Rex. Do you mind if I drink in the shower?"

I see her hand outstretched through the bathroom door. I placed the drink onto her palm and she disappeared like a magical fairy. I stood there imagining what she looked like in the shower. The sound of the fan is loud. The door is still open. I caught a glimpse of myself in the mirror. This guy is an idiot

"What the fuck are you doing?" said the other guy. "I'm taking over."

I took off my shirt and walked in. I heard the water running behind the curtain. I pulled it open a quarter and peeked. She was standing under the water sipping her Manhattan. Her hair was stuck to her back, forming a point on her spine. The water flowed down the divot in her slender back.

I looked at her ass. She turned around, still drinking, holding her hand over the glass like an umbrella to shield it from the water. I looked up while she looked over. She was humming some song while bobbing her head around. I kicked my socks and pants off, stepping on the crotch and lifting my legs out. I got into the shower. The water stung my arms which were still raw from the scrub. She wrapped her arms around my shoulders and stuck her tongue in my mouth. It felt just like I had imagined. Her mouth was cold. Her lips were warm. She was hot as fuck. She stopped to finish her drink.

She let me cum in her mouth. She knew that I loved doing that. She tried a trick she saw on the internet where she had an ice cube in her mouth while she did it. I didn't really notice a difference, but variety is the spice of life. I didn't care; I got laid.

We drank more that afternoon while she asked me more about my life. She wanted to know about my family, my hopes, my dreams. Why my bookshelf looked like Tetris. What games were on that xbox in the living room. Why I only had two glasses. I felt like I mattered. I felt like a king. It was like she loved me for me.

That night I took the mirror out of the hallway and placed it beside my bed. She wanted to try this thing where we watched ourselves fucking and pretend we're watching other people. It was hot. She put on more of a show when I was looking at her reflection. It felt good either way. Variety, spice, got it.

I slept like a baby that first night. I could see the outline of her slim ass under the sheets. The skin on my arms still burned. The faint smell of plastic was in my nose. She was giving off heat like a furnace, but I didn't want her to move. I felt a bead of sweat in my ass. This was as good as it got. I couldn't wait to have our first date the next day.

♦

GLO was packed. I was sitting at the bar. Jasmine was looking great as ever. She leaned in and tucked her elbows. Charli's eyes darted down to that grand Australian cleavage, briefly, then back to me.

"I'll grab us a drink then join everyone at the table. Hey Jas!"

"Rex, good to see you. The usual for you, and … what for the ladyfriend?"

"Yes, please, and this is Charli."

Charli was wearing a navy blue dress with a slit in the side that went halfway up her thigh and had stripes down the side. She looked like she could be the stewardess in a space airline. Her heels were high enough to put us at eye level. Her neckline was low enough for a half inch of cleavage. She barely had a handful but was willing to make the most of it. Sexy in just the right way to meet friends without being a distraction.

"I'll have a Manhattan, nice to meet you Jas."

"No worries. You two sitting at the bar?"

"Actually I'm at the birthday table today."

"Oh really? Special occasion?"

"Yeah, I'm turning 29"

"Well, in that case, I'll make you something special. I'll bring it over. Go enjoy yourself."

Charlie took my lead. I hadn't thought about it before this moment. Every woman I've ever been with walked in front of me, always Well, except for Kate. I moved slow as I was never in a hurry. Were they always in a hurry, or were they certain that they didn't need to be led? Like a shoveled driveway, no one notices until it's not done.

We had arrived fashionably late so Charli could finish her hair, something I wasn't used to accounting for. Most of the seats were taken already. Jason had managed to stay out of trouble for once just so he could come. He and Jullie were at the table. He was drinking a whiskey and she had something clear with a lime. Candus and Aaron were there with beer. Bethany and a new guy she was dating showed up. Her hair was bright pink on top and gradated to orange on the bottom. She called it an Ombre. I walked up with Charli. Everyone turned around.

"Fellas, Charli. Charli? Fellas." I waved my arm across the group and sat down at the head of the table. Charli set her purse down in the seat next to me and excused herself to go to the bathroom.

Candus leaned over and said, "When the hell did you get taste in women? This one's a looker. She the girl from the emails?"

"Yup. And, no kids. No fiance, and she isn't married to one of my students!"

"Stop smirking. And hey, you're welcome. Sara had nothing but good things to say about you."

"I'm sure she did. In fairness, she was the only girl before this who came to my place and didn't destroy something I loved."

"That's good. Hey, so you should let me talk to your little toy. I wanna see what she's like."

"We aren't going to share her, asshole."

"No no no, that's not what I mean. I've never seen you acting like this. It's like you're a different person. You're usually an asshole, and I mean this in a good way. Now you're just like a big softie and I want to see who made you change into this sweetheart."

"Oh, you don't have to worry about me. I'm always this guy, but I never trust women to act like this. I don't know if you know this, but some women can be absolute bitches and you have to be a little guarded, you know?"

"Oh, I know."

"But yeah. This one is good. I lent her my car so she could go shopping, and look what she came back with?"

"Yeah, it looks good. I'm just happy for you is all."

Charlie walked back, threw her arm over my shoulder, and leaned in to the conversation.

"Hey, you two, I have to steal my man for a bit. I promise I'll bring him back."

"You two are leaving already?"

"No. I just want a cigarette outside."

"Oh, well Rex doesn't smoke alongside, only foreign ports. Here, I'll come with you. I've been dying to meet you anyways, Rex won't shut up about you!"

Candus grabbed Charli by the arm and cajoled her out. Jason looked over. "Hey man, we have to take off," he said. "I hope you have a great birthday, man. Charli is a looker by the way."

"That sucks. It's so early. We haven't even had a chance to chat."

"I know. I'm really sorry. Jullie is kind of sick and something else going on. I'll tell you later."

"Jullie? Aww, cuz. Well, thanks for coming. Out of all my cousins I never knew I had, you're turning out to be one of my favorites."

She didn't laugh. She grabbed her jacket while Jason reached over to give her a kiss on the cheek. Jullie pulled away and walked to the entrance.

"What the hell was that, Jay? Is everything OK?"

"I will tell you later."

Even in the soft lighting, I could see he was pale as a ghost. I wondered what rattled him? Charli and Candus came back inside as I finished my drink. Charlie leaned over my back, her arms around my neck.

"What was that?"

"I dunno. Jason looks panicked over something."

"Well, hey baby. I'm freezing. Warm me up."

I rubbed her arms. They were bumpy and cold like glazed porcelain. That was the first time I'd ever felt someone who wanted my warmth, both inside and out. I just wanted to make her an omelet and a coffee and enjoy the day with her. I figured

155

I could have that now. For the first time ever, it seemed possible. It had been twelve years since Jon told me to get on a girl like a dirty shirt. Twelve years since I promised I would never be like that asshole. I was right. Finally, I could prove to that son of a bitch I was right.

I could feel her breasts against my back. She set her chin on my head. She was cold but all I felt was warmth. She rocked slightly in rhythm to the music the DJ was playing. Downtempo lounge, a slowed-down tune that would fit in at a jazz bar but with an EDM beat to accompany it. I loved its modern take on the classics. Everything was perfect. I didn't have to open her. I didn't have to tell her a story to build rapport. I didn't need to escalate. She was just into me. She got it. I didn't have to put on a mask. I didn't have to be him. She knew everything about me, and she was the perfect fit for all of it.

"Rex, you listening?" It was Charli.

"What now?"

"I'll grab us some drinks. Would you like the same one?"

I nodded. As she left, Candus came up and sat on Charli's chair.

"Hey. I need to tell you something, but you're not going to like it."

"Why? What's up?"

"I get she's hot. I get you're happy. But I think you're being had."

"What do you mean?"

"Well. I'm out there having a cigarette with Charli. She keeps talking about how she used to date some bad guys and how happy she is that she found a great guy like you."

"Who hasn't dated a dud? I know if I had a bunch of shitty dates then found me a good girl, I'd be happy too."

"No. You don't understand women. That's a huge red flag."

"It is?"

"Look. You know Aaron and I do our thing?"

"Yeah, I know."

"We used to date Sara before she found Webber. Once she

got engaged, she said the same thing. She used to date such assholes and now she found a good guy to settle down with. And well."

"Right, because Sara got him to take photos of you two fucking her, then Charli must be like that?"

"Whoa, don't be mean. I'm not trying to say that. It's not just that, either. My sister was the same way. My mom was like that. I was almost like that. I'm telling you. Go on, ask her."

"Ask her what? If she'd be open for a foursome?"

"No, idiot. Ask her what she was doing before you, and I bet you she tells you she'll have a story about some guy who was abusive, or manipulative, or controlling, or some other bullshit. Aaron saw right through it when he met me. He told me that I was just angry that he left me, and he knew I only liked him because he was the opposite of the guys I used to date."

"Oh I get it. So you can make a mistake and Aaron can fix you, but I'm just fucked? You guys worked out, why can't I?"

"Rex, you're not listening to me. I'm not saying that. Why do you think we swing? You think I'm just a whore because it's fun or something?"

"I don't care why you fuck other people. I just don't get why you're acting all weird and jealous about it now that I may have found someone."

Candus slapped the table. It got my attention.

"God, you are so man-brained. Look, do what you want. Have fun. I don't give a fuck. I am telling you when the love goggles come off with her, and it's going to happen sooner rather than later, she's going to get bored, and when she's bored, she's going to do something that's going to break your heart. All I'm saying is be careful."

"Fine whatever. Look Charli is coming back."

Charli handed me a martini. "Hey, baby. Brought you a Gibson! The tall blond girl at the bar said you'd like it."

"That's my Jas!" I look over to the bar and raise the glass. Jasmine nods and goes back to the customers.

"It's going to cost you, big time." She leaned forward and

closed her eyes. I looked behind us. Candus was watching Charli enjoy the moment and looked sincerely concerned. She whispered something to Aaron. I closed my eyes and ignored it. She's just pissed that I'm not going to share. Charli walked around the table mingling with everyone left. Bethany gave her a hug. They started to chat. Charli held Bethany's hair between her fingers and squeals. I felt a tap on my shoulder. I turned around and Aaron was standing beside me.

"Hey. Candus talked to you I take it?"
"Yeah."
"She brought up the assholes, right?"
"Yeah…"
"Hey, can we go somewhere? I know we weren't ever close, but I want to tell you something and I want it to stay between us. Come for a smoke?"
"I don't really smoke at home."
"Dude. Just come." He grabbed his denim jacket off the chair and put it on. I grabbed my coat, and we walked outside.

He pointed his pack of cigarettes at me, and I reached for one. He lit up. The lighter stopped working. He let me use his cigarette to light mine. Aaron took a deep breath in, held for a pregnant pause, then exhaled. He waited a beat before he looked me in the eye.

"I know Candus probably said some weird shit and pissed you off."
"Is that what she told you?" I asked.
"No. I just know what she's like."
"I can't tell if she's jealous or what. She told me that Charli had dated a dude who was an abusive asshole because that's what she's into, and that she only likes me because I'm nothing like the guys she usually dates, and when she gets bored of me, she will do something stupid, so I shouldn't trust her. And I'm pretty sure she's projecting."
"Oh dude. Of course, she's projecting, but she's not wrong either. Did she ever tell you why we swing?"
"No. I never asked either. Just don't care that much."

"Well, she says it's because I asked her to, but it's not, not really. I don't like doing it and I always tell her that I'm not going to watch her get railed by other dudes, only chicks. That's why she kicked Webber out that time."

"I thought that was because he was a dweeb and no one liked him?"

"Well, yeah, that too. But fuck. Look at me." He waved his hand across his body. Now that I looked at him, he had a similar build. Lanky, a hunch, bow legs. "I'm balding, that's why I shave my head. I look like a smashed can of assholes when I'm naked…"

"Is it a smashed can of assholes? I thought it was a can of smashed assholes."

"It's not about the fucking assholes. The reason I do it is because I was married before to a girl. She was just like Candus. She gave the whole speech about how she used to do all kinds of things, but she wasn't like that anymore, and she wanted something better and special and that I was the greatest guy and exactly what she needed. Do you know what happened?"

"Honestly, I didn't know you were even married before. Aren't you like twenty-seven?"

"Well, I was. And it started great. We fucked all the time. She would blow me in the shower. She loved the life of a military wife. She got to go to all the parties and hang with all the boys, and it was great. What you got is probably awesome right now. She'd buy me drinks and tell me I was special, and then six months in she changed. At first, it was just a little. She was always in the mood, then, eventually, things happened, and she was only in the mood sometimes, then barely ever."

"That's just what happens right?"

"That's what I thought. I figured everyone eventually slows down, like in their forties. But I was only twenty-five. And she started to get mean. She started to go out and didn't want me controlling her. Then, eventually, I found out she was fucking other dudes."

"Jesus."

"Yeah, Jesus. It killed me, but that wasn't the worst part. If it was someone wealthier than me, better looking than me, I mean I still would have hurt, but it would at least have made sense. When I caught her, it was some fat dude who dealt drugs out of his apartment. A real loser. That's what hurt. She fucked some fat loser and she couldn't stand me. I was boring. I was controlling. I was manipulative, and she said she never really loved me to begin with. So why do we swing? Because I saw the same thing in every girl I've dated. Every fucking one. They are great. Then they get bored. Then they fuck things up just because. With Candus, I just didn't care and thought, Fuck it. I'll fuck anyone and bring her along. And then when a half year came, she was still excited to see me."

"I had no idea about all this," I said. "So you swing to keep her from getting bored?"

"I do it to keep her jealous. For some reason, she loves having things she can't have. She likes to be treated like shit because she thinks she's a piece of shit, and if I didn't, she would think I'm lying to her, or that I was stupid and naive because I don't. It's why even if she's got a headache, she refuses to let me go to sea without fucking me the night before just so I don't forget what's waiting for me at home."

"You make her sound like the Dog Walker."

"The what?"

"Never mind, long story. Anyway, that's fucked up."

"You think I don't know that? Look, I'm not telling you not to fuck Charli. I'm not telling you not to fall in love with Charli. It's your life. I'm telling you that it's obvious to everyone but you what's going to happen, and I'm telling you because Candus calls you her best friend and doesn't want to see you turn into what I turned into after my divorce. Charli is going to get bored, and it'll happen with something small where she's not in the mood but she'll make it up to you later. Then it'll happen all at once. Once she calls you controlling for asking a simple question like, 'Hey, when are you coming back?' or something, just be prepared for what comes next."

"Ugh, you sound like my stepdad. I've been trying to get away from that shit all my life. There's a lot of girls out there. I had to get this one from eight hours away just so she wasn't like the girls we have here."

"Maybe. But you got two choices. You can either be like me, and understand what it takes to keep this thing going, or not, and roll the dice. Maybe you knock her up and buy yourself a few years before she starts getting bored, or maybe you find out sooner."

I looked over and Charli was still talking with Bethany. She looked back at me with a glimmer in her eye and winked. I smiled back. I looked at Aaron and his knowing stare.

"Thanks, Aaron, but I think I can handle this."

"Hope so, man. Happy birthday."

He jammed his cigarette butt into the ashtray and walked back inside. Jas approached the table holding a tray of tequila shots.

Charli shouted across the table, "Told you I had a plan. Happy birthday!"

Aaron grabbed two, handed me one. Jas walked around the table handing them out to everyone else. Aaron tapped his shot glass into mine and we took them back. He gave me a slap on the back and walked back to Candus and quietly joined her conversation at the other end of the table. The shot burned a bit. Cheap tequila always tasted like tequila. Good tequila tasted more like chocolate. I downed my Guinness to clean my palate then got up to take a piss.

Standing in front of the urinal, the smell of pink urinal pucks invaded my senses. The bottom of the urinal was covered in ice cubes. Behind me was a black guy sitting by the sink. He was folding paper towels and placing them on the counter beside a basket full of colognes. I didn't know how he did it. I couldn't sit there staring at men pissing all shift. The tequila shot was kicking in. I was starting to feel warm. In front of me was a digital ad on a screen set into the wall.

"Dos Equis, the most interesting man in the world."

An aged out James Bond looking guy in the ad was walking in the jungle, drinking in a bar surrounded by beautiful women drinking piss Mexican beer.

Then, "That was easy" with a big red button on a desk with a Staples logo. Office furniture ads filled my headspace while pissing at the bar. The man pressed the button and all his problems went away. I shook and went to wash my hands. The man turned on the sink for me then sat back. He handed me a napkin and it only dried my hands halfway before it's saturated. I waved them around for a second so they dry somewhat. He offered his basket.

"Would you like a spritz?"

"Uh, sure. Do you have Prada in there?"

"Oh, that one's popular. Everyone's had a bit of Amber."

The man rummaged around until he found it, a clear, square bottle with the familiar purple liquid in it. He handed it to me and I sprayed it once onto my neck. I reached into my pocket looking for cash. I found a five and put it in the jar by the sink. As I was about to walk out, I paused.

"Hey, can I ask you a question?"

"Shoot."

"Do you think women get bored when they have a life that's too happy?"

"I couldn't tell ya. You'd have to ask my ex-wife."

"Heh."

I looked at the table. Charli was sitting in my seat. Everyone still there was waiting for me.

"Hey, hey, hey! So Rex is almost thirty. And I know he's already the perfect man and the best sailor and he doesn't need anything, but I picked something up for him and wanted everyone to watch him open it." Charli pulls out a briefcase sized box wrapped with newspaper.

"How in the hell did you sneak that in here without me even noticing?" Charli is swaying and getting louder.

"Well, I grabbed it when I was shopping for dresses this morning and snuck it in your trunk. Candus kept an eye on you

162

while I grabbed it. Open it!"

"How many Manhattans have you had so far?"

"Like, six. Open it!"

I tore at the newspaper. Underneath is a thick, plastic square-shaped bag, a cardboard label in the middle. I looked at my gift. A full sheet set: "Espresso. 150 thread count. 50% Cotton/Poly."

It's the thought that counts. I told her I loved linens, but I never mentioned specifics. Even I knew that the way to a girl's heart is not by talking about thread counts. This was her best guess, I guess.

This was homely. I could see a life together on plain sheets like this. I was sure they'd feel scratchy, but I didn't care. This was as good as life got.

"I know, right? I saw you were down to your last set and you have a duvet on the bed with no cover, so I figured what better to get the man who has everything than a warm place to sleep."

"These are great. They are just what I need. Thank you."

She looked so happy and everyone around us was laughing. I can't see Rex in the mirror, but I can hear him clearly,

Of course, Rex would have liked a sheet set for his birthday. Who wouldn't?

Candus spoke up.

"Man, I knew you hated the sheets at work, but I didn't know you were the kind of guy who loved fancy sheets. I am just happy with a forty dollar set of flannel."

I opened my mouth and was about to talk at length about the different weaves of cotton, but the tequila was warming me up, and I couldn't stop thinking about the man by the sink and his answer. I couldn't do two things at once, so I let it go.

"What can I say? I make sure I have the best coffee and the best sheets and the best shoes because I can't stand the ship's boots, the ship's coffee and the racks."

Charli hopped onto my lap holding another Gibson. She brought it to my lips and tipped it into my mouth.

These sheets are going to pill in a few washes, I thought.

163

The Dog Walker | R.A.STONE

The color is going to fade, and it's going to look like baby puke. I'm going to sweat right through them in the summer. They won't last a year. Wait, what was I thinking? Fuck that. Aaron is an asshole and Candus is just jealous. The sheets will work just fine. I just have to be careful with them, and they can last. It's on me to make it work. I see that. Take proper care. I don't have to wash them each week, just when they are dirty. And I won't be having any more chicks over who will ruin them. Charli brought them to me. I didn't have to shop for them. They will be fine.

Melissa isn't coming back with her anemic ass. No single moms shooting milk onto the bed. No grass stains or any of that shit. These sheets won't have to put up with any of that crap. No more dreams about fucking lesbians. They don't have to be the best. They just have to be the ones on the bed, the ones I treat right.

When we got home, Charli ran straight to the bedroom and fell on the bed.

"Oh my god that was so fun. Happy birthday, Rex. I'm so drunk right now. The room is spinning." She was exhaling rapidly, humming something to herself, lowing imaginary bubbles into the air.

"Here, you're wearing your shoes to bed."

I reached down and detached the buckles from her heels. I placed the shoes on the floor and turned her sideways to unzip her dress. No bra. Or panties.

"I wanted to give you one more birthday present, but I think I'm going to be sick. Can we get a good night's sleep and I'll give it to you in the morning?"

"Of course. You're drunk and I don't want to fuck a passed-out chick."

"Rex. I love you. You're the best man ever. I'll make it up to you. I promise."

"I know," I said. "I love you, too."

Why did I say that? But I knew why: I didn't think.

I love you. Did I, though? I loved how she tried her best to please me, to make me happy. I loved how she was everything I wanted. I loved how she was perfect. I loved how she was a drunken mess and trusted me to take care of her. I loved how she tried a man she wouldn't have otherwise wanted and found out it was the best thing for her. I didn't know if I loved her, though. I looked at the other side of the bed into the mirror. Her back was to me, her face was in the reflection. She was already sleeping. She looked good, but her makeup was running a bit on the sheets. It was a good thing the new ones were beige. You wouldn't even notice it come off. She woke up a bit.

"You know. You really are just what I needed right now. You have no idea how bad my life was before I met you."

"What do you mean?"

"Oh, you know. Just, like before I met you. He was so controlling, so manipulative. And you're none of those things. You're just great. He was just abusive. I knew I didn't need…" She drifted back off again. And like that, it was just me in the mirror. A passed out naked girl in front of me and a new set of sub-par sheets in my hand. Maybe I just expected too much. Maybe they were good enough.

Charli's cell phone had fallen on the floor. I placed it on the nightstand. The LED light on the side was blinking. I'm tempted. I think about it. I picked it up. Fuck it. I put it back down. Candus was just jealous, and flannel sheets are redneck garbage. I'll bet Jon would have fucked her right here, figured if he fucked her hard enough she would stay awake. It's not fun for me unless a girl is into it. I took the duvet and placed it over her slender, sloppy body. It had been without a cover for so long, it was starting to fray. If it weren't for the flat sheet, it would be scratchy. My pillow was covered in makeup and mascara and lipstick. I hoped it wouldn't stain because it's my only set of three hundred thread count Egyptian cotton in the house.

I went into the living room and started up the XBOX. Maybe a few games before bed. Omelettes and birthday in the morning. It was funny. Kate used to go to the bar and get drunk then spend the night. She never drank too much and always made sure I went to bed happy. I don't think any other girl but these two ever spent the night. The Dog Walker would have, if I let her.

Charli didn't wake up till eleven. I had coffee and an omelet ready at ten. By the time she woke up, the coffee was cold and the omelet was rubbery. I was in my bathrobe watching TV when I heard the door to the bedroom open.

"Oh my god I drank too much," she said. "Thank you so much for taking care of me. You're so sweet."

"No worries. Thanks for a great birthday."

"I'm sorry. I promise I'll make it up to you tonight. My mouth tastes like an ashtray right now and I have a terrible headache."

"No, I meant thank you for the sheets. You had your makeup on last night and I have to change them. It was perfect. I made you a coffee, but you'll have to microwave it. There's an omelette, but it's also cold."

"Aww, thank you, but I'm going back to sleep."

"OK. I'm going to hop in the shower, I have to pick up some dry cleaning for the Christmas party tonight."

"I'll be ready."

♦

I looked dapper. I put on my evening suit, a midnight blue two-button. One hundred twenty thread count. Worsted wool. Double vent in a British cut. Underneath, a black shirt and a white tie with pink paisley. I had the military Oxfords spit-polished to a mirror shine. Cologne: Prada, Amber Pour Homme.

Charli wore one of those classic evening gowns you see in the movies. Spaghetti strap. Three inch heels. Her hair was up in some style she called a French twist.

It was exactly how I imagined it should go. Of course, I had mentioned it to her in an email a while back.

Most other sailors were dressed in their first suits since prom. Flashy, neon-colored silk shirts with open collars and black suits off the rack. Their wives and girlfriends looked good, but Charli looked better. She was thinner than the wives. She was much thinner than the female sailors. She was better dressed. Her makeup was subtle, but good. Great, in fact.

It was perfect, like everything. Everything went perfectly. She was charming with the captain, and his wife didn't feel threatened, so she liked us both. She laughed when it turned out the chief brought a prostitute who made out with one of the Hull Tech's girlfriends. Charli didn't drink too much. She held onto my arm when I needed someone there to flex and mingled when I didn't.

We went home that night and she took her makeup off in the bathroom before coming to bed.

"So I think one of your co-workers was hitting on me."

"Was it Webber?"

"No, I don't remember his name. He said he was an electrician?"

I was lying half-dressed on the bed. I could see another fifty years of banal conversation like this. I could live with that.

"Ah, that would be Maxime. I wouldn't worry about him. He's French." Charli came to bed. She had her hair up in a bun. She was wearing red panties and a matching top. She posed in the door frame.

"My god, where were you hiding that. It looks amazing."

"I've had it on this whole time. You told me how you loved red back when we first met."

"You remembered? I mentioned that like once in passing."

"I remember everything you tell me." She pulled down on my pants. I thrusted upward so she could pull them all the way off. She slowly climbed up my legs until we were face to face. She laid on top of me like a lioness over a wounded gazelle.

"You know, you're the first woman I've ever met who takes makeup off before they go to bed."

"That's disgusting. That's how you break out. What kind of girls do you bring home, sailor?"

"It's why I never have any sheets. I think you're the first girl who's ever bought me a set"

"Wait here. I have an idea."

She wandered off into the closet. I could hear her rummaging.

"You all right in there?" I asked.

"Of course. When you were in San Diego, you kept talking about sheets, and I thought it sounded cute."

She remembered everything down to the smallest detail about me. I'd never had a girl care this much about the details. She could read me. I was an open book. She didn't have any tricks. She didn't have the Cube or anything like I needed. All she did was listen to me tell her what I wanted then she told me what I wanted to hear. I didn't know what I did to get this lucky. She came back into the bedroom wearing my peak cap.

"I saw this in the closet and I had to see for myself. What do you think?"

My head was two sizes larger than hers so the hat was down on her eyebrows and tipped to the side. She gave me a horrible salute.

"It's funny. That hat has a lot of history."

"Oh? Go on."

She crawled up to me the same way as before. Once she got to my eye level, she slid down my side and moved her hand up and down from my shoulder to my leg. Every now and again she brushed up against my growing hard-on. It kept me excited.

"Did you see that ring in the middle on the inside? That was from San Diego. We were at a club, and the girls kept stealing everyone's hats, so we had to use them as coasters so we didn't lose our headdress and get charged when we got back to ship."

"Mm hmm."

She started making little circles around my nipple with her finger. She pressed her finger in my chest, right above my heart and held it for a beat.

"And that crack on the left side of the peak. That was when I was in Thailand. The wind picked up while we were at a diplomatic function, and it broke when it hit a pole beside the Thailand ambassador."

"Well, how many places have you been with this hat?"

She brought her hand down to my navel making a back and forth scissoring motion with her nails. It tickled a bit. I held back everything in my DNA to keep from throwing her around like a rag doll. I want to be on her like a dirty shirt, but this is new. I've never had a woman just listen to me before. Listen when I tell her the important things in my life. Just listen and enjoy seeing me happy.

"Twenty-four countries. Here, America, Panama, Gibraltar, Croatia, Italy…"

She leaned down to my waist. All I saw was the circular white brim. That little crack on the left, the only chink in the armor. I couldn't see what she was doing, but I could feel it.

"Mmhmmm."

"Dubai, Oman, Thailand, Japan, and Australia."

After Australia, I couldn't contain myself anymore. I grabbed her by the shoulders, brought her up and pinned her to the bed. She had a coy smile on her face. Was she predator or was she prey?

♦

We fucked all night til it hurt. I'd never felt so good in all my life. I have the stove on low. I've always wanted to make French omelettes. The technique was intimidating, but I felt like I could do anything. I wanted to take my time and get it right. The coffee was steeping beside me as I worked on the eggs.

"The trick is to keep whisking it so it sets without burning," I told her.

"Very fancy," Charli said.

She was sitting at my dining table. My hat sat on top of her duffel in the laundry room.

"Thank you. And with a flip, it forms a crescent shape."

I flipped it and it tore at the end, but I slid it into place with

The Dog Walker | R.A.STONE

a fork before it set. I grabbed the coffee pot and poured a cup. She was wearing my bathrobe and I was in my underwear, almost naked, but I didn't feel naked. I felt warm, safe, secure. She dove into her breakfast while I started making mine.

"So, hey. I have to leave you for a day or two. I have some friends in town and I promised them I would pay them a visit before I left. I'll be back on Wednesday, then I have to head home on Friday."

"Of course. Do you want me to come with?"

"No, it's okay. I know you have to work."

I didn't put nearly enough care into my eggs. I let them sit too long and the curds were too thick. I pulled the cooked egg to the side of the pan and it took shape as an American omelette. Crisp, bitter browning on the edges. I can cover it with cheese and I won't even notice. Minor adjustments are sometimes necessary to keep moving forward.

When I sat down with my food, she was already up. I made myself company with her plate and empty mug at the table while she went to the bathroom and started applying makeup.

I didn't like that she was leaving for a couple of days so soon before she would be getting back on that bus and going home, but it seemed a small price to pay to keep things positive.

"Well make sure to call me when you get to your friends' and let me know you're alright,"

"Uh huh."

Rex

Monday. I was at work. It was the early afternoon. She hadn't called yet.

"You're done on the bridge, then? So, how the hell did you manage to snag that looker? What was her name, anyways?" Laz was sitting at the Component Content Management System (CCMS) console, typing away.

"Yes PO. I figured I'd come down here and see what needs to be done. I don't know what to tell you. We met online if you can believe that. She bussed down here, and she's been staying at my place for the last week. Now, she's visiting friends and family til Wednesday. Then she heads back home Thursday."

"I figured you'd have to import a girl here. She planning on moving in with you or just visiting every few months or so?"

"Now that you mention it, we hadn't talked about it. I don't know."

"What does she do, anyways?"

"I'm not sure about that either."

"Well, what do you know about her?"

"Well, she loves that I'm a sailor. She knows the guys from work. She made me look good in front of the captain, and she just makes me feel good, you know?"

"Oh boy. Do you know her last name at least?"

"Very funny. Yes. It's Cappadonna."

"Oh, she's Italian?"

"I guess so."

"Well, you know Petty Officer O'Brien met his wife like that, right?"

"OB? I didn't know that."

"Yeah. He was in Dubai and she would email him a bunch. They met up at the Rock Bottom. After a few months he got her a visa and they got married a few years later. They've been together for 12 years now."

"No shit. Good for him."

"Well, yeah, but then there's petty officer Dixon."

"What, isn't he single?"

"Divorced. He met his girl. She was a doctor from South Africa. He was messaging her for months. She moved up here, same way. They got divorced in less than a year."

"Was that before or after he turned into an alcoholic?"

"Bout the same time. Did I ever tell you I was posted to a UN posting at Naples for a year?"

"No, but I heard that's where you were before you came here."

"Yeah. I picked up a little Italian, too. Do you know what Cappadonna means in italian? It's a hooded young woman."

"Interesting."

"Just make sure you take your time. O'Brien was smart. He was dating his wife for a few years before they got married. Dixon pretty much grabbed her straight off the plane and threw a ring on her."

"Ah, it's not like that. She doesn't strike me as the predatory type. Besides, she's born here, she doesn't need the green card."

"If you say so. Hey, head in the back. I need you to set up a circuit for ops. CCMS isn't accepting it so we are just going to patch it manually."

I stood in front of the patch panel. It was like the old school ones you see in the 1940s films. Multiple cables with two quarter-inch jacks hanging off it like spaghetti. It was a mess, but if you knew how it was set up, you could follow the circuit path from antennae to equipment to workstation. I was pretty good at it, definitely better than Jason was, but Laz was on another level above all of us. He could see this tangled mess and know in a second which circuits were patched where. I had to take my time, run my finger on the cable, read the alpha numeric codes on the side, go to the equipment rack and see the machine it was hooked into.

"Hurry the fuck up," Laz demanded. "The chief is getting pissed and he's calling again."

"Yes, PO," I said.

I took the cable hanging around my neck and inserted it into the socket thinking I'd had the right patch. Just then, the door flew open and Laz stormed over.

"Jesus Christ. I've showed you this before, now watch." He snatched the cable from the panel and plugged it in a few sockets away from where my guess was.

"Pay attention. Right now it's just an exercise, but if you're on deployment and this shit comes up, it can be the difference between us being able to follow a target in the box and losing a terrorist or a pirate who ends up blowing something up."

"Yes PO."

He was a great teacher, but didn't really care if he pissed you off during the process of teaching you. He especially hated if he had to explain himself more than once.

♦

When I got home after work, I spent the evening unwinding from my whirlwind romance. The place felt empty without her luggage everywhere, the smell of her clothes. She still hadn't called. I checked my messages on email and Facebook. I rechecked my phone. Nothing.

"Hey, Let me know if you survived," I typed into the messenger app. Then I made dinner. I left the phone beside the stove facing up just in case.

I started with some potatoes. I microwave them so I don't

The Dog Walker | R.A. STONE

have to wait 45 minutes for them to cook in the oven. That should keep me from being too busy to notice the phone ring. It makes them soft, but starchy. I should fry them afterwards so they are more palatable. The LED is still off on my phone. I add butter to the pan and let them sizzle. I turn off the stove. The sound was too loud, I could miss the phone call. I check my Seamaster. 20 minutes. Enough time for good enough potato's. Enough time for a fucking call.

It's not the same with just one dish. I should add something substantive to this. I'll sear a pork chop or something. That's loud though. I don't want to miss the call. I know, I'll boil it for a bit then broil in the oven. Quiet and seared. I check the Seamaster. 15 minutes. Enough time for seared pork chops. Enough time for a fucking text.

I could make a fruit sauce, that would taste great. Charli hasn't had that before though. What if I make it then I eat it then she calls and it's finished before she comes back? Naw. I'll use A1 sauce. It's good enough and I can save the fruit stuff for when she gets here. I check the Seamaster. 2 minutes. Not enough time for a call. I pick the phone up. I turn it on. It's got tons of power. I hit a few buttons and check the LED. It still works.

I finish the meal quickly. I look at my phone between bites.
You gonna inhale that pork chop, bud?
"I'm just hungry."
I can tell. Thirsty too.
"What's that supposed to mean?"
Nothing. Nothing at all. I haven't seen you eat A1 sauce. Not since you were eating minute steaks in the 8th grade.
"I just wanted to try something nostalgic, something with a good memory."
You could have seared the pork chop. You could have roasted the potatoes better. You could have made a blueberry sauce. It would have tasted great. It would look a lot better than the grey slop you're eating now
"It's fine"

Rex

I'm sure it's OK. Are you checking your phone?
"I'm expecting a call"
I'm not
"That's becuase you're an asshole"
I may be, but we both know she isn't calling.

♦

The potatos were kind of starchy. The pork chop tasted like A1. I could have done better. I've done better in the past. I took my mind off the worry and started up the XBOX and COD. I was met with the usual flashing text:
Waiting for players …

I kept checking my phone in between games. Still nothing. It was getting late, I had to go to bed and be up at six in the morning for work. I put the phone beside me on the nightstand and lay down on the pillow. There was no plug there for the phone so I was running the battery down to make sure I'd know when she got in touch, if she got in touch.

First game. Some guy in the lobby is calling me a faggot with a horrible KDR. I cuss at him then leave the lobby. I join another one, and another one. The phone stares at me, without judgment. I stare back, nothing.

I've placed dead last for the last 15 games. I can't hit anything, I can't react fast enough. I'm making stupid mistakes. Some guy named xXMilfslayer420Xx teabagged me. It's just pixels on a screen. The visual of someone crouching over my slain corpse while putting his digital balls into my mouth in high definition — it pissed me off.

I sat up, I punch the power button. I grab my phone and check the battery icon: 50%. Plenty of charge left. It only needed five percent of its battery on standby and twenty minutes to charge it enough to last the work commute. It stayed in a Faraday cage at work all day so it was always on airplane mode til after work, anyway. It'll last. Tons of time.

I stared at it like a guard dog watching his food bowl. The

175

The Dog Walker | R.A. STONE

LED stared back at me, blankly, no movement, nothing new. Eventually, it will flash. I drifted off and didn't dream. When I woke up it was still there staring blankly at me while I stared blankly back

♦

I was back at work. It was Tuesday. I was staring at the patch panel. I traced Laz's work from yesterday, from antennae to multiplexer. From multiplexer to the black path panel. From the black patch panel to the KG-84s. I checked the cryptography tapes. Made sure all the keys were valid. Worked the patch path from the 84's to the workstation. In so doing, I saw where I screwed up.

Laz walked in. I swore that coffee mug was attached to his arm like some Siamese twin. The wide bottom made it perfect for drinking at sea. It can't fall over.

"Well, where did you fuck it up yesterday?"

"I see what you did. I was so focused on making sure the encryption was perfect that I wasn't paying attention to the obvious. I bypassed the multiplexer and went straight to WADS."

"And do you know why that matters?"

"Yeah. If you go straight from the antennae to the patch panel your signal is just a mess. The power could burn out the 84's, and if it's sending audio then they won't be able to make sense of it, it'll be amplified to hell and kill the poor bastard's ears who's monitoring it."

"You learn fast. Don't forget."

It seemed obvious now that I knew where to look. At the time, I had it all figured out. Every single detail, but I forgot to check the most obvious thing. Follow how the signal behaved each step of the way, then it becomes obvious why something isn't working. I got ready and headed home with lessons learned: Stop looking for what I wanted to see, and start noticing what's actually there.

I got to my locker and grabbed my clothes. My phone's new

message indicator light was blinking.

My messages:

Hey, checking in to see if you're OK. Read

Let me know if you arrived all right. Read

Everything OK? Read

Her one reply:

Hey. I'm coming over for a bit. I need to grab some things then go see my cousin. I'll be back tomorrow, Mind taking me to the station after?

Thank god. She seemed OK.

♦

Charli wore a t-shirt and jeans and smelled like the chill outside. I gave her a kiss as she gave me her cheek.

"How was your visit?" I asked.

"Oh it was fine. I have to leave in a bit though, take a shower."

"When do you have to go?"

"Probably in an hour."

"Want some company?"

"It's okay. You don't have to. I have to shave my legs anyways. I haven't gone this long in forever."

She walked into the shower, and I heard the water run. She closed the door and started the fan. I went to the sofa and started the XBOX. I was a few games in when I heard the water turn off. I shut off the game and walked over to the bathroom and knocked.

"You okay in there?"

"Yeah, just putting on some makeup."

I opened the door.

"What's up?" she said as though it were a random day at work and she was busy.

"You're leaving in a bit," I said. "I've missed you."

I walked over and placed my hands on her hips. I nuzzled into her neck. She looked over, put her mascara cap back on the bottle and turned around.

"Okay. But we have to be quick."

"I can do that."

I have my hand on the small of her back as I lead her into the bedroom. At the edge of the bed, she turned around and lifted her shirt above her head carefully so it didn't touch her face. I unbuttoned my shirt and kissed her on the neck.

"That tickles."

"Sorry."

I set her down on the bed and pulled her towel to the side. She was completely smooth down there. I went down on her. She grabbed a handful of my hair and held me in place. I couldn't tell if she was enjoying it. She stayed still and made no noise. I couldn't look up to see if she's enjoying herself as her hands had me in a death grip, so I kept making alphabet shapes with my tongue on her clit. They told me that's how you keep it interesting and build a rhythm without getting boring. After the third wxyz my jaw starts to hurt. I looked up.

"Why did you stop?"

"I'm tired."

"OK come here."

She pulled me up on top of her then turned around and arched her back. She knew I never lasted when we did doggy. I tried my best. I thought about the patch panel stuff from earlier. I slowed down. I pulled out on occasion and let the cool air calm me down. She just reached back and pulled me in while rocking back and forth. It was a battle of wills, but I was strong though. I grabbed her hips and used that control to slow down her rocking. I brought my hand across and played with her while I tried to hold her stable. She leaned forward and lay on top of the bed closing her legs to increase tightness and friction. I was getting worked up, so I stopped thrusting to calm down.

"Are you done yet?" she asked.

I got angry. I don't know why, but I felt my body temp go up a few degrees.

"Shut the fuck up," I said.

Rex

I started fucking hard. I wanted to hurt her. Her ass jiggled a bit. Her tits rubbed against my sheets. Three more thrusts and I was done. She slid out from under me, gave me a kiss on the check and returned to her makeup.

I just lay there, confused. What just happened? Just two days ago she was like a panther pouncing on my dick. Now, she was like a prostitute doing a job.

Her phone went off. She rushed over to grab it, press a couple buttons, then said, "Rex? So I'm getting a ride, you don't have to drop me off" and disappeared back into the bathroom.

When she finished in the bathroom, she looked good, presentable. She was dressed in the same outfit she was wearing when I picked her up from the bus station. My laundry machine works wonders. Her clothes smell fresh as daisies with no Greyhound bus stench.

Before I have a chance to say goodbye, she grabbed her shoes and ran out the door, duffel bag in hand leaving me alone in the living room. I didn't want to sit down and play XBOX. I was confused and ran through what happened.

How did I find her online? Same way as Kate. She asked a lot of questions. She was the smartest girl I had ever met.

How do I know this? All she did was ask questions. What did I like? What was my favorite color? Do I find it hot when a girl wears this outfit or that outfit. She loved hearing about the military and what I did. Was she smart? Or was she just good at letting me talk about what interests me? Who came to pick her up? I never saw or heard a car pull into the driveway. Did they meet her on the street? Why did she ask me if I was done yet?

Fuck you, Aaron.

I paced around my house, running through the circuit from endpoint to endpoint. I knew her name and that she was from Prince George.

What did she do there? I don't know. Was she single, married? I didn't see a ring, but who knows anymore? I didn't think she was a mom. She didn't have any stretch marks or scars; that's a thing, right?

I couldn't figure out why I was acting like such a neurotic mess. She was coming home that night. Plenty of time to figure it all out. I took the day off so I could drive her to the station tomorrow. I looked at my watch: 1800. Three hours with her friends. Eight hours to sleep, Twelve hours for breakfast and conversation. Plenty of time. I sat down and went over it all again. Maybe I missed something.

Charli Cappadonna, hooded young woman. Hood woman. Heh. Fuck you, Laz. I know what I'm doing. I laid down and went over it all again. I looked at my phone. The LED stared blankly at me.

♦

I nodded off. When I woke up, I checked my watch. 2320. Odd. I checked my phone: no messages. I didn't get it. She had said she was going downtown for dinner and drinks with friends. She said she was just going to hang out. I should check. I dressed quickly. My shirt had some eyeliner smudge on the chest. I got in my car and drove while running through scenarios in my head:

Maybe she got in an accident.

Maybe her phone died.

Maybe they lost track of time.

Maybe I was being weird about it.

I was headed up Government Street then turned down onto Pandora, then Bay, then Wharf. The complete nightlife loop. I drove by all the bars. The Duke. Upstairs. The Carlton Club. The hotel. The streets were empty. After four laps, I was sweating. I pulled into the parking lot by the bridge, got out and leaned against my Sentra. I needed a minute. I checked the Seamaseter again: 0130. I could see the Duke a few blocks to my left, the Upstairs a few to my right. At the Duke, I saw two people coming out, a girl and a guy. They walked over to a maroon, mid-sized sedan. I walked towards them. They got in the car and began driving down Wharf. We crossed paths and I looked inside. The passenger's hair looked like Charli's. The other one, the guy, wasn't tall or athletic. He wasn't better dressed than me. The car cost about as much as mine. His has rust on the side and a dent which had oxidized from the neglect. He wore a ball cap and a polyester jersey. I couldn't make out the wording.

They drove by me and stopped two lights down. I couldn't tell if it was them in the car. They were too far away and my astigmatism adds bokeh from that distance. The car's tail lights were two glowing red stars, drifting away. I grabbed my phone and called Charli. It rang twice, then someone answered. He had a deep voice, deeper than hers but higher pitched than mine.

"Hello?" He sounded high.

"Hey," I said. "I need you to put Charli on. Is she there?"

I thought I had played it cool. I sounded casual. I knew she would get on the phone. What would she even say? Probably some crazy story that put me on the street at two in the morning, standing by the bridge, the same bridge I used to walk across with so many other women on our way to have a drink and fuck and break something in my house and stain my linens and then run the washing machine to make it like new again.

"Yeah dude. I'm not going to do that. Is that you in the parking lot back there? Go home bro."

I heard the disconnecting click and it was over. I sat down on the parking bumper beside my car. He was right. I'd been around these streets for years. The sky wasn't spinning. I wasn't lightheaded. I didn't smell like cigarettes or gin or sweat. I didn't have a pithy opener or a friend who taught me something and no one was there to ask them to describe their horse.

I was sober, lucid. One hundred percent aware of how dumb I was acting. Laz wasn't there to yell at me. Aaron wasn't there to tell me he told me so. It was just me, the nice guy, and I didn't like him.

All the sweat steamed off my body. A thin layer of gritty salt remained. It felt like I was burning underneath my skin. The temperature keeps dropping outside while the temperature inside of me was getting hotter than the stove. I started shivering but was still boiling inside. I had no one to blame but myself. Look at him, I thought, sitting there, my reflection in the window of some boutique store.

He wore some plain old henley with makeup stains. Dirty jeans. Tired eyes. He was still wearing my work boots which I hadn't bothered to lace because I had been in such a rush. I looked fit but worn out. I looked like someone who has known me for years and doesn't like me anymore and wants to give me shit.

"I don't want to fucking hear it from you. Not right now," I thought.

I don't want to kick you when you're down.

"Sure you do. You've been saying it for years. My stupid rules. My stupid promise. I'm just like him and I'm lying to myself. I fuck it up every time I have a chance to fuck a chick and have fun because I'm still that kid playing Nintendo listening to Mom bitch about Jon. Then I figured I finally had you beat when I thought I met the perfect girl. Why wouldn't you rub it in?"

Because that guy did you a favor. Go home.

"He was fat and sounded like a pothead. He was dressed like shit. His car was shit. You know, I could have understood if he were better than me. I'd still be pissed, but at least I would get it. But why him? He's worse than me in every way. Why did she fall in love with me only to throw me away for something that's worse?"

Same reason your mom stuck with Jon for twenty years and five kids and all the yelling and screaming. The same reason she complained about it to the only man who would listen, you. The same reason why half the town fucked a fat gruff bushman who smelled like diesel and ass.

"Because they are stupid?"

Because they aren't you. They don't want what you want them to want. They want what they want. They want to be excited. They want to be neurotic. They want to think they are ugly and don't deserve anything better and nothing pisses them off more when you lie to them and tell them they aren't. She's just like mom. She'd rather be yelled at and called a cunt and cheated on than be bored.

"I don't get it."

I don't get it either. But if they are happy with it, who are you to judge?

"I can be better"

How's that working out for you?

"Fuck you."

If you say so.

"So now what?"

Fuck do I know. Just enjoy yourself and stop trying to love them for what you want them to be. Learn to appreciate them for what they are. Who knows, you might be happier and have to do less laundry.

I got up, slapped the dust off the back of my jeans, rubbed the salt off my arms and face. I got into the car and drove home. She stole my fucking hat, too. I would have to borrow Jason's tomorrow for parade. He won't be there anyways.

"Hood woman. Fuck you Laz. And thanks."

I walked and sat down in my living room. College Fuck Fest. I put on the episode where the guy slaps the chick in the face and calls her a whore before he comes on her face. I never liked that one until today.

Megan

"Thanks for coming out tonight, Jason. I'm just in the mood to find something to fuck right now and I don't care what."

"Yeah no worries. It was nice to get out of the house, anyways. Lots of shit going on right now."

Jason's breath already smelled of rum. I was dead sober, angry, and horny.

We were at the Duke. Death Metal filled the background. All the tables were filled with people in black leather and official band merch. No one smokes anymore, so I could see the entire room from the entrance. One table stood out. Two girls dressed like they had no business listening to metal. That meant one thing: they want to have a fun night with cool guys in a way that their friends don't find out.

"Here. I'll get first round," Jason said.

He went to the bar. I went to the girls' table. The one girl didn't impress me. She was a normal-looking brunette with long hair and a tank top. She was running her finger across the rim of her highball glass like it was a Tibetan music bowl. Her friend did catch my eye, though. She had rather large, almond-shaped eyes. Clearly-defined clavicles. Her arms were longer than what seemed natural. She had bronze skin over a statuesque frame. I wanted to be on her like a dirty shirt.

"Hey, I have to get back to my buddy in a second, but I need you to help me win an argument."

I pointed at Jason. He wasn't not paying attention. The brunette scoffs, but the tanned friend smirks.

"Oh? What is that?"

"Well. We were fighting on the way over. He said his girlfriend just tried to break up with him because she thinks he was cheating on her. He tells me it wasn't because we were in San Diego, but I don't think that matters." The brunette acted bored, unimpressed, like any good cock block.

"Did he actually?" I know this shtick. I would have to win her over before she puts the bitch shield down.

"No, he didn't, but she was rather crazy. She used to wait outside the bushes and call his place to see who would walk over to the window and answer the phone. I'd rather he ditch her and meet a nice girl."

"Well, perhaps she needs better taste in men." The friend put her hand over the brunette's arm and gave me a look.

"No, I get it. I think if she's crazy like that, then that probably means she likes him, and is just worried about him but doesn't know how to say so. She's not crazy."

That was an odd answer. I've never heard that before.

"You know what?" I said, "I've never had anyone suggest something like that before. Interesting."

"But cheating is cheating."

"Hey. I have to go now. But, thanks."

"What did you win?"

"The next round, I think."

Jason left the bar holding two highball glasses. Dark. It'll be a rum and coke if he's ready to wing. It'll be Crown Royal if he wants to fuck with me. He handed me a glass. Tasted like rye.

"So it's one of those nights, eh?"

"Don't be a pussy. Did you talk to the girls?"

"Yeah. The white one is a little prickly, but she seems bored if anything."

"Oh, that's just what I'm good at. You know I got your back.

11 Megan

You interested in the native girl?"

"Is she? I couldn't tell if she was Filipino or what."

"Doesn't matter. Come on. Let's grab a cigarette then go over and talk to them again."

We walked out to the smoking area and set our glasses on the shelf beside the exit door.

"So whatever happened to that chick you had over to your place? She was a smoker. I figured she murdered you or something. You disappeared for like a month."

"I disappeared? You were sketchy, taking off like that and not saying anything."

"Well, that's because I think I fucked up."

"That's what you get when you stick your dick in crazy."

"Hey, she's your family."

"I know, but still. So are you ever gonna tell me what happened there?"

"You go first."

"Well, Charli happened. I figured she was the one. I was gonna stop sleeping around and settle down. She was perfect, you know? But then I realized that she wasn't perfect at all. I just talk too damned much."

"You? Talk too much? Let me guess. You started talking about bedsheets and all that gay shit you do to look like you're something special."

"Well, yeah, that too, but no. She just smiled while I talked about what I liked. She took notes, then later on she would follow the script. I was stupid and never realized she was reading me like a book. She said and did everything I told her I wanted, and then she got bored. I ended up wandering the streets looking for her. Turns out she was fucking some drug dealer dude. I felt like a fucking moron."

"Ah, what a bitch, man."

"I can't blame her. I wanted her to be something she couldn't be. And it wasn't that hard to get me. All she had to do was lie to me for a bit. I guess she just got bored and moved onto the next guy. Now, what happened to you?"

187

"Well, do you remember how I was saying Jullie was sick?"

"I don't remember."

"Well, turns out she was worried she might have been pregnant."

"You didn't wrap it up?"

"She said she was on birth control. Sometimes these things fail."

"Thank god. You're stupider than me! So, what? Are you a dad?"

"Maybe. I don't know. She did a test that night and it said no, but it's been a few weeks and she still feels weird. So we are going to the clinic tomorrow. They said I had to wait a couple of weeks before they can do an official test or something."

"Jesus. So what are you guys going to do?"

"Well, she wants to keep it. She says she's getting older and is worried this may have been a gift from god, her last chance."

"I mean, what are you going to do about it."

"Well. My dad was an asshole. I don't know yet. Here, can we talk about anything else?"

Jason kind of drifted off. He threw his cigarette onto the ground and ground it under his foot. We grabbed our drinks and headed back inside.

"Come on. I'll cover for you man. Just go get your girl."

We looked around. The girls were sitting at the bar ordering drinks. I muscled into the line up, bumping into the brunette.

"Here. We got the first round, on him." I pointed at Jason. The bartender leaned in. "Rum and coke," I said. "And for the girls," I pointed to Jason and I, then the girls.

"Gin and tonic, please. Singles!" the darker girl said. When she leaned in to grab her drink, her back leg kicked out for balance. She was wearing flats and taller than I thought. She looked over and said, "Thank you."

"No, thank you," I said. "You won me the bet."

The bartender set our rum and cokes on the bar then grabbed my cash off the counter. He went to the register and fiddled with some cash, then looked at me. I shook my head and he dropped my tip into the cup beside him. I guided this girl through the crowd, my hand on the small of her back. Jason towered over the brunette who followed him out of the crowd. He started running his mouth about something, the brunette looked less bored than she was a second ago. I turned to my target.

"So, you know I've been asked that before. Is it a line?" she asked.

Her drink was up to her lips while she played with the straw. The black lights in the bar made her drink glow blue, almost white. It also made the lint that was pilling on her clothes glow like static on a television. My clothes were pristine, as usual.

"Oh, of course. I find it's better if you make up a little game. If you just walk up to someone and say hi, they think you're a creep who just wants to stalk them all fucking night, you know? This way you know you have an out and you don't have to be rude if you're not vibing."

"That's very considerate of you. I'll bet you say that to all the girls. Are we vibing, you and I?"

I was on a roll. I barely noticed, but she was hiding something. I looked around. She's got to have some bullshit in her life. No ring. Maybe a kid at home? Maybe she's just a cunt?

"I don't know yet. You seem nice, and your friend and Jason seem to be getting along fairly well, so I figure we get to know each other and see where it goes."

"Jason?"

"Oh, my bad. Yeah. He's Jason. You can call me Rex." I smiled. I put my hand on her arm. She leaned into it. If the next two minutes keep going this well, I'll have to ask her about the Cube. "So I forgot to ask, how do you know your friend? Do you guys go way back or are you work friends or…?"

"So you don't remember me at all, do you?" she said. Suddenly, I felt like a bullseye.

"Wait. What?"

"I said, Don't you remember me?" she repeated.

"Have we met before?"

"Something like that."

"I'm sorry. I must have been drunk or something. I'm usually pretty good at remembering people. Did we get along?"

"I should fucking hope so. You were inside me."

"There's no way that's true," I said. "I remember everyone I sleep with."

I pulled away, took a step back. She must be lying. Did Jason put her up to this?

"Well, Rex, you were pretty drunk, so I can see if you didn't remember."

Can't be. I'm not like Jon. I remembered everyone. None of it was my fault. I was a good person. She had to be lying. She knew my name. Jason probably yelled it while we were at the bar or something.

"I don't think you understand," I said. "For me it's very important that I remember every girl. I remember every name, every time. It's a rule."

"It's a rule, eh?"

"It's a rule. There's no way you've been to my place before. I would have remembered."

"Well, you had a Chinese vase on your nightstand. You kept talking about your bedsheets, and you had a duvet on your bed that didn't have a cover. You made me a flaming sambuca."

Shit. She had been there, no doubt. I definitely slept with her. But who was she?

"Jesus, I'm so sorry," I said. Mom. I promised I wouldn't be like him. I'm just like him. I tried.

"You okay?" she asked.

Looks like that guy, that me in the mirror, had been right all along.

"Yeah," I said. "It's just kind of a big deal, not important. What happened, anyways? Maybe I just have it mixed up."

"Well. You were at the Upstairs. You asked me if it counted as cheating. I said no and you called me a dirty, fun whore."

"Fun, dirty whore."

"Right. Then we just talked. You put your hand on my arm."

Megan

She placed her hand on my upper arm, just like I do with them.

"You walked me through the crowd by the small of my back."

She demonstrated that, too, exactly how I do it.

"And then we just talked," she said. "You have a weird fascination with linens."

"Yeah. It's because I'm in the military and when I sail–"

She cut me off and finished my sentence:

"They give you the same sheets that prisoners have so you want to have something nice when you come home. I remember. It was actually kind of cute. I've never seen a man care so much about the most mundane details before."

"Jesus. I feel bad now for not remembering."

"Well. Then we went home. You poured me a sambuca and lit it on fire. I burned my hand and dropped the glass. It broke and then you told me, 'It's okay. I have to get a new set anyways. Most people break them.' Then you kissed me."

I kind of remembered cleaning up my floor a few weeks back, but couldn't remember why. It was just after Charlie broke my heart and I had been in a mood.

"Yeah. I remember a sticky floor."

"Then we fooled around. After that, you passed out, so I stayed the night because I didn't know where I was and didn't have a phone to call a cab."

"That was it?"

"No. In the morning you woke up and I asked you if you had fun. You looked up at me then ran into the bathroom and started throwing up. I thought you thought I was disgusting, and I started to cry a bit. But then you stayed in there so long I borrowed your phone and called a cab home. Do you really not remember any of this?"

"I kind of remember being really hung over in the morning and talking to someone. That was you?"

So there I was just standing there in the bar staring at her with a stupid look on my face. It was one thing to realize I had been outplayed by Charli. It sucked to get swindled like that.

But now? This was something different. This was about who I am. It was all lies. Mike was right. Worse yet, Jon was right. That stung more. I'd have rather been cheated on.

"Look, I was in a bit of a place that night. I drank way more than I should have, and I guarantee it wasn't because of you. You've actually got a very unique look. I don't normally go for dark girls but you don't look like any girl I've met before."

"Oh, good. I was worried you threw up because you didn't like me."

She giggled. Typical woman. I was sick as a dog, having an existential crisis and being sick and tired of my life, and she was worried about whether she's pretty or not. She walked over to Jason and her friend. I followed.

"So, now that you remember, are you going to stop trying so hard? Let's try a do-over," she said. "I'm Megan. Nice to meet you, Rex."

"Megan. I guess I have to relax. I mean, you know all my tricks at this point. I got nothing left. Except, one question."

"What's that?"

"What was your horse?"

"Chestnut brown, standing beside my cube. That shit was awesome by the way."

She leaned in wearing a smug look of satisfaction. I laughed, reached over and placed my hand on her face and kissed her. It tasted like gin. I didn't know why she put up with my shit. I knew better than to ask, but I just had to know.

"Come on. Let's get out of here. I live a short walk from here."

"I know. I remember."

♦

She was, OK. She wasn't particularly enthusiastic in bed, but she never said no to any ideas either. She was a blank slate, open for whatever I wanted. Most of the time she had her eyes closed enjoying the moment. I had never slept with a girl this dark before. Well, obviously I had, but I never knew I had before then. Her skin was burnt bronze all over. They are usually pink down there. David Attenborough would be fascinated. Her skin was soft but felt dry. Not quite leather, but not the soft supple feeling of white skin. It was nice. It was just different, smoother. She's sitting there watching me while I'm just running my hands up and down her leg like a science experiment.

"That tickles," she said.

"My bad. I like your skin. It's soft but dry, like felt."

"Is that a good thing?"

"I like it. It's just different. Normally girls are pink down there." Megan grabbed her shirt jacket.

"Are you leaving?"

"Not right away. I'm just cold. So why were you so drunk that last time?"

"I just got dumped by a girl."

"Do you want to know if it counted as cheating or not?"

"I bet you think you're funny."

"I kind of am," she said.

"No. It was definitely cheating. Or maybe it wasn't. I don't know. She just pretended to be the perfect woman, and I guess I just got caught up in the fantasy."

"Yeah. Melissa does that to guys, too. Not you though. You guys were weird."

"Wait. Melissa? How do you know Melissa?"

"I was her roommate. Didn't you know?"

"I know Melissa talked about a roommate, but I never actually saw you."

"Yeah. Every time you came over she asked me to watch Kaya so she could fool around. I had to hide in my bedroom with her while you slept with her upstairs."

"That didn't turn you off? I don't think I could ever sleep with someone that my buddy was sleeping with."

I didn't know why I just lied to her. I knew it wasn't true, but it felt like it should be.

"Not really. She kept telling me how hard she came with

you. I just wanted to see for myself. Plus, she's kind of a bitch, so I wanted to make sure I was better than she was." After a moment of awkward silence she continued. "Well?"

"Well what?"

"Am I better than her?"

"Yeah, but don't let it go to your head."

She squinted and did a little cheer inside her head.

"Melissa is anemic," I said. "She only lasted for maybe a minute in bed before she started convulsing. I couldn't even touch her. She was probably the worst woman I've ever slept with in my life."

"Yeah, but you guys got back together didn't you?"

"She had her tits done. I had to know."

"And?"

"False advertising," I said.

Megan slapped me on the chest.

"Ow!"

"Oh, I'm sorry." She rubbed my chest and laughed into my neck.

"It's OK," I said. "I'm just fucking with you."

Megan stopped laughing then gave me a look, more serious this time.

"So, hey," she said. "I don't want you to think this is a serious thing. I just got out of something serious and I don't want to get into one right away."

"That's fine. You caught me at a weird time, too."

"Oh, good." Megan reached over and grabs me underneath the sheets. She started jerking me until I got hard again, then she climbed on top of me, reached down, and put me inside of her.

A few minutes later, she was sleeping on top of me. For such a skinny girl, she was like a furnace. I slid out from underneath and quietly walked towards the kitchen and cooler air. I grabbed a coffee mug and poured myself a glass of water then went into the living room and stared out the window. The patio lights were off. The soft glow of the idle light on the television showed off my reflection in the window.

I'm naked, nothing left but the real me, that guy. I don't like him, but I guessed I better get used to him.

♦

My sheets smelled like sex and Prada, Amber Pour Homme mixed with something floral. That fucking duvet. I really needed to buy a new duvet cover.

My head was killing me. I didn't even know what time it was. I caught a glimpse of myself in the reflection on the glass of the patio door. I looked fit, but tired, vulnerable. I looked like someone who has known me my whole life and finally started to tell the truth about who I really was. I want to give him shit, but I'm tired.

You're just like him, you know.

"I know. I was always like that guy."

Do you even like Megan?

"She's not the best. Okay, but nothing special. She has nice skin and I don't recall dating many dark-skinned girls."

Well, what about Kate?

"Kate's great, too. She's cute. She goes out partying then comes home to me and spends the night. She makes me a burrito, and I make coffee, then she leaves. She's the only girl who's never broken anything here."

She's just another dog walker to you, isn't she?

"Naw. I can't get mad. She's just doing what she wants and enjoying life."

But she fell for your stupid tricks. There's no way she actually likes you.

"Maybe not. That's OK. I didn't like me for a long time, but you already knew that, didn't you?"

So, what's your plan now, tough guy?

"No plan. No plan, no rules, no justification. It's just you and me."

So are you just a villain now? Gonna be like Jon and fuck all the wives in the neighborhood, do a little coke, yell at scream at whoever when it suits you?

"It's a fair question. I hadn't thought about that. I don't think I will."

Sure you will. He did, all the time. It's what you know.

"Yeah, but I get it now. He yelled because he didn't know any better. It was what he knew. Mom always bitched at him anyways. Bitched and complained. She always made sure we had the newest shit, and when she found out a lot of it was stolen, she yelled at him some more. What would you do after years of that and two kids that you have to buy shit for every day?"

You're still a piece of shit. You fucked married chicks. You fucked Mike's woman. You fucked a single mom, a few actually. You fucked the worst girl in the world just because she got her tits done. You don't really care, do you.

"Well, I have to thank you, actually."

What did I ever do to you? You've never listened to a word I've said. You just argued and bitched and moaned and virtue signaled your bullshit rules.

"You said it yourself. Stupid rules that make me think I'm better than this. Everyone else is stupid and I'm smart. Everyone else is wrong and I'm right. But really there are no rules. No rules, no one cares, and none of this mattered."

Well, this is interesting for a change. Go on.

"I made all these rules, but I never told anyone else about them. They were just living their lives and having fun and making mistakes and moving forward. And when they broke my rules, I would get mad and resent them for it. Who knows. Any one of those girls could have been a great woman and we could have had a good time. I didn't break Rose's marriage. She did that to get it out of her system so she could give her man one hundred percent, right?"

I guess. Go on.

"Manjeet used to fuck all kinds of guys. Then she turned twenty-five and she settled down with a good Indian boy. I hear they have their first kid on the way. No one cares and everyone is happy. Maybe the rules aren't the problem. Maybe I'm the problem."

Well. I guess I better get some sleep then. Sounds like you have this all figured out.

"Hope so. Now I got to figure out how to get this girl out of my house. Kate is coming over today for a nooner."

A part of me didn't want to believe it. A part of my refused to accept that I had become Jon. A part of me was afraid to admit, I kind of enjoyed it too. I stared at the TV, just me, naked and alone. I felt good though. I climbed into bed and lay on my back leaving one leg outside of the sheets. It cooled me off a little bit. Megan put her arm across my chest while I stared at the ceiling and slowly drifted off to tomorrow.

Marie

All hands! Docking stations. Docking stations.

Return all gear. Man your stations.

We were close to port and the call to stations booming over the loudspeakers made me even more excited about getting into San Diego.

"I don't care anymore," I was telling Jason. "I'm going to add every fucking pic to the pucks before we get out of here."

"Rex!"

"What?"

"You know what I love the best about sailing?"

"Getting to look at porn for work? Hand me that puck."

"Ha, not that. I'm terrified they will slip a ladyboy in here and I won't notice till it's too late. No, it's that you get to have a whole second life out here."

"What do you mean?"

"Well, Jullie is at home. She's stressed out all the time. She's starting to demand all sorts of stuff that we just don't need, man. She keeps telling me to do more and more, and, finally, I just asked her, 'what exactly do you want from me?' and she doesn't have an answer. But a few hours after that, I get to be a different guy in San Diego, just for a bit."

"Yeah. I like it. After Charli, I was depressed at how easily I fell for her. For some reason, once we pulled lines, it was like she didn't exist anymore. For once, puking at sea was just what I needed."

"Do you have plans when we pull in?"

"Had. Did you know Kansas City Barbecue burned down?"

"What? You mean the Top Gun bar?"

"Yup. End of an era, man."

"That was the only thing I wanted to do this trip. Ah. You wanna just go drinking with the guys tonight?" Jason asked.

"I have a rule, man. Never drink within six miles of the ship. I don't want to get in trouble then have Laz find out about it before we even get back."

"Ah. It'll be fine. We don't have to go crazy, just have some drinks and talk about work."

Maybe it was the massive collection of porn in garbage stores. Maybe it was the smell of burnt plastic. Maybe it was the beer cans fermenting the air. But it didn't seem like a bad idea.

"Fine, but I'm going to shower here first. This stuff stinks."

♦

We went to San Diego's college district, fifteen bars within three blocks. The bar we chose had a surfboard behind it and a Molson Canadian logo across the front. What could be more Canadian than beer and surfing in a log cabin full of flannel-clad ladies?

I turned to Jason and said, "Hey. I got us a table. Get over here before we lose it."

"Yeah man. Hold up."

A waitress, dressed in her best Canadiana walked up with a tray of Jagermeister. She wore a red and black flannel shirt with tastefully exposed cleavage and synthetic yoga pants stretched over an ass that was superior to most white girls. She set the tray down, winked, and moved on.

"American bar. Californian surfboard. Jager shots. Waitresses in flannel, stretch pants, and Ugg boots. This is like if someone had to recreate Canada from reading it in a bad travel guide," I said.

"Oh, come the fuck on. Don't be such a bitch about it." Jason divvied up the shots.

"Cheers." Clink. One
"Cheers." Clink. Two
"Cheers." Clink. Three.

I tossed it back and winced.

"God. I don't know why German cough syrup is in the bar. Things never go well after Jager. I'll be lucky if I don't make a stupid decision. You'll be lucky if you don't black out."

I would wake up tomorrow with a headache and tasting liquorice and cigarettes.

"It's fine," Jason said. "There's enough people here that someone will make sure we make it home tonight."

Jason downed another few shots. He didn't usually go this hard, this fast.

"Dude, are you okay?" I asked.

"Yeah, I'm fine. I just want to get drunk tonight," he said.

"This trip has been a fucking slog. Everyone looks too tired to care." Jason shrugged. Behind us, we heard a familiar Canadian twang, almost like a duck who can speak English. Vocal fry, quacking in an almost feminine voice.

"What are you two doing here oustie!?"

We turned around to look.

"Oh my god. Jason, Reginald? I don't think I've ever seen you at one of these," she said.

I looked over and saw three of our officers: The combat officer, Brad; the logistics officer, Steven; and the communications officer who does double duty as my divisional officer, Marie. I had only ever seen her hair in a regulation ponytail before. Now she had it down. It was thin, stringy, albino blond with a wave to it. She was wearing makeup for once. She had changed completely. Whereas at work she would look plain and homely, beady-eyed with thin eyebrows and thinner lips. Here, now she looked like a woman. Overly rouge'd blush, still paper thin eyebrows, but darker. She must have put on contact lenses. Her eyes looked even beadier. In my Jager'd state I mistook it for sultry.

"Sirs!" Jason said as he shoved Jager shots into the officers' hands and pushed their hands up to their mouths. Steven handed his shot to me, but Brad and Marie obliged.

"Thanks, Jason. Do me a favor this time. Don't end the night with a message on my desk tomorrow with your fucking name on it, okay?" said Brad.

"I will do my best, sir."

"Brad."

"I will do my best, Brad."

Jason grabbed Brad's hand and shook it like he was jerking it off. Marie got between Jason and I, picked up her glass, and said, "Well, well, leading seaman. I wasn't even sure if you drank let alone left the ship. We've worked together what—"

"Two years now, and you can call me Rex."

"Two years, Rex, and this is the first time I've ever seen you out of uniform."

"Yeah. Laz trained me well. Work hard, play hard. I don't mix the two unless I have to."

"That's not what I heard. What's this I hear about Webber and a bachelor party?"

I rolled my eyes. "It's been a year now, and still this is the only thing people remember about me. I didn't actually fuck Webber's wife." Marie was responsible for monitoring my career. So what does she know about me? Not my exemplary performance. Not my dress or decorum. No, just the time I fucked some cuck dude's wife during her stag.

Marie laughed.

"Well. I'm just saying. Word even got around to the wardroom. Well, that and the time you brought a bunch of girls into the wardroom and had them dancing on tables. You know you are the first to have an open invite to the wardroom? Even the cox'n doesn't have that."

"Well first off," I began, "it was only two girls, Kate and Terrin. Secondly, they weren't naked. They were wearing wife beaters, and it was a cowbell-themed party, so that's totally normal, and, thirdly, one girl had never been on a ship before and the other one loves officers, so it's not my fault." She continued to stare at me,

"And I didn't fuck his wife!"

"Sure you didn't. And she even left her clothes at your place and Webber had to go get them?"

I punched Jason on the arm.

"Yeah. I wonder who keeps spreading these rumors?"

"What are we talking about?"

"Webber's wife."

Jason laughed. "Told you no one would believe you," he said then returned to his drink.

"So this Terrin and Kate. Are they your girlfriends then?" Marie asked.

"No no. I'm dating Kate casually right now, but it's just so she has a place to sleep after the bars close. And I lost my old roommate. Terrin is going to move into my second bedroom. She's like a sister to me."

"That's nice. You know, Laz speaks very highly of you. You're supposedly very good at your job."

"Careful with the compliments. I've been drinking and it will go straight to my head."

"Well, we wouldn't want that, would we?"

The bar was so loud that she had to shout when she spoke which emphasized her voice's quacking quality. When I was a small boy in small-town British Columbia, I believed that French girls had sexy accents. Then, having met a few French Canadians, I came to hate it.

But she was asking about me, and it's hard not to take an interest in talking about myself.

Another tray appeared. More shots. Jason's eyes were glazing over. Brad left for a cigarette. I joined him.

"You know, Brad, I love going out for a smoke back home. The bar is sweltering, and it's a nice chance for some cold air. In Diego, it's even hotter and muggier outside. I don't know how you do this."

I motioned to his pack. He offered a cigarette and I took one.

"When did you smoke?"

"I don't." I lit mine and puffed quickly. "Unless I'm in foreign ports. I just never got addicted like people do. But when I'm in another country, I'll smoke like two packs a night then quit before we head home."

"That would be nice. It's a shitty habit and you shouldn't start."

"Everyone says that and never quits. Besides, it can't be any worse than the asbestos inside the bulk heads or the chillers making me deaf in the shack."

I looked up and exhaled. It was pitch black without a star in the sky. I sometimes forgot how quaint of a city we lived in. Too many lights in California. Nothing to look at when the Jager hits. I didn't notice that my head was spinning. The sail was supposed to help me forget. Brad finished his cigarette, grinned, then said, "So uh, you and Marie seem to be having fun."

"No, she's not my type."

"Too French?"

"Too heavy."

Brad laughed. "Jesus Christ, guy. I mean, fair enough. Besides, I've seen your type, remember? How is Terrin, anyways? Say hi from me."

"She's my new roommate. Will do."

"Yeah though, Marie? She's not anybody's type. Just be careful with those French girls. They can be dangerous."

"If you say so."

"I'm serious. Do yourself a favor. Don't let word get around like with you and Webber's wife."

"For fuck sakes, why does everyone bring that up?"

"It was the first thing me and the captain learned about you. And, I never said this, but that Webber guy is kind of a dork. I'm sure you weren't the first guy."

12 Marie

"The only reason people think this stuff about me is because it's more interesting than what actually happens. I'm a boring guy, and I don't do half of what I'm notorious for."

"Whatever you say. I'm taking off. Do me a favor and make sure your little buddy Jason there gets back to the ship all right. I'm not joking. I'm tired of seeing his fucking name in a folder on my desk."

"I'll do my best, but he's, like, fifty pounds heavier than me, so no promises."

Brad half heartedly waves as he walked to the street. A row of cabs was there with a group of drivers lounging around beside them. He walked up to one and they took off. I looked back and, suddenly, Marie was standing beside me.

"Jesus, you scared the hell out of me. How did you get out here without me seeing you?"

"Jason is inside and he gave me three more shots," she said. "I had to get out of there. Where's Brad?"

"He said he had to go."

"Well, that's annoying. Are you going back to the ship tonight or did you guys get a hotel?"

She took a step towards me.

"Ship tonight. I had to otherwise Jason would probably sleep in and we would leave without him."

I took a step back.

"Good call. Brad has been very unhappy with me. I've had to bring a file in on Jason three times this year already."

She stepped closer. I turned to face the street, looking around.

"Here, you hungry? I want a hot dog."

"Sure."

We walked across the street to the street vendor. He's been cycling up and down the street all night in his little rusted out cart. In big letters that I should have read, it says TACOS in big letters. Beside the S is a comically large, poorly drawn sombrero.

"Mexican hot dogs. They're the best," I said.

In the cart are dented buffet trays. Shredded meat, sliced

cabbage, shredded cheese, and a brown soupy sauce. He pulls out strings of meat and places them into a corn tortilla inside of a napkin and hands them to us.

"Eww, what's that brown stuff?"

"It's called mole. It's like a savory chocolate sauce, and here."

I see poblanos sliced in a bin with a set of tongs standing upright. "These are poblanos. They aren't spicy, but they have a great texture to them. Put them on top like this."

"You seem to know a lot about Mexican food. You know how to cook?"

My foot touched the edge of the curb and I lost balance. Marie held me by the arm and pulled me back onto the sidewalk. She kept her arm there an extra beat.

"I do. I've always had to. Ever since I was a kid my mom taught me to and told me, 'These bitches don't know how to cook, so you better.'"

"Ouch,"

"Yeah, she's kind of old school. What about you?"

"I couldn't even boil water if I had to. My mom thought it would be horrible if I ended up like her and had to cook for a man."

"I've noticed that. You know I've only ever met one girl who was able to make so much as a sandwich."

She shrugged her shoulders, leaned in, and took a bite of her taco. Round cheeks, small lips, and beady eyes. Something about that image taking in a whole taco like that just turned me off. Then again, she did look rather sultry.

"I figure you don't need to cook to land a man."

"So what do you do then if you like someone?"

"I'm in love with the sea."

"I can feel your sarcasm from here."

"Seriously, I just talk to them. Isn't that what you're supposed to do?"

"Well, fuck, I should have been a girl. It sounds easy."

I ate my last bit as a loud, cracking sound from across the street startled Marie. I wiped my hands with the napkin and looked over.

"Is that Jason?" she asked.

"Yeah. It looks like it."

I wasn't surprised. His pants were around his knees, and he was lying on the street. Two police officers were holding him down. One was holding his neck while the other had a knee in his bare, hairy ass. They were yelling something incomprehensible at this distance. Marie blinked in bewilderment.

"We were only out here for five minutes," she said. "What could have possibly happened in such a short time?"

"I don't know, but there's nothing we can do for him here other than get arrested with him. Let's head back to ship. We can tell the cox'n and our supervisors so they don't have to find it out at 0800 for muster."

"Brad is going to be pissed. God damn him."

I gave the cop's a wide berth and wandered over to the cab area and got a ride to the base. Marie followed behind like a puppy dog. I felt in control, but it was taking effort to pay attention to what was going on.

I was looking out the window and caught a faint reflection in the mirror. I looked like a mess. This was a guy without any fucks left to give, and I thought, I'm over it, all of it.

They don't cook. They don't even bother to learn.
They lack charm. They just show up and bring beer.
They wreck all my stuff. They don't even care.
They don't have rules. They just follow their feelings.
Fuck it. It's all pink man.

♦

We crossed the brow and give a drunken, half-hearted salute to the ensign. The watchkeeper looked up, nodded, then went back to his log book. I should have gone and woke up the boss, but instead of walking through the hanger to get to the chief's mess or the control room, I opened the hatch to the aft lower desks. Marie followed behind me. The diesel smell was overpowering.

I walked into the hatch combing and entered the reserve space. We had converted it into a makeshift gym. It's tiny, only eight feet a side containing just a dip bar pulling triple duty as a squat rack and bench press, and a bench with hard worn leather underneath. I turned around and Marie was right in front of me.

"Fuck it."

Normally, when I go in, a girl closes her eyes. Some look downright beautiful when they are getting fucked. Some girls get really ugly, which is so much hotter. Marie did none of that. She didn't crinkle her face with sex wrinkles around the eyes, forehead, or mouth. She didn't get soft and sensual in the moment. She was bland, awkward, more like she was going through the motions than enjoying another successful hunt.

I gave her what she wanted. I just wanted to get another girl under me. One more pussy of separation from that train wreck, Charli. I would have done this in the control room if it weren't manned. No chance of getting caught over there. This was the only private place with any softness to it. The smell was industrial, and so was her performance.

"Ugh, you're like fucking a doll."

"What?"

"Never mind. Shut up. Turn around."

It was ten minutes, at most. I didn't bother to check the Seamaster. What the fuck else better did I have to do? She fucked as well as she cooked. I didn't cum and neither did she as far as I could tell. She fucked like she spoke. It was sexual vocal fry and when it was over, she just put her clothes back on and waited for me to do the same. She waited until I opened the hatch and walked onto the lower decks. When we hit the first ladder she looked back.

"I'll go up here and let Brad—let LT Peats know about Jason's arrest," she said.

She turned to face the ladder and walked up as per safety regulations. I went to the chief's mess and knocked. A muffled voice called out,

"Come in."

I cautiously opened the door and peeked inside. The chiefs were all sitting around drinking together. Laz was in the back laughing at the cox'n telling a story,

"PO Lazaroff? I need to see you for a second," I said.

He grumbled, set down his beer, and walked to the door where I delivered the news.

"Jesus, fucking christ! Chief!"

"What?" The cox'n looked absolutely blitzed. He was placing a stack of beer cans into a pyramid shape as he looked over at me and Laz at the door. He knows when they use his rank in the mess, it's something he's got to deal with.

"Chief, can you come here for a minute?"

"Jesus fucking christ. Leading seaman, this better be fucking important!"

"Yes chief. It's Jason. He did something stupid."

♦

Late the next day, Jason was back on board and confined to the control room. Laz was in his civilian clothes checking emails while Jason stood at attention beside him.

"Until I can sort out what they are going to do with you, you're staying in here. I'm giving you this duty watch."

"Yes, PO."

"So how in the hell did you end up in prison?"

"They don't have a drunk tank in San Diego, PO, so they processed me into general pop."

"Well, the combat O and the cox'n aren't happy with you. The only reason they aren't madder is because you looked terrified in your orange jumpsuit."

"Yeah, they put me with the Mexican gang. Those guys are scary."

"Well, Rex. Jason is taking your watch today. Enjoy the free day off." Now's as good a time as any, I thought.

"PO?" I said.

"What now? Do I need to get the chief again?"

"No, no. Nothing like that. I figure now that things have died down, I have a problem. I don't know what to do or who to ask."

Laz took a sip of his coffee and waited for the news.

"Okay," he said. "But please just tell me I don't have to do any paperwork."

"I slept with sub lieutenant Orleans last night."

"What? Marie?"

"Yeah."

Laz laughed until his eyes started blinking from his throbbing headache.

"What the fuck did you do that for? Jesus. Are you trying to fuck everyone and their wife on board?"

"I didn't — ah never mind PO. Like, is this a problem? I have my professional review next week, and I know in the SOPs there's the section about fraternization and she's an officer and–"

Laz motioned for me to stop.

"All right, all right. Calm down."

He laughed for another minute.

"Look, don't worry about it. And I'll tell you something. When I was your age, I fucked my combat officer."

"Wait, aren't you gay though?"

"I'm not saying I liked her, but it was just cool to fuck an officer. My yeoman gave me a high five, and that was the last I heard about it. Besides, you've done a great job here. You'll be fine. Treat it like a slumpbuster and move on."

He put his hand in the air and held it for a beat. I slapped it.

"So what the fuck were you thinking? She's horrible."

"Charli kind of fucked me up. I just wanted to fuck something, anything."

12 Marie

"Well, next time you'll listen to me and you won't have to fuck a fattie."

"Yes, PO."

13

Kim

I was at the Fleet Club. Jason was released from birds, or confinement to ship. Finally, he walked in.

"I'm here," he said. "Thanks for giving me a ride, man."

"No worries. We have to wait a bit before we can go, though. Two weeks isn't so bad for getting locked into general pop and requiring the command team to bail you out. Here buddy, to freedom," I said. I sat down and handed him a bottle.

"Thanks but no thanks. I think I'm done drinking for a while."

"What exactly did you get arrested for, anyways? I never asked. We only left you alone for maybe five minutes. I had a taco, and then I looked up and you were getting arrested."

"Yeah, thanks by the way. It's not like I needed help or anything. Some camaraderie."

"What were we supposed to do? Wrestle two cops so we can run back to the base for the MP's to arrest us later? The way I saw it, the best thing I could do was head back to ship so I could let Laz know before he found out from someone else."

"Yeah, you'll forgive me if I don't say thanks. General pop sucks."

"You look good in orange, though."

"They even took my shoelaces, man. What, did they think I was going to hang myself with them?"

213

I sipped my beer as the door opened and in came Candus, Aaron, and three other sailors from the tanker, two girls and a guy. A whiff of fresh salt air followed them in. I didn't recognize any of them. Mike wasn't there. Candus was holding a bag under her arm.

"Jason! We heard you were getting out today. How was your time in the slammer?" Aaron said. He laughed as he spoke,

"Oh, god. Fuck you."

"Relax. I heard they treated you really well, gave you a tear drop tattoo and everything. And here. The techs got together and got you something. Laz told us you're ordered to wear this at the next ships banyon on the quarterdeck."

She handed Jason the bag. He looked inside and laughed. Faintly, at first, then louder.

"Are you fucking serious? Have a party at sea and make me stand there wearing this and looking like an idiot?" He pulled it out and unfolded a large orange t-shirt. He held it up and stared.

"What is it?" I asked. He turned it around for me to see the words:

Property of LA County, #00069

Jason grabbed his untouched beer from the table and finished the entire thing in one tip of the bottle.

"Do you guys know everyone?" Candus asked us. "This is Kim, Fred, and Joanne."

Kim was a tomboyish blond wearing a t-shirt and jeans. Fred was a skinny guy in a denim jacket and blue jeans, and Joanne wore a denim skirt and a black, long sleeved shirt. I noticed a ring on Steve's hand. His other hand held Joanne's. Jason's eyes were glazing over. "Fuck you guys," he said, then, "Hi."

And the night began.

♦

I looked at my Seamaster. It was still early. Ten-ish. Jason

Kim

was more subdued than usual.

"I think this is the first time we've drank together where you weren't three drinks ahead of me."

"I don't think you understand, man. There were Mexican gang members in there. I am not a small guy by any stretch, but man they have some big Meixcans in there, and I thought I was gonna get cornholed."

"Could be worse," I pointed out. "At least you're not pretty and that scar on your face must give you some street cred."

"Yeah. Laz took me aside and had a talk. He told me I'm gonna take over the mids watch when I get back. Says he wants me to have more responsibility and straighten me out."

As I watched him slouching back in his chair, staring at his feet, almost remorseful, I got angry.

"Well, that's fucking great."

"What?"

"Well. I've never missed a day of work. I know that shack better than anyone. I've held together the watch and been fucking perfect. They even threw an above average ready for promotion on my PER, and now they are gonna give you the watch as a reward for being a drunk?"

"Oh, I'm sorry man. I didn't know."

"Ah, fuck it. It's not your fault. It just pisses me off, you know? I did everything right. I worked my ass off. I didn't just do it by the book; I wrote the fucking book. And, in the end, it didn't even matter."

Jason didn't know. How could he? He had barely paid attention to what was going on half the time. He was just going with the flow, enjoying himself.

"Well, fuck. Had I known the reward for working hard was more work, I'd have taken MDMA at that party with Rose. I'd have slept with Webber's wife. I would have been on a cute latino girl in San Diego like a dirty shirt instead of fucking my boss."

"Ah man, shit happens. Stop worrying about it. Wait, you fucked Marie? Eww."

"Fuck you, convict. It's better than Jose with the face tattoo. I've been working too hard fighting for something that isn't even real. If they wanted me to do the right thing, they'd have rewarded me for it. Time to let go, man. Enjoy what's right in front of me."

Jason raised his glass, and I tapped it with mine. Candus and Aaron joined in. Candus rubbed my back.

"Rex, don't sweat it."

"Ah, I'm over it. Just have to stop caring too much."

"So, Rex, you don't remember me, do you?" Kim said.

"I don't. Were we on course together?"

"No. I was at fleet school when you were teaching. I was in one of the other classes. I'm friends with Matthew."

"Oh, yeah? I haven't seen him since graduation. I hear he got posted out east."

"Nope. He switched spots with someone from Halifax who wanted to go there. Plus, he's married, so they try not to split families up anymore."

"Oh? So he and Melissa are still married?"

"No, actually. They divorced last year. You should see her now. She ballooned up, hard."

"Oh, that's too bad. She was a looker back in the day."

"Yeah, I heard."

"No. I didn't mean that."

Candus whispered something to Aaron. It caught my attention. Kim briefly looked at them, smiled, then turned back to me.

"I'm just fucking with you. We used to roast him about it. 'What's it feel like to know the instructor banged your wife?' He hated that shit."

"You guys are savage."

"And then Candus tells me that you know Sara?"

I looked at Candus. She looked back and winked.

"Oh? And what all did Candus tell you?"

"Just that you knew her. Why, what did you think she said?"

"Just the rumor that's floating around that I slept with her during her husband's stag party."

"Oh, yeah, she said that. I just assumed he was cool with that."

"I don't know who is cool with what anymore," I said.

Kim laughed and raised her glass, I tapped it with mine and we had another drink. Candus interrupted.

"Well you should see Rex's place. It's pretty swank."

"What, like milk crates and a big TV?"

"No. I mean like really nice. He has this giant sofa, white leather and–"

I finished her sentence. "White Italian leather," I said. "Sectional."

"Yeah. And the mini bar," Candus continued. "I've never seen a sailor actually keep full bottles in the house, but he manages to do it."

"Really? Not bad," said Kim. She turned toward me. "Impressive, even."

Candus continued,

"Wait. Watch, this. Ask him about his sheets."

"Oh. Rex, what about the sheets?"

"Candus…"

"Come on, tell her." She is grinning from ear to ear.

"They are custom made. Three hundred thread count sateen with a goose down duvet. But it's not as good as it sounds. I'm down to my last set, and I've needed to replace the duvet cover for a long time now, so it used to be a lot better."

"Well, I'll tell you what. You make me a drink sometime and you can show me. Maybe I'll take you linen shopping and we can buy you another one."

"I can't tell if you're being sarcastic or not."

"Of course I am! I'm into girls. I don't buy fucking bedsheets. I look like a horse girl for fuck sakes."

"Wait, you're a lesbian?" I felt more at ease. All these questions sounded like Candus was setting her up on a reconnaissance mission or something. After all that, I realized she was just one of the guys.

"You didn't know?"

"I never ask about that shit. Well then, to muff!" I said, and raised my glass. The rest of the table raised theirs, and everyone repeated, "To muff!"

I looked at Kim. "What are you guys up to after this?" I asked.

Steve, who had been sitting quietly this whole time, listening, went first.

"Jo and I are headed home. I have to work in the morning."

Then Candus said, "Aaron and I are going to drink here for a bit then head out later."

"I'm going home, man," said Jason. "The last thing I need is another confinement."

"Kim?"

"I was probably going out with Candus and them later, why?"

"I wanted to go on a date later on today with this girl, but I was going to invite everyone over for a drink at my place before you head out."

"Aaron and I are good. We are waiting for some people anyways. Kim, why don't you go? You live near, don't you?"

"I'm like a five minute walk from here, but I drove today," she said.

Candus picked up Kim's jacket and handed it over. Aaron grabbed her clutch from the table and tossed it into Kim's lap.

"Go grab a drink? The gang isn't getting off shift for another hour. Grab a drink or two then come back."

I wasn't drunk, the room wasn't spinning, and I assumed she was still a lesbian. This was nice. No cunt taking advantage of me. No slumpbuster to get over her. It was a date, but she was just one of the boys.

Back at my place with Kim, I went straight for the mini bar to play host.

"This is just what I needed," I said.

"What is?" she asked.

"Just a drink with one of the boys. What are you drinking?"

13 Kim

"What do you have?"

"I have everything."

"Gin and tonic then"

"Liquid panty remover, nice choice."

I grabbed an airport-sized tonic bottle and began to mix. She sat down on the sofa and looked around.

"This place is nice. Do you rent it or is it yours?"

"It's mine."

"Geez, you pay your bills on time and everything."

"I know, right. My milk crate days are far behind me. Just wait till you see the patio furniture. It's wicker and forms a golf ball when you put them together. They're like Legos."

"I just want to see these sheets that Candus was talking about."

"Yeah, that was weird. She's never been over to the house before. I didn't even know she knew about them."

"Oh, that's because Sara told her about it. She wouldn't shut up about how nice the linens were. She tried them out and said it was like sleeping in a cloud."

"Oh, they are. Here." I handed over her gin and tonic.

"Can I bring my drink?"

"Sure, just don't spill it."

Kim was tall. Tall as me. No makeup. She had good bone structure. She stood straight and stiff next to the bed like a professional diver, then fell back. The air shot out of the duvet on all sides as she landed on the bed. A few down feathers fluttered around.

"Oh, my god. It is like a cloud!"

"Yeah, after the fire blanket and our prison sheets on ship, I've grown fond of the nice linens."

I looked down at her. She had her eyes closed, lost in thought. She said she was a lesbian, but I had to know how much of a lesbian she really was. I was on her like a dirty shirt.

I kissed her, one hand braced on the bed to hold myself up, the other hand outstretched awkwardly to keep my drink from tipping. She didn't stop me. She didn't grab me either. She just laid there and kissed me back.

I pulled back. She opened her eyes a bit and looked at me. I set our drinks on the floor. She pulled her shirt over her head, all business, as if she were getting ready to have a shower. No sensuality, no seduction, no leaving anything to the imagination, just clinical. Efficient. I unbuttoned her pants while she pulled her sports bra down to her waist. She had an athletic build like a farm girl. She unbuttoned my shirt and I pulled away to go down on her.

"No," she said. She pulled me back up then slid under me grabbing my hand and placing it on her inner thigh. "I'm on my period."

♦

And like that, it was over. It wasn't bad. It was rather nice, actually. In a word, efficient. She knew all the motions, all the sensitive spots.

"Have you always been a lesbian?"

"Naw. Only for the last five years. I had boyfriends before, but it always felt weird. I figured it out after I joined the navy."

"You never came."

"Oh, I don't need to. I had to see for myself."

"What did you see?"

"Why there's all these stories floating around about you. Sara, Candus, even the officers ask if I know you."

"Yeah, I don't even know half of them. People are just bored. What exactly do they say?"

Kim already had her sports bra on. She grabbed her shirt off the floor and picked up her drink, taking a swig.

"Just that you're a lot of fun, and not like a lot of the other guys they meet. You see, a lot of guys are nice. They are too nice. They want to get married and have a family and cuddle on Fridays, and it's just so boring, you know? It's like the only thing they want is to make an omelet in the morning and pour a girl a coffee in the morning, you know?"

"They do?" I said, but I got it. When she looked at me, she saw the other guy.

"Meanwhile, some guy like you shows up, and it's something different. I don't know how to put it. You're not mean, but you also aren't nice. You're…"

"Interesting?"

"Yeah. Like, I didn't know that dark skinned guys are brown. I thought everyone was pink down there."

"You're not the first one who has said that, you know."

"I'll bet. Sara is just miserable, too. She wants Webber to be interesting, but he's just always so nice. It's like she can't do anything to him and make him mad. Did you know she told him to give her parents his car?"

"I've heard. He brags about a lot of weird stuff."

I grabbed my glass and headed to the bar.

"Want another?" I asked and reached for her glass.

"Yes, please."

She still hadn't put on her pants. All I could see were thin panties and muscular legs. I couldn't stop staring at the small fold where her ass met her hamstrings. The space between them made a little diamond.

"You know you're kind of wasted on women," I told her.

"I know."

I returned with two more drinks. No ice this time, and they are both triples.

"So, Candus showed you the way, huh?"

"Candus and I fooled around once and it just kind of felt good, you know?"

"I don't, actually."

"You've never slept with Candus?"

"Naw, she's more of a little sister to me than anything."

Hearing that, Kim slammed her palm on the sheets.

"Oh, that bitch! Now I get it!"

"What?"

"She kept pushing me to come out tonight. She told me I had to see you. When we were at the bar, she made me sit beside you. Didn't you notice she basically told me to come over and have a drink with you?"

"What, does she think we are monkeys you just put in a cage?"

"Well, I mean, she wasn't wrong."

"Yeah. I was on you like a dirty shirt."

"What?"

"Never mind. It's an expression. That little bitch is running reconnaissance. If she thinks I'm going to sit there and take pictures of her and Aaron going at it she's got another thing coming."

"Well. It wasn't bad. You're pretty good. You said you have a date later? Sure you don't want to come out with us?"

"Naw. I promised."

"What's her name?"

"Kate."

"Cool. Well, if it goes south, give us a call. We can always use the company."

She finished off her gin then finished getting dressed.

"Wait," I said. "I have to ask."

"Oh, you're plenty big," she said. "Don't worry about that."

"No, not that. I don't care about that."

"Really? I thought guys–"

I cut her off. "Fuck, you're such a lesbian. No. Did you ever consider switching sides tonight?"

She paused and smiled, somewhat coyly, I thought.

"Just for a second. I'm still on team muff, though. Got to go. They are waiting for me at the Fleet Club."

"Sounds good."

I grabbed my shirt and draped it across my torso.

"You haven't seen the kitchen yet. Want something to eat before you go?"

"Eww, no. Why in god's name would I want to see a kitchen? Bye!"

She ran out the door. I put my pants on and walked to the living room. I passed by the mirror and looked. Just my reflection. A few down feathers in my hair. My shirt was unbuttoned and my pants looked fine. The phone rang in the bedroom. When I walked over and answered, I saw a small red stain on the pillow.

Lipstick! Fuck!

I looked at the phone. It was Kate. I yanked off the pillow cover and tossed it into the hallway.

"Hello, babe," she said.

"Took you long enough!"

"I had a really crappy date yesterday. I need a drink. Where are we going tonight?"

"The Duke."

"Fun! I'll be over in a bit."

14

Jason

Jason was pale as a ghost and sober as a Mormon. I heard beeping on the console. It could wait.

"Jullie is pregnant?"

"Yeah man, and she wants to keep the baby."

"I don't know what to say. Was this an accident or were you looking forward to this?"

"Oh, don't get me wrong. I've always wanted to be a dad. I just assumed it would be someday that's not today with a woman who doesn't stalk me."

"Well then, I don't know whether to say 'I'm sorry' or 'Congratulations.'"

"You know what? I'm sure it will be fine. You know this was how my parents got married? I guess they hooked up and mom was already pregnant with me on their first date or something."

"Well, glad to see that runs in the family then. So they got married, you were born, and you all lived happily ever after?"

Jason laughed. "Oh, god no, dude. I don't think they lasted six months. I don't even see my dad. I think I've met him maybe twice in my life. Fuck that guy."

"I feel that. My parents split up when I was five. Jon stepped up. I still don't know how they found each other."

"I remember mom telling me I would be the man of the house when I was old enough to walk. I promised myself I would never put a woman through what he put my mom through, you know?"

"I know. We all make our promises. So what does this mean?"

"Well, I guess I'm getting married and I'm going to be a dad. And now that I'm getting married, you two," Jason pointed at Webber and me, "have to make sure I don't have a miserable time with it. Let's do it this weekend cause I'm pretty sure I have to start doing doctor's appointments and looking for a house and all the other shit you're supposed to do. I'm freaking out, and I need a day to just relax."

I looked at Webber.

"I want to come," he said, "but Sara feels sick today. I have to take care of her. I'm sure you guys will understand." Just when I thought I couldn't have hated this guy any more than I already did, he pulls this.

"I should have fucked your wife, you asshole," I said. Then I heard the loudest, most gravelly laugh ever. I didn't know Laz was in the room.

"Oh, whatever, man. You didn't have a chance. She's mine. I'm really sorry, but Jason will figure this out soon enough, too. He's going to be a husband now, too. You don't get to do things sometimes."

I looked at him, all smug, talking like he's part of some golden brotherhood. He looks like he's chewing his own face. God, he was just a dweeb. I couldn't worry about that right then. Jason was sitting down at the console, sweating. Even thinking about what he's about to become looks worse than what he was in for in San Diego.

"Jason, I have a plan."

"You have a plan?"

I slapped him on the shoulder. "Yeah, I have a plan. Hopefully, Mike will talk to me."

"What, is he still raw about that Alyssa chick?"

"I guess I'll find out. PO!" Laz looked out from behind his desk. "I need to run some errands at the tanker. Mind if I skate for a few hours?"

"Is the traffic distributed?"

"I can handle that, PO," said Jason.

"Fine then. Just be back before end of day."

I headed to the brow and off to the tanker.

They had the best dock. A-Jetty, right by the parking lot. I walked past dry dock. The submarine was still there. It had been under repairs since I joined, SSK 876 HMCs Victoria. We nicknamed it "Building 876." It was a good grift. The engineers would verify parts with a twelve month certification, but the construction guys took thirteen months to construct everything. They'd start on the bow and work to the stern, but by the time the stern was finished, the bow required recertification, so they took it apart and the engineers would start again. No one seemed to catch on to the pattern. They must have made a fortune doing the same thing every day. It was the nautical Sisyphus, but profitable.

Patterns were everywhere. You just had to look.

All they needed to do to finish was have one officer who was in charge of the project come down and take stock of what was going on and make an executive decision. Skip the certification. Skip the rules. Just put the fucking thing together and take it out to sea. Could have saved a ton of effort and millions of dollars. I guessed everyone just loved going with the flow, enjoying the work. It was the story of a submarine that had a shitty ending, but everyone knew how it worked. It would have been a far better adventure if they had changed what they had been doing, but who knows? Maybe it would sink and those certifications were more important than I'd thought. Not that it mattered. Their rulebook was why I was staring at a giant black dildo half assembled in dry dock instead of hunting with the carrier group in the straits of Hormuz. Things would have been so much easier without all the rules and regulations. They should have focused on what they were trying to accomplish.

After all, it was working for me.

I stepped onto the tanker's brow and saluted the ensign. The watch keeper handed me a pencil.

"Can I get you to check in? What can I do for you?" he asked.

"Can you pipe leading seaman MacDonald to the brow? Also, who is in the shack right now monitoring comms?"

"That would be leading seaman Douglas."

"Oh, good, Aaron's on board, can you pipe him too please?"

The guy walks to the PA and piped the general call.

"Leading Seaman Douglas, leading seaman Macdonald, brow."

Mike came up first. He saw me and scowled.

"Mike. Hey, how's it going?"

"What can I do for you, leading seaman."

"Oh, come the fuck on, don't be like that. It's important."

"I don't care man. I got nothing to say."

"Jason's getting married. He's going to be a father?"

"What? No shit? I didn't even know he was dating anyone."

"He sort of is. Remember Jullie? He knocked her up and he's trying to do the right thing, but right now he's looking rough. I want to have a bachelor party for him this weekend before he has to start doing pregnancy stuff with the doctor and buy a house and everything."

"Didn't he take care of Webber for his stag? Why isn't he going?"

"Sara is sick. He has to stay home."

"What a fucking dweeb! Good thing you fucked his wife."

"I should have. Anyways, I need your help. Do you still talk to Alyssa?"

"Yeah, you didn't hear? We got back together."

"Oh really?" That explained why she stopped answering the phone.

"Yeah. She told me she was just angry at me for fucking around and pretended to date you to make me jealous."

"Oh, you thought we were dating?"

"Well, what am I supposed to think? Every time I tried to get a hold of her, she said she was coming over to your place.

What was I supposed to think?"

"Oh, love at first sight obviously. You know how well I got along with her after we first met at my place."

"Oh shut up. So do you fuck anyone ever? Or is it just stories of girls blueballing you at home and guys like me telling everyone you're a fucking savage?"

I didn't have the heart to tell him. Then again, neither did the fucking Dog Walker. She probably tells him how she's in love with him, and how he makes her so happy. I checked my watch: 1430. Aaron came out of the hatch and walked over.

"So, look. It's two-thirty now. Can you call her and ask if she still has that friend who does the stripping thing? I figure we bring her to our place and we set up a poker game, then we all head out to the bar. Jason's chick is a bit of a psychopath and will probably lose her shit if we take him to a strip club or something. This way he can have as much fun as he wants without having to deal with any bullshit in the morning."

"Who's having a bachelor party now?" Aaron asked.

"Jason's gonna be a dad. Shotgun wedding," I said.

"No shit?"

"Yeah. Candus is off today, but you two want to come and help? I want to make sure he enjoys himself. He's been panicking ever since he found out."

"Of course he is. Candus and I had a scare last month. I was almost a dad too. I just about threw up."

And so the plan was set: bachelor party, stripper, poker, drinking. It's probably better if Webber isn't there. I'd have probably punched him in the mouth if I got drunk and he started bragging about getting pegged or some other bullshit.

♦

As I arrived back on our ship, I said to Jason, "I got a plan. It's handled. You'll love it."

Laz stood up and said, "Leading seaman, come here for a minute."

The Dog Walker | R.A. STONE

He walked me to the back. He had a folder in his hand and Marie was beside him. He handed me the folder. Inside was my performance review. Marie didn't even make eye contact preferring to stare at her clipboard. I read my review.

Potential: 60%. Performance 40%.

Final assessment: Above average, can be considered for merit board and possible promotion.

I signed the bottom and handed it to Marie. She place the file onto her clipboard and shuffled out of the office.

Laz: "Thank you Petty Officer."

Me: "Ma'am."

Laz was straight-faced, but I knew what he was thinking. Was the performance review a performance review? Or was it a performance review–wink, wink; nudge, nudge. After way too long of a pause he said, "Happy?"

"Yes, PO."

"Questions?"

"No, PO."

"Carry on, then. Also, your posting message is in. You're going to the shore office. You did good."

Finally! A much needed break from the chaos. I went further in my career by fucking the boss than by being the perfect employee. Easier to promote me and shuffle me along than to have a conversation with command. They needed to promote more women anyways, and being dicked down in the reserve space isn't conducive to the military's goal, I guess.

♦

My new roommate hadn't moved in yet, so the spare bedroom was empty. I had to move my Italian white leather sofa into there so we could set up the poker table. I was impressed. The place was called HighLifePoker and they thought of everything. Two guys came with a professional-looking table and installed it in the living room along with a set of comfortable, brown leather chairs. They had no arms which I assumed was

230

14 Jason

to facilitate lap dancing.

"Sign here, then here," the guy in charge said. "My name is Doug, and I'll be your bouncer tonight. I'll be back with the girl around nine. Her name is Jade."

"You're smaller than I thought you'd be. When they said they provided a bouncer, I figured you'd be some three hundred pound black dude or something."

"Ha, everyone says that. Frankly it doesn't usually matter. The kind of guys who can afford the party tend to have good jobs, something to lose. Just having me here as a witness is enough to keep things civil. Most guys just want to see tits that don't belong to their frumpy wives. If anyone gets drunk and belligerent, the host does most of the dirty work. I'm just there to remind him that I can put HighLifePoker or HighLifePokerGirls on the credit card receipt."

I scribbled my signature, and he took his clipboard then handed me a couple boxes.

"Here. Two boxes of chips, they are complimentary. We don't handle any money. Thats entirely on you. Feel free to give these out for guys to take home. Our number and website are on the back, so it's good advertising for us. Guys tend to love the reminder of the party. And if Jade makes any other arrangements with anyone for extras, that's nothing to do with the company. We have a strict no extras policy, but we also have a no tipping policy, so…"

"Got it. One thing: I have my mom coming over the day after for lunch. When do you guys come pick this stuff up?"

"Anytime you're awake as long as it's before noon. We have another party setup for Sunday. Otherwise, we will have to charge you for another day."

I'll throw fifty at him when he's on the door later. I didn't really feel like getting a lap dance or, god knows what, extra services, but I was sure Mike was just the kind of shit bag who would. I peeked into the box and saw five different colors of chips. On the front of each was a 1940s-style pinup girl and, on the back, their business information. Clever.

231

♦

He showed up on time wearing a tuxedo t-shirt, tinted sunglasses, and black slacks. We shook hands and walked Jade. She was fairly tall at five feet seven. In heels, she stood almost six feet. She wore a plaid skort and a white t-shirt. I felt like I was coaching her for a tennis game. After introductions I handed the guy two twenty dollar bills and a ten.

"Hey, thank you so much," I said. "I hope you don't mind, but I just wanted to say thanks."

"Not a problem, sir."

I turned to the girl. "So, you're Jade, right?"

She looked at him. He nodded, and she turned to me. "Yeah. So, who's the bachelor?"

"His name is Jason. He's stressed as hell as this is a last minute thing. He doesn't know what's going on, so it's going to be funny to watch his surprise once you start dealing."

"OK, so here's how it goes," she began. "Once you give the word, the guys will have a seat at the table, and I'll start distributing chips. I'll do all the bartending so that you can all just sit back and enjoy. Pretend like Doug's not even here. He will mostly hang at the door and will only come over if someone is at the door and wants to come in. I don't handle any of the cash, so you have to sort that out beforehand. Do you have a spare bedroom? I know some guys like a private dance so I only take cash and it's one hundred for a fifteen minute dance. No hands. Any questions?"

"Nope, sounds great," I said. "All I ask is you don't fuck up my sheets. And for the bar I have pour spouts on all the bottles. It's about three seconds an ounce. Jason is a drinker so try not to over pour him too much. Don't forget, and watch out for my coffee table. It's glass."

She took her bag into the bedroom.

"No cover for the duvet?" she asked.

"Oh, right. I had one but it got ruined. Just throw it on the floor. The sheets are Egyptian cotton, sateen. They're good."

14 Jason

♦

I was sitting at the poker table. I hated poker, never had the attention span. Jade walked up with a tray and placed my Gibson in front of me.

"There you are sweetie."

Those tits were amazing. They reminded me of Melissa. No stretch marks on the stomach. I wonder if she lasts longer than a few minutes? Jade was a little weathered in the face, but her bangs swooshed in a way that covered a lot of the problem.

Jason was losing his mind and already down a hundred bucks. Mike was laughing. Aaron was quietly working the table, his chips stacked neatly in front of him buttressed against our attempts to have fun. Jason turned his chair outward and slapped his leg.

"Jade! Bring me a rum and coke, then come have a seat here," he said.

Jade smiled then shuffled off to the mini bar. Her ass tried its best jiggle as she went, but she was pretty skinny so it looked stiffer than it should. She came back, drink in hand, swished her hair to the side and sat on Jason's lap. Aaron was chatting with Candus and watching his cards. Candus was out a long time ago.

Mike smirked at me. "Alyssa pulled through after all, eh?" he said.

Jade tried pouring Jason's drink into his mouth, but he was moving around and some of it splashes onto the floor

"Yeah. Hey, Jade. Watch the floor. I just had it installed!"

Jason took the drink out of her hand and threw it back. She stood up, leaned into him while placing both her hands on his lap, and said, "You did good, babe. Am I going to have to cut you off soon? You don't want to wreck these lovely looking Home Depot floors now."

Two dollars a square foot, and how did she know I got them at Home Depot?

"Hey now. They may be Home Depot showroom floors, but

233

they are mine," I said.

Mike slapped me on the back. Jade had a seat at the head of the table and dealt another hand.

Candus didn't last but fifteen minutes. She was the most impulsive person I knew. I lasted almost an hour. Mike played aggressively and I kept folding. But Aaron, he was a shark. I should have known he wasn't fucking around when he started shuffling his chips. One handed. Two stacks into one. Shuffling chips like they were cards. Splitting them up, checking his hand, then doing it again. He and Mike were so enthralled in the game, they were barely looking at the tits on the table. When Jason finally lost his last hand, he ended up sitting on the floor by the coffee table.

"Hey babe, want another drink?" Jade asked. "We can't have the man of the hour sitting there doing nothing."

"Now you're talking!" Jason said.

Jade set the deck down. Aaron and Mike stared at each other, placing bets. Mike was still aggressive, but Aaron wasn't backing down. Then Jade appeared with another drink. Jason stared blankly. The room was warm with all the bodies, booze, and boobs everywhere, and we were all sweating. Then Jade sat on her knees, suggestively, on the other side of the coffee table from me. She leaned forward, arched her back, and put her ass in the air as her breasts slid across the table top, slippery from the sweat underneath. I wanted to stare. She looked hot, but then I saw the streaks and smudges her tits made like large fingerprints on the glass.

"Jade, goddamnit!" I yelled. "You're leaving tit prints all over my glass table top. My mom's coming over tomorrow. Her dad's a preacher. What are you doing to me, woman!?"

The room erupted in laughter. Jade sat up and Jason hopped to his feet. He walked over and whispered in my ear, "Hey. I'm going to take her in the room. You okay with that?"

"Oh, yeah, man. We already talked about it. No hands. A hundred bucks. I got this one. Have fun."

I gestured to Jade who nodded and grabbed Jason by the

hand leading him into the bedroom. She closed the door. Behind it, I heard the sound of a stereo playing Brian McKnight, Back to One. God, I hated that song. A girl once broke up with me on that fucking song. I looked over and Aaron slapped his cards on the table.

"Three of a kind. Eat it!" He slid the rest of the chips over to his side.

Mike was laughing. "You, dumbass," he said to me. "I couldn't think straight watching you yell at Jade about your stupid coffee table."

"Well, look," I said. "Two streaks looking like giant alien snail trails across the whole fucking table with a little nipple bulge at the top. Now I gotta go clean that because if I don't, I'm going to forget, and my mom's coming over tomorrow."

"Yeah, don't want your mom to find out you are hanging with strippers, ya idiot."

I dampened a cloth at the sink then wiped down the table. I got Doug's attention and said, "Hey, after this we are going out. You guys are more than welcome to join. Drinks are on me."

"Mind if my girlfriend joins us?" he asked.

"Not at all. More the merrier. She must be a pretty special lady to stay with a man guarding tits all day."

Jason came out of the room buttoning up his shirt. He walked over, opened his arms, and gave me a big hug.

"Man, thank you," he said. "I needed this. I really did."

"Don't sweat it. I figure it was better than feeding you rusty nails then throwing you in a cab. Here, we are going out now, get your stuff."

When Jade came out of the bedroom, everyone made their way towards the door and began putting on shoes. Jade pulled me aside and said, "Hey Rex. I'm sorry about your table. I don't want to get you in trouble with your mom."

"It's fine. I gave it a wipe but I'll just Windex it tomorrow. You wouldn't believe how hard it is to get tit smudges out. They are worse than fingerprints."

"You know this?"

235

"Well, you're not the first girl I've had over at my place," I said and laughed. Jade looked confused.

"Well, here. I feel bad. Tell you what, let me make it up to you." Jade grabbed me by the elbows, spun around, and slid her hand down my arm and into mine. She walked us past the group. Mike gave me a look.

"Hey, meet you at Upstairs?" he said.

"Yup. I'll be right behind you," I said as we entered the bedroom.

Jade closed the door and dimmed the lights. She bent over and pushed the button on her music player in her bag, and Brian McKnight started playing.

"Hey, can we listen to absolutely anything else?" I asked. "I fucking hate Brian McKnight."

"My god, you're such a grumpy bastard, aren't you?"

"Yeah. I got dumped to it once."

"Fine, I got something else." She pushed the forward button a few times and a slow techno song came up, one I didn't recognize.

"Thank you."

"Shut up. Sit back." Jade pushed me onto the bed and slipped into character. In the dim lights, her face softened right up. She looked twenty-one. She began dancing in front of me, touching herself, sliding her fingers up her torso, pausing on her breasts. I didn't know what to do with my hands, so I placed them behind my head. She tried to unbutton my pants seductively, but the button on the Jeans was too rough. She grunted and finally undid the button. She taps me on the hips, I lift, and she pulled them off.

During the song she unbuttons my shirt and strips off my underwear.

"Don't forget. No hands. I'm in charge."

"Yes ma'am."

"Ma'am? I'm not 40"

The sheets felt soft and still very warm from Jason's body heat. We didn't say anything and, for the next few minutes, she moved her body up and down mine. Her breasts slid up my torso, stopping just short of my face. I looked down, but she put her hand on my chin and lifted my head back up.

"Like I said, no hands, head up."

I was rock hard, standing in all my glory and she knew it. I had never just laid back and paid attention to what was going on before. I'd fucked a lot of girls on that bed, those sheets, but I was always preoccupied. With Rose, I was worried about getting to work on time. With Melissa, I never even had a chance to enjoy myself. With Kelly, I was trying to get my routine right. The Dog Walker wasn't even a person. I got off on the idea of fucking her like I was getting revenge. She was such a bitch. Charli made me happy, but it was mostly me being happy at being happy instead of enjoying the moment. But now? Just some random woman I had just met. I wasn't fucking her. I didn't want to fuck her. Yet, I'm enjoying myself and focusing on everything she was doing. And her breasts were amazing.

"Are they real?"

"No, but this job paid for the expensive ones. They place them under–"

I cut her off. "Under the muscle so they just push your real breasts up and out so they feel real," I said.

"How do you know that?"

"You're not the first girl I've had over."

"Well, you seem to get around, don't you, you little man whore."

"Yeah, and I used to be such a nice guy too."

She laughed, turned around, and arched her back. She rubbed her ass against me. It was small but flawless. Sara was all awkward without rhythm when she was doing it, but Jade was smooth and followed the beat. I bet she was laughing to herself, enjoying my predicament. There was no way she couldn't tell I was rock hard. She held herself upright by resting her hands on my hips, her hair draped across her back like an artist's brush. A few strands stuck to her sweaty back.

"So you don't have a little lady waiting for you once I leave?"

"Not anymore. We split up."

"I'm sorry to hear that."

"Don't be. I learned something important. They only love you when you're the asshole."

"That's not true."

"Oh? A few minutes ago I was yelling at your tits for being on my table."

She spun back and laid on top of me. We barely touched.

"It's not that. It's not about being an asshole. Do you remember when your friend was wanting me to sit on his lap and pour his drink and stuff?"

"Yeah, that's your job. So?"

"Well, he kept telling me how beautiful I was, how great I am, and how he always wanted a beautiful woman to help him drink. I don't know if you know this, but I hear this all the fucking time. Like all the fucking time."

"Well, aren't you supposed to?"

"Yeah, but I'm not pretty. I know they are lying to me. They just want to fuck me so they say what they think I want to hear, so, hopefully, I fuck them. But you? You didn't."

"Right. I yelled at you for spilling drinks on the floor and smudging my coffee table."

She stopped dancing and sat on my lap. Her breasts sat between her face and mine like she's some giant Amazonian lording over me as conqueror or conquered. It felt honest. She was naked, but then again so was I.

"I know, but that's because that's what you honestly felt! I don't have to think if you are just trying to fuck me, or if you're lying to me. You looked at me and you were honest. And yeah, it hurt my feelings a bit. I am used to these puppies helping me get my way. You didn't care about that though. And, it's kind of hot."

"I just don't get it. Every woman I've ever met seems to love complaining about shoddy treatment. And now you're here telling me you think it's, honest."

"Yeah, well that's fun too. I loved complaining about my ex

when we were dating. It was frustrating, but also kind of exciting, you know? I felt like he pissed me off so much, but it just made things, exciting."

"You were married?"

"Yeah, I married him right out of high school, but it didn't last long. We broke up last year"

"Wait, how old are you?"

"How old do you think I am?"

"I thought you were thirty."

"I'm twenty-one."

"I'm sorry. I just assumed."

"No, it's okay. I did a lot of drugs. That's why I have a twenty-one year old body and a thirty year old face. I know I'm not the prettiest. So, when some guy tells me what he thinks I want to hear, I know he's lying to me. And if he's lying about that, what else is he lying about? He doesn't know me. He only thinks he does. And I've dated guys like that. They get really mad when you shatter their illusions."

The girl with the fake tits was more honest than all the real tits I've known. I didn't count anymore but I knew it was more than 27. Jade was excited. I don't want to lie to myself anymore. Everything made sense now. I grew some perspective. It was more than just being Jon or the stupid rules. The other girls clicked into place.

Rose was in love with her man, sure. But she was excited with me. I just wanted to fuck her, but I was honest and it was exciting and she got that bug out of her system before she settled down with the guy who called her beautiful.

Melissa couldn't stand me. I was too easy. She caught me with little effort and I was always nice to her. I wasn't nice because she deserved it. She was a single mom and a sailor. She knew I was lying, that I wasn't really there. I put my hand on Jade's cheek.

"Hey, your boss said no touching, so you can slap me If you want, but…"

I kissed her on the lips. She closed her eyes, waited a beat, then puts her hand on my chest and pushed back,

"Whoa, I'm on the clock, but I tell you what. Let's go meet up at the bar. I'm off work at midnight, then we can talk, okay?" I hopped out of bed and headed to the bathroom. My foot got caught in the duvet on the floor, and I tripped. I almost slammed my head into the wall. Jade laughed at the spectacle. I turned around to give her shit, then paused. She was putting her clothes back on. I could see the lines in her face as she zipped up her skort. I closed the bathroom door.

"Let me take a piss, then we can head out."

"Oh, one more thing," she said through the door.

"I know. Money is on the table in the living room, right beside those smudges."

A Choice

My shore posting was perfect. I got off work around the same time the bars gave last call. Kate loved it. She got a place to sleep and I got a woman to sleep with. It was a match of convenience. I'm ten years older than her, but we are equally experienced. I could have been insecure about her skill, but I could also be thankful for her training. It's a choice. Once you start seeing and understanding the patterns, you start gaining perspective.

Kate called me at the office. "Hey, are you coming out with me tonight?"

"I can't. I have to work till 0400."

"Oh, right. Another midnight shift?"

"They all are. Mids watches. Two days, two mids, and five off from now until forever."

"Well, leave your door unlocked. I'm coming over when they close. Mind if I stay the night? I don't want to have to drive all the way home while drunk."

"Park in visitor parking and help yourself."

The Dog Walker | R.A. STONE

I went to work looking at consoles and crypto tapes and old chiefs who just want to go home every night and hopefully salvage their marriages whereas I got to go home to a drunk woman in my house without first having to endure the ringing of an EDM beat or the roar of a chiller in my head to get her there. No broken glasses. No stained sheets. I could have nice things again.

When I did get home, Kate wanted out of her bar clothes and her commute, and I wanted out of my uniform, and both of us needed a shower. Then we would fool around. She would make burritos. I'd make coffee. Then we'd part company and go to our other lives. It was the perfect marriage. Better than leaving the money on the table.

As for work, Jason was now my supervisor. The added responsibility really got to him. Laz promoted him, and we both got sent to the shore office. On his last day before parental leave started, for laughs the chief told him to wear his prison shirt from San Diego. I had just hung up the phone when Jason looks over and said, "Hey, I'm going to take off in a bit. You going to be fine taking the rest of the watch?"

"Leaving early?"

"No one is going to care, and if they want to charge me, who is going to hold that paperwork for a year?" I looked at his shirt, Property of LA County. Jason shrugged. "Besides," he said. "The best way to learn the boundaries is to test them."

"Fair. I have to stay up, anyways. Kate is coming over after she hits the bar tonight. I can handle changeover myself."

"Oh, you two are still seeing each other? I thought you were dating Jade from the party?"

"Yeah. I'm kind of dating both right now. Which is fine. No one is exclusive. Kate just likes how after the bar she can walk to my place and sleep there and doesn't have to catch a forty minute cab to her parents' place then come by the next day to pick her up her Bronco."

"Well, that's good to hear, then. Just make sure you wrap up."

Jason wanted to say something else. He was waiting just like my mom used to. I was playing with the crypto loader, but set it down to play this game instead.

"Yeah, I know. Looking forward to the leave?" I asked.

"I'll tell you this much. I'm almost a dad. She's expecting next month. I'm freaking the fuck out."

"Why? I thought you were looking forward to being a dad."

"It's not that. Remember what I told you about my dad? I'm worried I'm going to turn into him. I don't want to be that guy."

"Yeah. We all get that same feeling. I used to be the same way. My stepdad was a womanizer and a piece of shit. Then I realized something."

"What was that?"

"You can just do the good parts and ignore the rest. That and most of the stuff I saw him do that was so bad was really me assuming that just because a woman is complaining, then something has to be wrong. But I figured out that they don't get to tell me how to live. Once I figured that out, the stress went away and I could just choose to do the parts I wanted that I thought were good and ignore the rest."

"What does that have to do with being a dad?"

It was looking what Jason really wanted a sympathetic ear to listen to him complain. I continued.

"I'm saying it's all the same shit. Keep what worked and discard what doesn't. You'll be fine."

"Yeah. Easy for you to say, though. You're not the one who stuck his dick in crazy and now has eighteen years to live with that."

"No, you dumbass, that's not what I mean. I mean that I realized my mom bitched a lot about how bad Jon was, but she always stuck around. She complained a lot, but she always stuck around. And then I realized, I was a kid. I didn't know that women love to complain. I thought she really hated the guy. Then I realized she stayed with him for twenty years because she was just into that shit."

"That's dark. Are you trying to make me feel better? Cause

you're not."

"No. What I'm saying is Julie was obsessed with you, borderline crazy, right?"

"Yeah, thank god she got pregnant. It calmed her the fuck down."

"Well, it's not like you're hiding who you are. She probably knows that you're the kind of guy who would leave. She fucks you like a maniac, right?"

"Oh, yeah, man. I feel bad sometimes. She's like eight months pregnant and she still gives me blowjobs like twice a week."

"See what I mean? I think she enjoys working to keep you loyal. I think she appreciates that even if she doesn't know about your dad. And if everyone is okay with whatever the situation is and just decides to make it work, is it such a bad thing?"

"I guess not."

"Look, I know it sounds stupid, but the way I see it, she's working to keep you happy, and you're working to stay loyal. You don't have to leave if you don't want to. And if she doesn't want to keep you around, then so be it."

"Is this the part where I kiss you on the mouth?" Jason grabbed me by my shoulders and leaned in,

"Why did you have to go and make this moment weird, dude?"

I shoved him. He bumped into the rack of crypto equipment. We almost took out the entire west coast search and rescue communications network with that dumb maneuver.

"I get it. I'm probably just being a bitch, anyways. But hey, I'll see you when I get back."

"Naw. I'll stop by when you have the kid. I'll bring you a set of poker chips as a gift."

"Don't you fucking dare. Julie would stab me with a fork in the neck if she knew."

"I'm joking. See ya."

Jason grabbed his beret and headed out the door. The security lock slammed into place behind him.

15 A Choice

The shift passed by so quickly I didn't even notice. My relief came in at 0350. I saluted the ensign in the lobby and walked over to my car to drive home. I loved these drives. No one on the road and I was alone with my thoughts. I got home and my door was unlocked. She always locked it when she came over. I couldn't remember if her Bronco was outside. I didn't think it worth looking.

I set my keys on the kitchen counter and walked down the hall. No one in the living room. No one in the bedroom. Back to the kitchen. I poured a glass of water. She must have found someone else's bed that night. I took off my jacket and unbuttoned my uniform, grabbed my bathrobe off the sofa, and sat down at the xbox. I realized I needed to piss first, so I got up and walked to the bathroom. The seat was down. The frosted glass shower door was closed. I always left it open to prevent mold in there. I finished peeing, washed my hands, and headed back to my game. I started Call of duty and waited for a lobby, but I couldn't shake the feeling that something was off.

Waiting for players…

Something's definitely off. I put my controller down and went back to the bathroom. I looked at the door again, something pink behind the glass door. I slid it open and Kate was there, naked. Her mouth was wide open, her makeup dripping like some kind of psychotic clown, her hair piled against the back of the tub. It was damp, almost dry. How long had she been sleeping there?

I closed the door and laughed as I walked back to the couch, pressed the X button in the middle of the controller to turn it on.

Waiting for players…

I paused again and returned to the bathroom.

"Ugh, you're like hauling a waterbed," I said as I grabbed her arm and pulled her out of the tub and over my shoulder. She was limp, dead weight, muttering nonsensical whatevers. I walked her to the bedroom and rolled her onto the bed. A spritz of water from her hair hit my face as she landed flat on her back.

245

The Dog Walker | R.A. STONE

Her tongue was flapping against the back of her mouth. It was loud, and I started to worry. I grabbed her arm and pulled it across her body, put my other hand on her hip and pulled her into the recovery position. I tucked her hand under her face. She stopped snoring.

It was probably the sweetest thing I had ever seen. The mirror was still against the wall. I hadn't moved it since Charli. I felt like a peeping Tom in my own room, a voyeur watching her sleep naked in my bed, her ass on display in the mirror like it was a window in someone else's house. I looked down at her. She was sleeping ugly. I wrapped her in the duvet like a burrito.

Players found...

♦

I slept in til eleven the next morning. I had a date with Jade that night. Kate wasn't awake yet. I started up the stove and put the kettle on. I was spooning some grounds into the french press when I heard a knock at the door. Still in my robe, I answered. It was my neighbour, and she looked pissed.

"Hey, hows it going?" I said.

"Did you take a shower last night?"

"No, I was at work. I had a friend housesitting for me though."

"Well, your friend used all the hot water in the building. I turned on my shower this morning and it was ice cold!"

"Oh no. I'm so sorry. I didn't know we could even do that."

"We have an old boiler in the building. I don't know how long your friend had the water running but in this building it's never run out before. I'm going to complain to management. This is the rudest thing I've seen."

"Look, I'm sorry, I didn't know. I'll have a talk with her when she wakes up. I promise it'll never happen again."

"See that it doesn't. I've put up with a lot from you since you moved in. The noise. The parties. I think I've been very fair, but it stops now."

"I promise. Thanks for understanding."

She walked off flashing a look of defiance. She had moved in last year after her divorce. I felt bad, but I knew she had some shit to work through, so I always tried to be polite.

The kettle whistled in the kitchen, and I prepared a pot of coffee. I poured two mugs then walked into the bedroom. Kate was scowling at all the noise. I set a coffee down on the nightstand for her.

"Looking rough. Here, I got you a coffee."

"Awww, how sweet."

Her voice sounded gravely. She sounded like Laz.

"So I found you last night in the tub," I said.

She jolted upright as best she could. Well, her head moved a few inches, anyway.

"Oh, my god, I'm so sorry. I didn't mean to. I was just so drunk I took a shower to sober up for when you got home. I must have fallen asleep. Was I out very long?"

"I don't know. I just had the neighbour come in, though, and complain. I guess you used up all the hot water in the building. Which is impressive. We have forty-four units here, so you must have had a very long shower." Kate buried her head into her hand. Shaking, as if to make everything go away.

"I'm so sorry. Oh, god, I'm so embarrassed."

"Relax, it's no big deal. I thought it was hilarious. I came home and thought you found a different place to stay. Then I went into the bathroom and saw a pink blob behind the shower glass, found you passed out in the tub. I was going to leave you there. You looked so peaceful!" I laughed. She didn't.

"Oh, you asshole!"

"No, it's fine. I figured that probably wasn't good for your neck, so I threw you into bed. The sheets are a little wet, though, so once I get you out of here, I got to do some laundry."

"Well, here. I was the one who wrecked your sheets. I'll do them before I go. Thank you so much for the coffee. And to make it up to you, I'll go buy you a duvet cover."

"Raincheck on that. I have to leave a little later. Next weekend maybe?"

"Can't. I'm going to Vancouver that weekend. We'll figure it out though. Thank you."

Kate sipped her coffee holding the cup in both hands for warmth. She had been shivering most of the night even under the duvet.

"I was going to make some breakfast. You want an omelette?"

"No, I'm vegan."

"I didn't know that about you."

"Yeah, but if you give me a minute I can make us some hash browns."

"No chile rellenos?"

"I'm in no condition for that."

The rest of the morning was uneventful. Her head hurt so she didn't talk much. I let her wear my robe while she washed her clothes from the night before along with the sheets. Thirty-minute cycle, just enough time for hash browns.

"Are you okay if I stay here for a bit, nurse this hangover?"

"Sure. Long as you're out before dinner. I have some things to do."

"Thanks. You're the best. I tell you what. While you're out, I'll clean up the place for you. Do you have stuff to clean with?"

"Rags are on the table."

"The table with the streaks?"

"Yeah."

♦

Jade fucked like a maniac. I could get bored of the sex and she would go back to blowing me. She had a weird fascination with anal sex. I never liked it but I also wasn't no bitch. Man's gotta do what a man's gotta do. I'm sure that the reason she acted so out of control was because she couldn't just ask for a hate fuck. She had to earn it.

She gave everything I wanted from a woman sexually. All I

A Choice

had to do was keep her from blacking out from drugs or booze. It was harder than I expected.

"How many pills did you take?" I asked her.

Half a tit was hanging out of her top. I could see the areola, but no nipple. She was smudging my shirt with her tit juice.

"Like, one. Maybe two, or three. Hold me."

She went limp in my arms. I could squat twice her weight, but this was impossible. The squat bar would stay still, but she flailed about. It was like holding on to a waterbed. I had to get her home but the tricky part would be to convince her.

"You're probably done for the night," I said. "Let's get you home."

"Let go of me!"

And like that she was on her feet in the bar.

"Rex, come on. Let's dance."

She grabbed me by the arm and pulled me onto the floor. She waved around, oblivious to the beat, waving her arms in the air one minute and falling into me the next. Her skin felt warm and damp. She was slippery at first, but then the salt in her sweat stuck her to me like flypaper. I felt a tap on my shoulder and looked back. It was the bouncer. He wasn't impressed.

"Hey man, you got to get her out of here before I have to kick you both out."

I hated that I always had to pay a fifty dollar surcharge just to get a heads up, but it was better than being dragged out by the neck.

"Yeah, I get it. Thanks for the warning."

"No problem. Enjoy your night sir."

He stood behind me as I made my way to the exit.

"No. I want to keep dancing," she said.

"You can't. We just got kicked out."

"No!"

Jason was the new father, so why was I having to convince this girl to go to bed? Jade jumped onto my back and I grabbed her legs. A piggy back is the best I can hope for. This is going to be the messiest fuck I've had with her since the last one. If this were baseball, a three hundred batting average would get me to the World Series. For me, it meant I was getting blown a third of the time and cleaning up sheets the other two thirds, and I didn't even like baseball.

The bouncer reached above me and grabbed the drink out of Jade's hand. I nodded. "Thanks."

We made it out the door and I got hit with crisp air. It was freezing outside. Steam was rising off of us as her sweat evaporated. I leaned her against the wall so she wouldn't fall.

"Stay here. I have to get our jackets. Don't move."

Jade looked up like a four year old who just got in trouble. "Okay," she said, pouting.

I walked back to the bar entrance. The bouncer stopped me.

"Sorry, man, you're not coming back in."

"I get that. I just need our jackets from the coat check."

I reached into my pocket and pulled out the two tickets and a ten dollar bill. "For the girl," I said.

He leaned inside. "Lindsey! Can I get you to grab some coats for me?"

"Appreciate it," I said, then I looked over at the wall where I left Jade. She wasn't there. Fuck.

"I'll be right back," I said.

I started looking around. A few doors down was a doorway for a boutique. It was inset from the sidewalk and a couple of guys from the bar were standing there staring at the ground. I followed their gaze and spotted a familiar shoe. She was laying on the ground, asleep. I looked at the guys. They looked drunk and hungry, maybe desperate. They were talking amongst themselves. I couldn't hear what they were saying.

"Excuse me," I said. I walked in front of one guy and grabbed Jade's arm.

"Hey man, you know her or something?" said one of the guys.

I looked at them. They were sizing me up. They weren't very big and were a few years younger than me. I couldn't tell if they were Indian or what, but they have those pencil thin beards that

A Choice

Indian guys love to sport. Back in my home town, the Indian guys had farmer's builds. These guys looked more like druggies. I braced myself and hoisted Jade onto my shoulders. One movement into a fireman's carry, just like they trained me on firefighting qualifications. The heels on my Chelsea boots made my lower back hurt.

"Back up. Thanks guys," I said.

One guy raised his hands to indicate there's no problem, and they continued walking down the street. I couldn't tell, but I was pretty sure that errant tit had fully flopped out of her top. I didn't even care. I hauled her back to the bar where the doorman was holding our coats, her thin leather riding jacket and my American Navy Peacoat. What's another twenty pounds of wool at this point? I motioned to my shoulder with my head, and he threw them on top of Jade.

"Thanks."

He nodded and went back to the door. My car was across the street in the parking lot. I hadn't had a single drink on a date with Jade yet. I put her in the back seat to keep her from possibly playing a drunken joke on me and pulling the gear shift into neutral or jerking off the hand brake and putting us into a ditch. She mumbled something, but I didn't care what. She fought me trying to pick her back up when we got home and I pulled her out of the car and was helping her into my house.

"I can do it. Let me go. I can do," she said.

But she couldn't do. She banged into the hallway like a bowling ball off the bumpers in a kids' lane. My neighbors hate me enough already. Even I want to hate me, too. Once she got into the house, she ran straight to the bedroom, shoes on. She fell onto my bed and rolled over. I saw a smudged face imprint on my pillow, mascara and foundation and lipstick all on that beige pillowcase. I hated Charli, and I hated those sheets, but they are my last set, so I can't get rid of them. They reminded me of her. They reminded me of all these fucking chicks now.

"Hmm, cmom hr."

"What are you babbling?" I yelled at her while she sloppily

reached into my pants. Her hand didn't fit while my jeans were buttoned up. I unbuttoned them and her nails stabbed into me. I was still flaccid. She jerked it a couple times and then made a disappointed face.

"Awww, smesee not ready," she mumbled.

When Jade drank, it somehow accentuated the lines in her face. When I was a kid, my mom used to listen to George Jones sing, "I've aged twenty years in five." I don't know why, but I miss listening to that tape. We'd be driving to the store to rent a video game for the weekend and that tape would always be playing. It was always about the patterns.

Jade stopped jabbing her nails into my pelvis, and I started to get hard. She tried to talk, but it was just babble. I could feel her breast on my leg. She had pristine tits, a tight waist, and thin legs, better than Charli. When she was lucid her blowjobs felt like heaven. At times like these, it was just sad. I was the human pacifier. It was nap time. I pulled her up. Her eyes were closed,

"Do you think I'm pretty?" she asked. Her mascara was running. Was she crying?

"I think you're wonderful," I said, "but you're drunk. Go to sleep."

"Hmmam, rn."

She was laying on top of my duvet, so I rolled it over her in thirds. I didn't even look in the mirror. She was wrapped up like a burrito. I grabbed my pants, buttoned them up, and walked into the living room. I turned on the XBOX and looked for a lobby.

Waiting for players ...

♦

Next morning, I was up early. I was still in my bar clothes from the night before. Jade was sleeping in the bedroom. Ordinarily, I'd have gone in there and woke her by taking off her panties and fucking her, but I wasn't feeling it. She would already be wet and grab me the moment I went in. At least, she had been every other time I had done it.

It was a game. She wouldn't open her eyes. She loved it. It made her feel like everything was forgiven and that she was still worth a damn. But not today. Today, she ain't shit to me. I wasn't in the mood and my back hurt and my boots had gotten scuffed on the street the night before. I walked in and watched her laying on my bed. My pillow looked like a Jackson Pollock. She was draped across my sheets like a sloppy mess. She must have awoke in the middle of the night and stripped down to just her underwear. Her arms were holding those amazing breasts. Even now, they were perky and tight.

I went to the bathroom and turned on the shower. My pants smelled of gin and my shirt had the faint smell of cigarettes. My neck was stiff from sleeping on the sofa, and my back felt weak from too much lifting with my back instead of with my legs. I had a bruise on my arms, and I didn't remember how I got it. The water was scorching hot and turned my skin red. I stood underneath, my head tucked into my chest, water pouring down. I hadn't touched a plastic puck in a year, but that smell of burnt plastic and sight of ass is all I can think about. I wanted to soak up all the hot water in the building and rest on the cast iron tub, but my balls hurt, so I jerked off instead.

I grabbed some clothes out of the dryer. Jade was still passed out on my bed. I grabbed my keys and headed out. I didn't put on the Seamaster. I didn't care what time it was. I'd be back when I was back.

I wore sneakers so my feet didn't hurt. I figured I'd buy a book and get a coffee at Starbucks or something. I just didn't want to be at home. They sold these mini egg bites. They tasted good, almost as good as a breakfast burrito. I hadn't read fiction since I was in school and devoured the Hardy Boys anthology.

The eggs took a minute to cool down, so I grabbed my whip-creamed sugar coffee and scanned the bookshelves across the room. The nonfiction section was as good a place to start as any.

The Dog Walker | R.A. STONE

The only book that appealed to me was by Christopher Hitchens: Letters to a Young Contrarian. He was drinking a glass of scotch on the cover. I liked scotch. The blurb on the back:

"A series of missives exploring a range of contrarian, radical, independent or dissident positions, and advocating the attitudes best suited to cultivating and to holding them."

I was having my own dissident moment, so I figured why not? How else could I explain the fact that I had left a naked stripper at home just to jerk off and eat egg bites, or that I had a job that I performed to the highest expectations, without fail, only to get promoted so my divisional officer wouldn't have to explain why she let me rail her next to the squat rack? My phone buzzed. Kate was texting.

"Ugh, I wish you were downtown right now. I just had the worst date ever."

"I am at the Starbucks on Government Street, actually"

"Oh? I thought you had a date."

"Yeah, but I kind of ditched her."

My phone rang as I sent the last message.

"Oh my god, I was just having the same thing. I'm driving over, meet me in 5."

I guess Mr. Hitchens would have to wait. I scarfed down the egg bites and went outside to see her Bronco. I hopped in. Kate was sitting there in that same white skirt she was wearing when I had met her along with a pink hoodie, half zipped.

"Aren't those your bar clothes?" she asked.

"They are nice enough. I don't want to get into it."

"OK, whatever. You smell like cigarettes. Where are we going?"

"I don't know, where do you want to go?"

"You're the man. You pick," she said.

"Well, I need a drink, but it's like eleven, so head towards Oak Street Village. I know a brunch place that serves Caesars."

"Can I drink those?"

"Probably."

A Choice

The island never had any seasons. It was always fourteen celsius and cloudy with a drizzle of rain. Shorts or a short skirt and a sweater made sense. There was no urgency, no upcoming winter to prepare for, no upcoming summer to get hyped for, no upcoming fall to sit back and relax to. Every day was the same. You just had to find the patterns and sync to them.

The difference was, this time I was breaking the patterns. I should have fucked the passed out stripper in my bed, then made her a coffee and done some laundry. I should have bitched about dirty sheets while I was on her like a dirty shirt and done it all again next weekend. I should have done my best at work and gotten passed up for a promotion again.

Instead, I fucked my boss and got promoted. I left the stripper and jerked off in the shower. Instead of smelling like Prada, I reeked of cigarettes. I was on a date at eleven in the morning. I checked my wrist. No watch. Nothing but my own choices ahead of me. Time didn't matter. Only one moment to the next.

I know that having Caesars at eleven in the morning at brunch with a girl I only kept around for sex was a small choice, but at this point, who cares?

"I'll have a Caesar, and a hamburger with home fries. Thank you."

"And for you, miss?"

"I'll have one too. For my meal, can I get this avocado salad? No mushrooms, no tomatoes, and no tofu. I'm a vegan."

"You know it comes with cheese, right?"

"Yeah, that's fine. I can eat cheese."

The waiter turned our order in and brought our drinks.

"So, you've never had a Caesar before?"

"No. My parents raised me in Mexico," she said. "They don't have these down there."

"Well, it's clamato and vodka. They add worcestershire sauce and celery salt, then garnish with a pickled vegetable. It's great to nurse a hangover or get some quick calories into you after a night of drinking."

"I'm sold. Why do they call it Clamato?"

"It's just tomato juice with spices and clam broth. So what happened with you?"

"Like, real clams?" Realizing she's a vegan, I say,

"No, the spicey. It's like how pumpkin spice isn't actually pumpkin."

"Oh. Well, I was on a date. You know that band who does that song that goes, 'yeah, yeah, working for the weekend?' Well, it was one of the guy's kid's."

"Working for the Weekend is Loverboy. BTO is Taking Care of Business. Is the band Canadian?"

"Yeah, whichever, you know the one. Anyways. I'm on a date with the main guy's son and he started getting all grabby. Then he looks at me when I get creeped out by it and starts by saying 'do you know who I am?' and stuff so I just smacked him in the head and left. Then I texted you cause I wanted to complain about it."

"I notice you only call me when you want to complain about a date or spend the night and go to the bar."

"Yeah. It's not the same. You're just more fun is all."

I set my drink down. The waiter put our food on the table, and I looked at Kate. I really looked. I was looking at Kate. She was looking at me, smiling. There was no pretense. We had no serious issues. She had no kid at home. Her nipples weren't lactating. She didn't have a drug addiction. She wasn't leaving to go fuck a fat drug dealer or taking notes on my inner desires for later. She wasn't about to get married. She had no fiance at work. No one was bleeding from a head wound beside us. I won't get a promotion for fucking her. There was simply no bullshit. Nothing.

And she was smiling, smiling for no reason other than she was happy. She had been miserable a second ago, and she got over it. Her eyes were smiling, too. Ten minutes later and she's happy about something else. Were her eyes always green? I hadn't noticed before.

"What are you looking at?" she asked.

I had been daydreaming longer than I realized.

15 A Choice

"What?"

"You've been staring at me for like a minute. What are you looking at?"

"Your eyes. Were they always green?"

"You never noticed my eyes are green?"

"I remember you telling me they were green. I remember telling you about the movie. I remember they are green. I just never paid attention and actually looked at them. See, I tend to just go through the motions, figure out the patterns, and I've just always worked that way. I never pay attention."

"That's weird."

"Yeah, but I kind of realized something here while I was drinking this Caesar, before they gave me my burger."

"Oh, yeah? What's that?"

"Remember when I asked you what your favorite horse was?"

"Oh yeah! This mean you want to start dancing for me now?" Kate starts to make dancing motions with her hands as hooves.

"No. Ha, no. It's just, no one has ever asked me what my horse was."

"Well, what's your horse? Close your eyes, wait a second, now tell me."

"A white horse with green eyes. Her skin slightly oranged from a tanning bed. Easy to get along with. Doesn't hold a grudge. Isn't an alcoholic or a single mom or crazy. Do you know where I can find a horse like that?"

"Aww, shucks, I'm glad this old mare can still do it for ya."

"Look. I've been dating a lot of women over the years. We've been seeing each other casually for, what, a year now?"

"Bout there."

"And this whole time, you're the only woman I've ever known who has never done anything crazy. No red flags. Never pissed me off. You've never destroyed anything in my house, and I've had most things in my house get utterly wrecked by women. You're the only one who has so much as made me a fucking sandwich. I've been dating you for a year now, and I have literally nothing I can say about you that isn't great. So, I want to ask you something."

"Well, I don't know what to say."

"Why do you let me treat you like this?"

"What do you mean? Treat me to lunch?"

"No. I mean, I've never once tried to commit, to try to lock you down? Have you ever been curious?"

"Not really. I told you I got out of a relationship just before we met. I've been happy just doing my own thing. He never paid bills on time. He never paid rent on time. He was always doing drugs. It was just nice for a bit to live like a normal, functioning adult."

"Yeah. I was thinking the same thing. Here, let's do a trial period. Ninety days. Proper dating. If it works, great. If not, one of us can just call it there and no hard feelings."

"Yeah, sure. Why not?" Kate gave it less thought than she gave her salad.

"You clearly love that salad given how fast you're eating it. Gonna take a breath?"

"It's so good."

I grabbed my burger and took a bite. It was nice. The two of us just ate. Not saying anything for the next ten minutes. I finished my burger. Kate took her time with the salad after my jab. When she was finished she set the fork down on the inside of the bowl.

"There is one thing though. If we are going to date, you have to buy a duvet cover, because I'm tired of getting scratched up with goose feathers."

"That's fair. When do you want to do that?"

"Right now. Finish your drink, then we are going shopping."

"Fine, but we aren't going to Walmart or Zellers or some shit. I don't want some cheap one hundred fifty thread count bullshit. It costs more, but it's got to be three hundred thread count Egyptian cotton."

"Oh my god. You have no idea what you're talking about,

do you? Six hundred thread count sheets. If you want soft, that's what you want."

"See, that's a common thing people do. They assume more threads equals better threads. It doesn't. Egyption cotton threads are an inch longer than normal cotton. That's why they can weave them thinner than normal cotton. But once you get past three hundred, they mix other fibers in there to strengthen the threads. They are too thin at six. The sheets end up being about the same softness but they rip so much faster."

"Yeah, but they are still one hundred percent cotton," she said.

"That's how they get you. Trust me. My mom used to be a seamstress. I know. What they do is they use rayon or something in the core. Then the fibres are still one hundred percent but with a synthetic core. And the synthetics rub the cotton causing it to wear faster. So yeah, three hundred thread count is the best."

"Well, then, you'll have to show me."

The waiter came by and handed me the bill. I handed him my Visa.

"You're not going to look at how much?"

"Unlike the guys you're used to dating, I don't need to worry about lunch, or paying bills or any of that stuff. Ready to go? You're driving."

I took a chance. We pulled up to the Linen Chest and walked inside. Kate went straight to the bedsheets and duvet covers. I looked around to see who was working.

"Here, three hundred thread count, cotton. What color do you want?"

"White or ivory. If they have navy blue for the flat and fitted sheets, that works, but the duvet has to be white."

"Why white?"

"So I can tell if it needs to be washed."

"Oh, so you have clean sheets too?"

"I will. I've been putting this off for a long time."

Kate grabbed two packs off the shelf. We walked over to

the desk which is when I noticed that Kelly was working today.

"Hi, Rex."

"Kelly."

"Hi. You guys know each other?"

"Yeah, Kelly and knew each other a while back."

"Will that be all?" Kelly asked as she scanned my sheets then placed them in an oversized bag.

"Yes."

"That'll be $245.39." I placed my Visa in the machine. Approved.

"It was good seeing you again Kelly," I said. "Take care."

"Enjoy."

As we walked to the Bronco, Kate stopped. She placed her arm on the hood and looked at me.

"That was weird."

"What do you mean?"

"Well, you said you knew her, but she just kept glaring at me. Why? What were you two?"

"We used to date for a bit."

"Oh? She's cute."

"Yeah, it's a long story. I'd rather not talk about it."

Kate got into the Bronco and we drove to my place. I didn't think anything of it until we parked in visitor and started walking towards the entrance. Oh shit. Jade.

"Maybe we should come back later."

"What do you mean? I want to see these sheets in place."

"Yeah, but I should probably wash them first. Maybe later on we can–"

She interrupted. "Oh, whatever. So you have dirty sheets on your bed or whatever. It'll be fine."

She snatched the keys from my hands and put them in the door.

"You forgot to lock your door, Rex."

As she walked in, she saw Jade wearing my bathrobe. Jade stared back at her holding a beige pillowcase covered in makeup and what looked like a little vomit.

15 A Choice

"Oh, hello."
"Hi, who are you?"
"I'm Kate. Who are you?"
"I'm Jade."
"I was worried you were still here. We need to talk."

1.6

Keep the hat on.

Thirty days after that and I was sitting on the sofa. A Mexican blanket was draped over the chaise lounge where Kate was lying down reading a book. I was on the computer reading a blog post by this funny guy who talks about sex. He calls himself Chateau Heartiste: Discovering a Girl's Soul with One Simple Question.

Kate and I had a new tradition: Lazy Sundays where neither one of us plan for any activities or work or projects or parties. We just sit there and veg out as she calls it.

"Imagine you could only go to one of two places for vacation. One is Spain. You can have coffee in the cafe, lounge on beaches in the sun, hang out at the museum, dance and drink the night away. The other place is Antarctica. You can be alone with the wonder and power of nature, your breath taken away by awesome sights and see glaciers crash together all day from a rocky beach where the water is filled with sharks and the shore is home to penguins and polar bears. No stress, and you feel alive. Which vacation do you choose?"

"What? Is this another question from that fucking blog?"

"Which one?"

"Well, Spaniards speak Spanish like they have a lisp, and I love sharks so, clearly, Antarctica, why?"

"It means we can keep dating."

"Oh, fuck off. Stop reading that crap. You're supposed to be looking through Jason's baby registry for a gift."

"I already did that. I'm going to buy a few jumpers so that he has four sizes, and they will last him the whole year."

"Look at you, thinking ahead."

I got a message on Facebook and recognized the profile picture. Charli.

Her message? "Hey."

That was it. Just a "hey." Not a, "Sorry for fucking you over." Not a, "Sorry for using you like some kind of weird experiment." Not, "Sorry for fucking some drugged up asshole and lying about it because I felt like it?" Nope. Just, "Hey."

"Hello, how are you?" I replied.

"Oh, I'm fine. Just sitting here. I am moving soon to a bigger place and I was just thinking about you so I thought I would say hi. I miss you and had such a great time when I was with you."

"That's good to hear," I typed back.

I wanted to call her a bitch. I wanted to yell at her and bring up all the dumb shit I was going to bring up that day when I was freaking out in the street. Most of all, though, I wanted to know why I didn't feel like it, didn't care. I should have been angry. I had every right to be angry. I wanted to be angry. I just wasn't angry, but I was curious. What could she want by reaching out like this?

"So, what's up then?"

"Well. I was packing things up and I realized I had your hat here still. I figure you talked about how much you loved the thing, and how you took it all over the world and maybe I'd just send it back, or bring it to you. I'll have to make it up to you for keeping it for so long." She ended her message with a winking smiley face and a set of lips.

I hadn't forgotten the hat. I remembered the little ring stain on it from when I would keep a drink in there so that the strippers in San Diego didn't try to steal it and wear it on stage. I remembered the crack in the plastic rim from when the wind picked it up in Thailand and it hit the ship and almost fell into the water. I remember when she wore it half-cocked while she fucked me in my bed on those lackluster sheets she bought me. That hat had been around the world, and she had it. That hat was the culmination of every ding, dent, and scratch I had received in my entire adult life up to that point. That hat was as much me as anything was.

I should've missed that hat. I wanted to miss it, but I didn't really care. I had a new hat. That week she'd left, I'd ordered it from Logistik Unicorp. The new one had nothing wrong with it, but I didn't parade anymore. It was newer, younger, and pristine. No marks from drinking. No stains from strippers. No memories from the past. It was just a peak cap. It looked good and did its job without all the saltiness from the war. The only things cleaner than this hat were my sheets and that duvet cover. Kate washed them more than I used to.

"You know what?" I typed back, "That's okay. You can keep it. I have another one now."

"Oh, well, thank you. Hey, I missed you," she wrote.

"Good to hear. Nice catching up with you."

She left a smiley face emoji and that was that. I got up and went to the bathroom. As I pissed, I stared at myself in the mirror. Blue jeans, grey henley, scruffy face. I looked fit, happy, rested. I looked like someone who has known me for years and he's happy for him.

You're just like him, you know.

"Yeah, but only the parts of me that work."

So, you finally get it.

"Yup. I get what you were trying to do. Thanks"

I wasn't trying to do anything. I was being honest, being me. You were the one trying to be something else.

"Well, thanks anyways. It took me a while to understand. I'm slow, but I learn."

Learned what?

"Not loving chicks for what I wanted them to be and just accepting them for what they are."

The Dog Walker | R.A. STONE

A lot of these broads were train wrecks. You had your work cut out for you.

Kate yelled from the living room, "Who are you talking to in there?"

"What? No one," I yelled back. "I'm just thinking out loud. I want to show you something."

I went into the living room and got back on the computer.

"Sure, what's up?"

"I am confused. This chick I used to date way back before I met you just tried to reach out, out of nowhere."

Kate walked over to the computer and looked at the messages.

"What's she look like?" Kate asked.

I clicked her profile picture.

"Oh, she's cute."

"Yeah, but she's insane. She was borderline or bipolar or something. Worst girlfriend of my life."

"What's this bit about a hat?"

"Oh, she's talking about my peak cap from work. She stole it from me when she was here and says she wants to give it back or something." Kate walked off into the bedroom and came back with my new peak cap wearing it canted to the side. It was so big on her that the extra head space has it sitting low enough that she can barely see out of it.

"You mean this thing?"

"Yeah. That's the one."

"Yeah, she doesn't really care. She's just bored. She wants to see if she can pick up the phone and you'll entertain her, keep her occupied or hook up or something. She doesn't want you. She wants to know if she could have you again."

"Is that how you girls think?"

"That's what I would do."

"I'll never understand you chicks. Come here."

I grabbed Kate and brought her in to kiss her. She reached up to take off the hat.

"No," I told her. "Leave it on."

The
Dog Walker

R A Stone

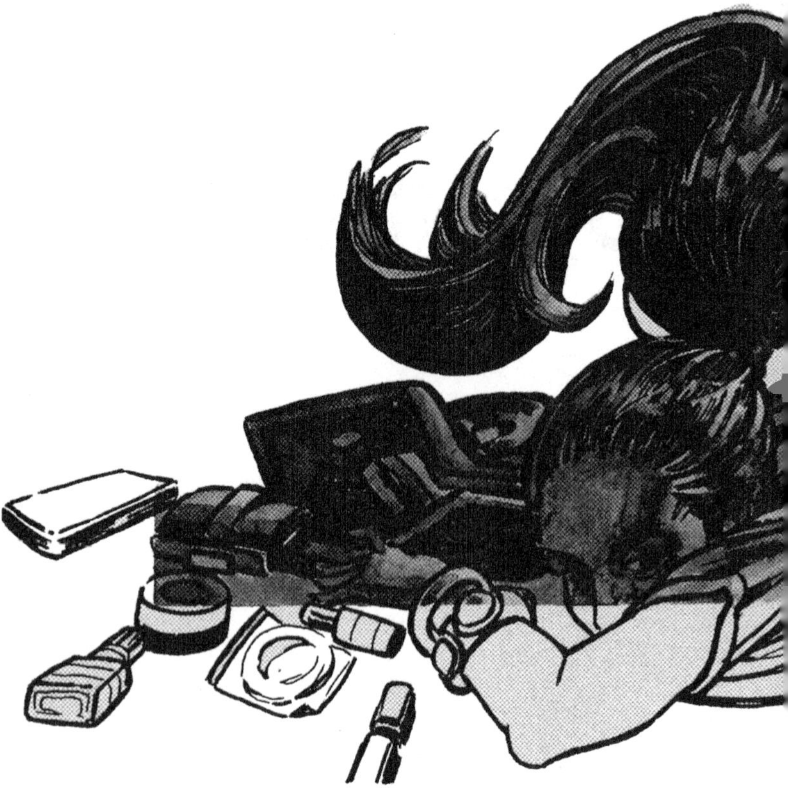

rayrayisHAPPY

Printed in Great Britain
by Amazon